T0204893

BLESSED
NOWHERE

A Novel

GUERNICA PRIZE 6

Guernica Editions Inc. acknowledges the support of
the Canada Council for the Arts and the Ontario Arts Council.
The Ontario Arts Council is an agency of the Government of Ontario.

We acknowledge the financial support of the Government of Canada.

CATHERINE BLACK

BLESSED NOWHERE

GUERNICA
EDITIONS

TORONTO • CHICAGO
BUFFALO • LANCASTER (U.K.)
2024

Michael Mirolla, general editor
Lindsay Brown, editor
Interior and cover design: Rafael Chimicatti
Cover images: JannHuizenga/iStock (front)
and Andrea Brambila/Unsplash (back)

Guernica Editions Inc.
1241 Marble Rock Rd., Gananoque, (ON), Canada K7G 2V4
2250 Military Road, Tonawanda, N.Y. 14150-6000 U.S.A.
www.guernicaeditions.com

Distributors:
Independent Publishers Group (IPG)
600 North Pulaski Road, Chicago IL 60624
University of Toronto Press Distribution (UTP)
5201 Dufferin Street, Toronto (ON), Canada M3H 5T8

First edition.
Printed in Canada.

Legal Deposit—Third Quarter
Library of Congress Catalog Card Number: 2023952486
Library and Archives Canada Cataloguing in Publication
Title: Blessed nowhere / Catherine Black.
Names: Black, Catherine, 1975- author.
Description: Series statement: Guernica prize ; 6
Identifiers: Canadiana (print) 20230620175 | Canadiana (ebook) 20230620183
ISBN 9781771839112 (softcover) | ISBN 9781771839129 (EPUB)
Subjects: LCGFT: Novels.
Classification: LCC PS8603.L246 B54 2024 | DDC C813/.6—dc23

For Mom
In all her love and grief

A single person is missing for you, and the whole world is empty. But one no longer has the right to say so aloud.
— PHILIPPE ARIÈS, *Western Attitudes Toward Death*

La muerte no se reparte como si fuera un bien.
Nadie anda en busca de tristezas.
—JUAN RULFO, *Pedro Páramo*

PROLOGUE

THIS IS A LIE I TELL MYSELF: once I figure things out, I'll go back home.

However long I've been away, I can still see home as clearly as if I was sitting right there at the kitchen table or hanging up my robe or lying in the bath looking at my toes in the reflection of the faucet. I can be staring at some painted-over graffiti in a Mexican hotel room, closing one eye and erasing it with my thumb, and then a phone rings in the hotel office downstairs and I'm back home again: the telephone ringing at the bottom of a drawer of dishrags, the full ashtray, all those boxes of kids' cereal in the cupboard, and my mother plain-faced across from Gloria with her own plain-faced look. Mother all tight-lipped, scratching behind my dog's ears and saying something about how I've run off to the middle of blessed nowhere. My sister shaking her head. They both sigh the same way—that slow leak from the very bottom of their lungs where all their disappointment lies.

I'll go back home when I get my head straight.

Before that it was I'll go back home when the drought breaks. And then the rains came, so naturally the story changed.

It had been three long months of breathless heat in Tadeo. This is what it looked like: the fountains all over town were filled with grit and garbage, and all those poor dusty street dogs were snarling at each other for bits of food dropped at the taco stands. In the hotel room next door, my neighbour Mojo couldn't fall asleep. I know so because I could hear her Spanish language records and Mojo's drowsy voice repeating common nouns.

The day the drought broke, I was lying in bed with my feet up the cool wall, listening to Mojo learn words. Thunder rolled way far off, sounding like a yawn in your inner ear. When I got out on the balcony, I saw the sky was full of all these thick, cottony clouds that draped right over the Sierra Madre Oriental mountains, and everything felt so still and so charged, like the ground underneath your feet could leap up with electricity and zap your ankles. Then wind. Little bits of broken glass scuttling along the street—you couldn't see it, but you could hear it. Grackles on the telephone wires tipped their beaks up to the sky, just waiting. I'd never seen anything like it before. You couldn't believe the anticipation. The rain was probably only a few miles from Tadeo, maybe only half an hour down the highway in a town where the religious fanatics whipped themselves and walked around on their knees. I could imagine it already raining there, washing all that blood away, mixing it with sand and turning it to terracotta mud. I wondered if it would get as far north as Texas and wash the dirty windshield of my dead car, or maybe it would rumble all the way to Canada—flood our city streets and Joseph's kiddie pool.

Then the tarpaulin of sky split right open before I could even duck inside, and I could have sworn I heard the whole town draw a breath—that sound a crowd makes for fireworks or a high wire act. The spouts from the balcony pissed warm rain onto the street while overhead gutters spewed water in wide arcs. I rubbed my hands under them and you could smell the street, a good smell as pure as earth. Then Mojo came out next door.

The rain flattened her crazy curls and her mascara started smudging all under her eyes in a mess. She was still in her bare feet, grinning and holding her palms out.

Out in the street below, the two hippie girls had come out of our hotel in big, vaulting strides, leaping gutters. Vula started to twirl with arms outstretched, while Sue struggled to tie her skirt in a knot above her knees. They were always like that: invincible and defiant in that way that young girls are, laughing at the old perverts and cops who ogled them, dancing with skirts held in tight fists, and talking in clicking whispers with their pierced tongues. I was starting to love those rotten little girls.

Vula was scooping and splashing from the rushing gutter, her hair all plastered to the sides of her face, while Sue shrieked like crazy. Handfuls of filthy water. They were running down to the bend in the street, climbing into the fountain where donkeys were usually tied up. Just two of our big nomadic tribe of outcasts and fuckups, unwashed and unlovely and unloved. Somehow we'd each found Tadeo for a while, whether we were broken and worn out or burnt out or whatever. Most of the time we tried not to think about what landed us here in the first place.

Then as suddenly as it started, the rain eased and then stopped. Left behind was the scent of earth, wet animal, leather, all of it hanging there in the humidity. The girls in the fountain looked up and said Hey like someone had just unplugged the cantina jukebox. Then they started wringing out their skirts. Mojo shook her curls, wiped under her eyes, smiled and shrugged at me. I ran my wet hand all around my neck, to press the memory of water deep into my skin.

The birds had left the wire, and the potted succulents dripped water from their tips. I stayed out a while longer watching the girls leap up on the high ledge of the fountain while a taxi from the big town nearby jostled through the pooled potholes and splashed them. Both the girls swore like crazy in perfect Spanish slang, even though Sue is Boston Irish and Vula's French Canadian.

Then everything changed.

The taxi stopped a few buildings away from our hotel, and the driver squinted like he was trying to make out street numbers. It came closer, door-by-door, until it stopped in front of our hotel.

When I first saw her—sensible shoes swinging out of the cab onto wet stone, pressed pant legs dipping into the gushing gutter, spindly grey ponytail—she was just a collection of separate parts. Those were my mother's shoes. Those were my mother's skinny legs under that cheap material. Those were my mother's hands gripping a glossy magazine and that's the big amber ring my father bought her the

Christmas before he died. That was my mother's face, too, looking older. She appeared as a collection of small, nonsensical details. Just as the whole world had become without Joseph.

In that moment, I felt startled into being, like being woken by someone snatching the covers from you. I thought I'd rush back inside the hotel room, just scrape the doors of the balcony shut, sleep her away, sleep her gone. But instead I just watched with my pulse beating in my cheeks as she struggled to lift her suitcase from the trunk, the driver stepping in and hoisting it out for her. Mother, looking confused, fingered the coloured peso bills and stuffed some into his open hand. Then she dragged her vinyl suitcase on its useless wheels topsy-turvy over the cobblestone. It twisted and capsized in the gutter and she strained to get it upright.

I said something then. The only word I could.

I said Here.

She turned her face upward, and I could tell she couldn't make sense of me either: her scrawny wayward fuck-up daughter standing there in the middle of nowhere-Mexico, drenched in what had been the first rain after a very long season of drought.

I.

IN RETROSPECT, the city had been an easy place to leave. In the heat-wave, it stank of chlorine and dishrags. Downtown with the garbage strike on and the trees of heaven blooming, the dirty chlorine smell was almost too much to take. So I smoked as I pedalled my bicycle, until my legs and lungs burned equally.

The busiest streets were lined with bursting garbage bags that seemed to be filled with cotton rags used to clean up after bodily discharges or surgeries or something. The water from raw chicken. It closed my throat up tight to think about it.

Those weeks before I left, I rode my bicycle everywhere. Every day. No stopping. When I rode around at twilight, people on our street looked the other way or smudged their sad little smiles and almost made me sick with their pity. Mother said something about it, of course, when she came over with Gloria to make dinner one night.

"You're riding around a lot these days," she said, in this particular tone of voice that implied an ellipsis at the end of the sentence. Dot dot dot.

Gloria left the room. I listened to the balls of her feet on the wood stairs. She always went up two-at-a-time, just like when we were kids.

"Yep," I said.

"You have better things to do, Abby."

"Like what?"

"Oh I don't know. Work. Get the house together. You were never interested in bicycles before, it was your sister, and now suddenly you're always on it. Pedalling around ..."

So I said that's what you do on a bicycle. Pedal around.

"I'm just saying," she said.

"Saying what?"

"It's unusual." End of conversation. Unusual. Like she was being generous with me when what she really wanted to tell me straight out was she thought I was fucking nuts.

A few minutes later, after she lit a cigarette at the kitchen table and coughed deep and wet into her closed fist, she said out of nowhere, "It makes people uncomfortable. It makes them wonder if you're all right. Like if it's some kind of a neurotic obsession or something."

I stared at her.

"I've always biked," I said.

And that was that.

Frankly, it didn't matter what anybody had to say about it because when I thought about it hard enough I could still feel Joseph with me when I was on that bike, like when he was really little and we'd ride all the way uptown together, him strapped into the baby seat, me not believing my luck that this kid was all mine. And God, wasn't I stupid then. Thought we could see the whole world that way. I'd show him Europe and America and India by train, by bicycle, the two of us together. I didn't know the world would take him. Suck him from me. That he was never mine to begin with. That he was just passing through this life. Now when I pedalled I had to imagine his weight making my legs work harder, his body making the turns more solid and more precarious at the same time. I had to try hard to remember that feeling.

I wore my knapsack and pedalled to get groceries at dusk.

The world was all purple-bruised and empty at that time of night. It gave up nothing and cooked its hotdogs over coal and stank up the neighbourhood with the scent of summer parties and family dinners. I hated the smell of suppertime but biked through the streets anyway, past houses busy with chopping and rinsing and the setting of places at a table. Enough to make you feel eleven years old and already delinquent. I wanted to throw bags of dog shit onto their doorsteps, over their miniature picket fences. And I knew it was crazy, but I wanted to see into their basements, see if he was down there, and sometimes once the sun finally went down behind the rooflines I'd stop to take a look. I'd roll my bike up their skinny driveways, crouch down and look into those dirty windows past laundry baskets and over tool benches and I'd cup my face to peer behind furnaces and cardboard boxes marked ATTIC or BOOKS. Once in a while I'd try the window but they were usually nailed shut. I knew he wasn't down there. I understood that, but I had to check anyway. You just have to. Just in case.

So every night around dusk I'd ride to the corner store for a pack of cigarettes, and once a week I'd ride six blocks to the supermarket, fill two mesh bags with groceries, and weave home through traffic. Cereal and Tang, juice boxes and cans of alphabet pasta hanging from the handlebars. The wheels would swish faster and the chain of the bike made its quick clicking noise as I'd push to keep up with the cars, snaking in and out of traffic with people blasting their horns, cutting across intersections against the lights, busting over lawns and curbs, the groceries on the handlebars swinging, hitting me in the shins. I'd pass by home three or four times before I went inside.

I'd assembled everything he liked: fruit leather, popsicles, cookies and Redi-Whip, all those things I'd never let him have—tooth rot stuff. Now I stockpiled all that crap in my cupboards and fridge like some kind of magical bribe for him to come home. I never told anyone this. Especially not Mother or Gloria. I'd keep the cupboards closed when they came by so they wouldn't see the row upon row of the backs of cans and sugar cereal with the front of the boxes turned the other way so I didn't have to look at that rainbow and the leprechaun.

My dog would always lick his lips at the sound of the can opener but he'd never touch anything I put out for him to eat. We're both going to starve, I thought. His dog food was forever crusting over on a plate in the corner of the kitchen, I thought that maybe he'd be okay if I just found him the right thing. I tried kibble, the kind with meaty middles and the kind shaped like tiny bones. I tried canned meat that opened with an aluminum key. I even tried cooking hamburger—not interested.

So there the two of us would sit. I'd watch kids' shows. Smoke.

The telephone would ring. Most of the time I'd forgotten where I'd buried it—a kitchen drawer or under the sofa pillows.

Three rings and over to the answering machine. Always Mother or Gloria. They were beginning to sound so much alike. Pissed off I hadn't called back: three messages now, one of them said when I played them back. Then words about a lasagna. Enough to make you pour yourself a stiff drink. Or two or whatever.

I'd been pouring myself vodkas the night I got the idea to call Joseph's father to tell him what had happened. I had this promotional bottle Gloria let me take home from the tavern where we worked and I usually just mixed Tang crystals right into the vodka and breathed tap water over it. Stirred it with a finger. Fancy-shmancy.

As I drank I got thinking and obsessing and going over things, like you do, watching this game show where people looked sweaty and eager for money. They laughed too easily and rubbed their palms into their hair as they guessed at letters and a wheel whirled and they won thousands, thousands upon thousands, and the audience clapped at their good fortune. The music was maniacal and twizzled round and round too. It would make your heart race if you were there in the middle of it all. I remember turning the sound down as they spun the wheel again, and it occurred to me that I'd never bet on anything in my life. It occurred to me that I'd never even tried to win a prize, not even at the midway at the Canadian National Exhibition. But I almost went to Vegas once. I guess I started thinking too long and too hard about it, about how Joseph's father and I had sat in the tavern after my shift and had fallen in love or something like it. And how when he had said to me, "Let's go to Vegas and get married, Abigail," he didn't even know me well enough to call me Abby, like everyone else in the world.

As I sat there drinking Tang and vodka, my lips all puckery with powdery orange, I could almost imagine what the gaming tables would have been like under my fingers, the green felt, and I thought about winning triple-cherry slots, quarters pouring out for five minutes straight. That's what being in love felt like.

"Let's go to Vegas right now," Joseph's father had said to me and it made my blood twinkle. "Tonight. Come on, don't you want to do it? You been to Vegas?" Even all these years later, the idea still made me feel effervescent inside.

He had a car and I had a credit card and I had really honest-to-God thought about it. Sailing down the winking neon strip in a convertible, sitting on top of the seat as he drove, my feet on the edge of the windshield. God, imagine that. I even pictured the chapel and a little silk bouquet of sweet pea roses, and Elvis asking me if I did or didn't and I'd thought, seriously, that I just might say I do.

But I didn't say why not or let's go or even let me pack first. I said, "Vegas is far." Then hated myself.

Martin didn't have a convertible anyway. Just a van with fuzzy seats and nothing in the back but a mattress with some sound equipment piled on top, squishing down the bed that was squishing down a shag rug. So instead of Vegas we just went back to the van with the shag rug and fucked twice. It was fine. Then the next day he took off for a sound check at the next dive he was playing. I thought he might stop by the tavern after his gig. Maybe he'd show up like a rock star and the other girls would raise their eyebrows as he took me by the hand and led me out back to kiss me in the alleyway. I was a sucker for all that Sid and Nancy shit. Romance and grit and all. But he didn't do that either. He didn't show up. And his gig was cancelled because of an electrical short.

We saw each other a couple of times after that. Nothing serious. Except one night after shots of Jägermeister and some B.C. hydroponic we became convinced we could read each other's thoughts. Even with our psychic connection he was surprised to learn, six weeks later, that I was pregnant. And I never would have guessed that he already had a kid, "somewhere," he said, and didn't want another.

After that, Martin just drifted.

But Joseph, he lived in my body like a seed of mercury. Like my own pinch of magic.

I still remember the feeling: I loved waking in the morning with the knowledge of him inside, sleeping, growing, nestled and good. For a while, I didn't tell anyone about him and was in love with the secret of him, and with the ridiculousness of my motherhood. I knew nothing. And the idea of all I still had to learn, and learn quickly, terrified me, thrilled me, made me smile to myself as I served tables of terrible food and cheap booze and rode my bike home from work in the middle of the night. Somehow, it made everything so suddenly hopeful.

When Mother found out she came over daily, like she'd miss something if she didn't. She gave me back my own miniature clothes that smelled of mothballs, and a ratty bassinet and woolen hats, so many woolen hats some old friend of hers was always knitting, and weird plastic and rubberized things she had to explain.

"A breast pump. This is your new best friend, Abby," Mother had said. Or: "It's called a Jolly Jumper. You loved it. Kept you busy for hours while I cleaned houses. I'd just pop you up in a doorframe and voila, instant babysitter." I had imagined my very own baby in a doorframe, churring and giggling, barefooted.

Voila!

That was then. Another then.

But the night I decided to call Martin to tell him what had happened to Joseph, I sat there thinking all that through again. By the time I got up the nerve to do it, the host of the game show I was watching was shaking hands with one of the contestants. The contestant was licking his lips, laughing, clapping his hands together and grinning like he was some kind of Hollywood big shot. The spokesmodel stood beside them both, and the three of them looked ridiculous together—the host and his big square teeth, the contestant in his sweaty shirt, and the spokesmodel in her Barbie doll dress wanting to be somewhere else.

Joseph's father was like that contestant. Thought he was such hot shit when really he was just a nobody who'd had his fifteen minutes of fame. He took his time to vanish too. First he'd be on the road for a week, then I'd get a call every month or so, and when the baby was born he held him in the hospital room, posing for the requisite snapshots while I struggled to stay awake and tried to shift as carefully as I could over my stitches. Then that was it. No one in the neighbourhood ever saw him again, and Joseph never even knew him. Now, wherever he was, he didn't even know his son was gone.

I took the phone book from the bottom drawer in the kitchen. Thumbing through the pages, I looked for Martin Jones. There was one listing. I couldn't believe it. Martin D. Jones on Duplex Avenue. I went in search of the telephone.

The man who answered the phone sounded like a nice guy, but I was suddenly aware of how much I'd had to drink, and tried to enunciate, but the vodka had made the words all slippery and my lips and tongue felt bigger. Anyway, I told the man on the other end of the line that I was looking for Martin Jones, about thirty-nine, forty now, lived in Kensington Market, a singer, played harmonica. The man laughed and said the most he'd ever sung was in church on Sundays, and that wasn't in key. Cheesy, but he sounded like a good guy. He said he was sorry, he wasn't my man.

There were over sixty entries under M. Jones, and even more with middle initials, so I started dialing M. Joneses on the Lakeshore and in the Beaches, and up and down Bathurst Street. And across town on Shuter. Wives and kids and boyfriends and fathers answered the calls. There were a few dead M. Joneses, and a bunch of female ones.

My name's Abigail Walsh, I'm looking for a Martin Jones, someone I lost touch with. I was wondering if you might know him.

No one did.

I got tired around the seventeenth call and it was getting late. The sky outside the kitchen window was bruised-looking and it made me rush hot and cold with fear of all those empty hours ahead. So I watched the TV on low, and finally, when the windows were just reflections of the kitchen, I rested my head on the table and slept halfway through the night.

I woke up with this clear, piercingly clear thought that I should take out an ad in the classifieds to look for Martin. So as the sun came up I wrote it out on the back of the telephone bill. Wrote it and rewrote it until it was perfect.

At Dolly's Corner Store and Deli, I watched Seymour through the storefront window as he twisted and strained on his leash until some children approached him with their palms up. I bought the weekend edition of the newspaper and headed outside. The kids wanted to pet Seymour. He was soft and nervous, with his ears folded back. I felt sorry for him. One of the kids, one I'd never seen in the neighbourhood, stopped to ask, "Why's he so skinny?"

I couldn't tell him, so I said, "He's a just a picky eater."

It would have scared the hell out of them to know it was because he was starving himself for Joseph. So instead I lied. I said, "He only likes pizza. Can you believe that?"

And the kid said, "Pizza ..." through his missing teeth.

I tugged on his leash. "Come on Seymour, say goodbye."

His unclipped nails clicked beside me, up the sidewalks north of Christie Pits Park. Nearing home, I felt around in my pockets for house keys, which I'd left in the front door of my house again. They were always there when I got home from Dolly's or wherever else: hanging there from the front door lock like they'd lost their purpose. Like a tassel. Like nonsense.

Inside, I read ads celebrating fifty years of marriage, a first birthday, thanks to strangers for help after an accident, Lost items like wedding rings and lovebirds and gold watches. Chihuahuas and tabby cats and long lost friends.

The Found items gave me a funny feeling, a kind of hopeful-painful feeling. People couldn't be all that bad if they returned glasses and pets and wallets and things. It gave me a lump in the throat to read those ads, and the ones written to saints, too. Quaint, superstitious-sounding prayers to Saint Jude and the Holy Spirit, all a little different but with the same refrain: pray for us. I read one all the way through. Here's what it said:

May the sacred heart of Jesus be adored, loved and preserved throughout the world, now and forever. O Sacred Heart of Jesus, Pray for us, St. Jude, worker of miracles, Pray for us.

The ad went on to say that if you recited it nine times a day for nine days, your prayer would be answered. Guaranteed. So I read it eight more times and then phoned the newspaper, read my ad from the back of the phone bill, and made them read it back to me punctuation and all:

Martin Jones period. You lived in Kensington Market comma, played harmonica and sang in a band period. Abigail Walsh is looking for you dash urgent exclamation mark. Call: then my number.

I'd wait now. Wait for his call.
In the meantime, I'd read classifieds about people staying married and losing their lovebirds and praying to Saint Jude for a miracle.

II.

BACK UP. It was winter. December 1997. Sixteen days after Joseph was buried. I was on hands and knees combing the carpet for a new moon of a nail clipping. My fingers were raking the roots of the carpet fibre as I picked at little things, bits of waste, dirt, gravel from a shoe tread. I smelled deep into his bedclothes, his hairbrush, but needed and wanted a real, hard, sharp scrap of him, so I lifted the velvet-lined cardboard in the bottom drawer of my jewelry box and found the only baby tooth I'd saved. Now it rattles in a silver locket I wear around my neck, a gift from my dad on my sixteenth birthday. His photo is in there with Joseph's tooth.

Anyway, there I was on my hands and knees and suddenly I sort of woke up and thought, Jesus, what am I doing down here? Things like that were starting to happen more and more often. Like I was some kind of a sleepwalker in my own life. And it terrified me. The waking, that is. If only I could stay under, it might be alright.

Back home that winter, I'd been manoeuvring my way around his world without disturbing any of it: the Christmas tree we'd decorated with dollar store glass birds and plastic beads, the packages underneath the tree, the one he brought home from school, tightly wrapped by teacher-hands. His toys: armoured action figures with spiked maces and helmets and whatnot, bright Lego blocks that pierced the sole of your foot, stuffed animals with those sad glossy eyes. I stepped over them like they were landmines or something, or like casualties. I hadn't even realized it until Mother came over and started tidying up. She stopped and stared at the Christmas tree and all those wrapped presents, like she was wondering where to start. And I said, "Just leave it." And Mother nodded and kept cleaning but she couldn't look me in the eye for the rest of the afternoon. She doesn't cry, you understand. She looks the other way and gets busy.

Twilight was when nothing worked. Not the Valium Gloria gave me, not the giddy sounds of kids' TV shows playing in another room, not the pot smoke in my lungs. I tried different rooms, lying in the empty bathtub with a drink trying not to fantasize about the water swirling with blood, lying on the sofa bed with a pillow over my ear blotting out God knows what sound in that quiet house. Blotting out the quiet maybe. Then just before morning, I'd lie awake in Joseph's bed, watching his balsam wood airplane turning on its fishing line.
Round and round.

When other people were eating dinner and dozing off in the blue of their TV screens, I'd walk the busier streets of the neighbourhood past shop windows filled with flowerpots and shrunken trees and used books. I needed the herbal medicines behind the dirty glass window, the cafés where all the old men got together to play dominoes and drink beer. All that stuff. I'd stare in with my coat collar held tight at my chin reading and rereading the titles of books in messy piles in a particular store window. Some part of me thought maybe there was a sign in the author names or in the titles, some sign that Joseph was coming home. Sometimes I wondered if he was just somewhere else, like if he'd slipped through some loophole in time and was just beyond reach, or maybe life was going on totally intact in some other plane of existence: me and Joe at the kitchen table eating chicken fingers.
Then this one night I was standing in front of the glassed-in slope of all those unwanted books, looking at all the titles for the hundredth time: *An Introduction to Iridology, Lessons in Ballroom Dancing, Literary Criticism Before 1900,* and *A Topographical Guide to the Americas.* I found myself thinking about the texture of the pages of

that last book, and imagined my fingers on it, tracing over its mountains, dipping into lakes, slipping over the dotted borders of provinces, states, and countries.

The store was closed but I tapped on the glass with my mitt and this delicate-looking man with a cloud of white hair got up from his seat behind the counter to unlock the front door. His eyes were still on the tiny television screen as he spoke to me. Someone was playing poker and it seemed like he didn't want to miss the hand.

"I know you're closed," I said. "I should probably come back tomorrow."

"Good thinking," he said, and began to shut the door.

But I asked him if I could come in for just a minute to see that atlas. The topographical one. The guy thought about it for a moment before letting me into the shop.

It was dim inside, warm and musty, and I felt sort of excited while he lifted the atlas from the store window.

"You're a geographer?" he asked.

I said no.

"An explorer?" He smiled in a twinkly kind of way.

"No. I just like the book."

So I sat in a corner of the store on a footstool and felt the places we'd never visited, Joseph and me. My fingers trailed over the Appalachians, sank into lakes, traced the routes of wagons and horses, and skimmed along the plains of open nothingness.

The storeowner made this sort of exclamatory sound from time to time, I guess in response to an unlucky hand or a bad play or something. He let me sit and read over that atlas in his store until he turned off his television set and very quietly made a phone call to another country—his rotary phone hissing past so many numbers. After that, the storeowner poured me a cup of sweet Turkish coffee and I closed the atlas and decided I needed to take it home.

"There's no price on it," I said, turning it all around.

"Fifteen dollars."

I offered him ten.

"Robbing a poor old man," he said, but smiled again and put the atlas into a plastic bag.

The walk home along the icy peaks of people's frozen footsteps was a walk on the white caps of atlas-mountains, going snow blind, getting lost. I imagined taking out my atlas and retracing my steps. I imagined drinking sweet coffee from a thermos in my bed of evergreen, in my dugout in the snow bank. Then I would sleep, curled beside Joseph, and the cold would take all the fear from me. The dogs wouldn't find us. We'd sleep, and we'd be preserved for years and years under that thick drift of snow, until we were both totally forgotten.

Spring came anyway. Right along with its rain and birds and mud and kites and people feeling better and better about their lives. Season of evaporation. Everything misting into nothing. Hours, days, weeks were hazy and indistinct. And on days when that infuriating light rain dampened the whole city, I thought even I might be dissolving right along with the skyscrapers and the swans.

And in the gritty tunnels of the commuter trains, I looked for him. In the silver domes of the underground safety mirrors that made my head and eyes enormous, I looked for him. There was the flash of subway glass reflection, again and again. I looked for him there. Please, I'd think. Let me see him for a second. There were sleeping pigeons under the bridges where we'd walked together. All of nature heavy and waterlogged with thoughts of him. Sleeping birds in the girders of the overpass: Joseph. The locked gates of the abandoned stockyard: Joseph. The traffic and the puddles and the strangers going home.

III.

OUT OF NOWHERE the tavern let me go. I'll be fair and tell you that when Bruce came up to me I'd been staring at the TV screen way back at the far end of the bar, watching some show on the monarchy in Great Britain. I couldn't hear what was being said, but was totally entranced by those wide panoramic shots of the castles and all the green, sculptural gardens. There was something so remote about the pale princes and muscled horses. Some fairy tale kingdom that belonged to other people. Not real people.

He just said, "Take the rest of your shift off." And he clapped me on the back just about making me jump out of my skin. He was always too hard touching people, like, the kind of guy who crunches your rings into your fingers when he shakes your hand.

I remember turning around to see my customer in the far booth waving a bill that he'd had enough time to fold into a miniature fan. And again, I'd forgotten to refill the water mugs and clear the dirty dishes. I felt this rush of blood to my face when I realized that. I started to fumble through my change belt like an idiot, but Bruce squeezed my shoulder. Too hard.

"Go with her," he said, gesturing at Gloria, and he didn't even look me in the eye.

Gloria went all weird and quiet as we drove to Dolly's for the luncheon special. She played the car stereo over-loud, overcompensating until I had to reach for the dial to turn it down.

All I said was, "Jesus ..."

26

And she was all over me. "It's country!" she said. "You love country!"

When I didn't say anything and the car was silent, Gloria just stared straight ahead, rubbing her lips together, mashing her lipgloss, until we were parked at the deli.

"You used to love country," she said.

Inside the deli, I had no idea what to order. I just couldn't think about that shit anymore, so I ordered exactly what Gloria was having: onion rings, Banquet Burger, extra pickles. Like when we were kids. I took my burger apart piece by piece as Gloria watched.

Finally, quietly, softly, all serious she says, "We've been talking, Abby, and we all think you should take some time off. Just to get back on track."

She was reaching across the table to clasp my hand in her own. Gloria's hands were always warm, so I let her hold my hand for a second because it felt good, and when she let go of it I just kept taking apart my burger, lifting the lettuce leaf from the sticky patty. Gloria was making me feel all crawly. I could tell the conversation was going nowhere good.

"You could go on a holiday someplace nice," Gloria said, smiling, rubber lipped.

I was getting dizzy because of my breathing and I asked her for a sip of her milkshake. I kept trying to eat like everything was cool: biting along the edge of a pickle or whatever.

"How 'bout you go on vacation?" she said. "You know? Take a holiday."

Gloria was all mouth and eyebrows when she was trying to be earnest. "You haven't been on a holiday since when?"

"Mm-hm," I said, licking ketchup from my fingers like I didn't give a shit. Then all breezy I asked her, "Should I go south?"

"Yes!" Gloria said, flattening her hands on the table. "Someplace in the sun! Someplace fun! One of those all-inclusive places. You've got enough money for that." Gloria looked around the restaurant then gestured firmly at a poster of Greece that the owners had framed on the wall.

"Greece!" she exclaimed, with a little piece of food flying from her mouth.

"Not south," I said. I stared at Gloria.

Gloria's expression was somewhere between hopeful and desperate. Then her face loosened up and kind of collapsed and she told me Bruce was letting me go.

I couldn't fucking believe it.

For what? I honestly couldn't think of a good reason.

"For what?" I asked her again.

"I know," she said, "But listen. In the big picture it's probably the best thing that could happen, right? Abby, you started working again so soon after everything, you know? You just didn't take any time to process."

"Process? What does that even mean, process ..."

And Gloria said, "I mean now's when you take care of you." She held my wrists, reaching across the table. "Okay?" Gloria smiled and I noticed that all her lip-gloss had worn off onto the straw of her milkshake.

I nodded just to get Gloria off my back and thought about picking up the new classifieds on Saturday morning. Find a new job. A better job. I wiped my hands on a paper napkin.

"I'll figure it out."

"Exactly," Gloria said and sounded relieved. "You'll figure it out, Abby, you always do." Gloria smiled. "We'll have our old Abby back in no time."

IV.

I THUMBED THROUGH the papers that weekend, past all those inky notices for cheap airfare and then past job ads marked with triple dollar signs. I seriously thought about answering those sex-calls people make, but decided there was no way I could stand all the greedy sounds, all that awful grunting and breath and all. Then I found a small ad seeking Polite Professionals, so I called.

They wanted to meet me.

I tied my hair back in a scarf and pulled on a blouse I hadn't worn since my cousin's wedding. I rubbed the oil stain with some salt and water and dried it with a hairdryer and most of it came out. I borrowed a pair of low heels from Gloria and went to the interview wearing a bright shade of lipstick that Mother insisted made me look more cheerful.

"Just fake it, Abby, even if you don't feel it," Mother said, Gloria nodding behind her with her eyes closed. That whole act of theirs drove me crazy.

The big boss in the brown suit asked all kinds of questions about my experience; he even asked how I'd handle an abusive caller, say, someone who used profanity, someone who called me rude names. I needed to know what kind of rude names, but he wouldn't give me an example. "You know. Rude words or what have you."

I told him nothing really gets to me.

The boss nodded and put his pen to his pursed lips. He kept doing that. Then he asked me about my experience with cosmetics—if I'd ever used their hair dye (no); if I'd ever called a complaint number (no). So many questions. My eyes were getting tired-out by the fluorescent lights that were fluttering above the boss' desk. Then finally he got around to the personality question. Gloria had warned me about this. What did I consider the greatest accomplishment in my life. Gloria said he'd probably go with what my weaknesses were, so I was prepared to say punctuality.

Greatest accomplishment.

I didn't answer right away, even though I knew exactly what I wanted to say. I took a second before I said it.

"Raising my son."

"How old is your son?"

"He'd be ten in two weeks."

He wasn't listening.

"Mine," he said, "are eleven and thirteen." He smiled, folding his vinyl-bound clipboard with its embossed logo. He turned the framed photos on his desk to face me. So I looked at them. Nodded. Smiled. Because that's what you do. He pointed to the girl. "Eleven." Then to the boy. "Thirteen." Like I didn't understand English.

He told me they'd call later that day with their decision, and then ushered me out into the reception area where two nervous-looking people sweated in their rumpled pants and borrowed blazers.

I waited.

No call from Martin. No call from the boss with the fluttering lights and the two kids: eleven and thirteen.

When Joseph's birthday was in a couple of days, I went out and bought an ice cream cake, coloured candles, and tucked them away in the freezer just in case. It was good I didn't get that stupid job anyway. Maybe we'd go away for his birthday. Go on holiday someplace in the sun, maybe. I lay on his bed and thought about it. Couldn't tell anyone, of course. They'd think I was nuts. Mother especially, with her daily visits to the grave, all those disgusting flowers and wreaths and stuffed animals and all that shit. My child wasn't there.

He was elsewhere. Maybe, I thought, he'd even be home if I just went away and came back from someplace else, like starting all over again. Rewind. Press play. I was beginning to suspect time was like that: looping and flexible. If he was gone in one afternoon, then maybe he could come back in another. I remember thinking that and then falling asleep across Joseph's bed that night, after a slice of mint-chip cake and nine novenas I could now say by memory.

Here's how I left: on a Sunday, not meaning to, in a mustard-yellow Volvo I'd bought with half of every tip I'd earned in the past four months. It looked to me to be the kind of car that would take you places, not high-end places obviously, but far and wide places. It was a road trip car, a station wagon that could be loaded down with luggage and picnic baskets and a slobbering dog, and you could drive it to Florida or Banff or Algonquin Park and back if you wanted to. I liked the idea that the car had already travelled more miles that I'd ever seen in my entire life and I remembered stroking Joseph's forehead before he'd fall asleep, telling him, "We're going to see everything, Joe. We'll see mountains and deserts and oceans and forests, we'll see rivers and valleys and rolling green hills ..." An endless list of places until his eyes blinked slower and slower and finally shut.

A week before his birthday I circled into the parking lot where the car was parked and laid my bike down to talk to the guy. Negotiate a good deal. I didn't want to get taken, wanted to look like I knew what I was doing, so I got right down on my back and kind of shimmied under the car looking for God knows what. Then I looked under the hood, checked the oil, noticed a missing cap. I asked the guy about it and he said, "What top?"

I told him, "The missing top there."

"The coolant cap?"

"Yeah."

"You don't need that," he said.

"No I know, but it should still have one."

"Well, it's a five-hundred-dollar car," he said. "With all the money you'll be saving you could get yourself a new cap."

A real smartass.

Before I laid down the cash, I checked out the interior, got right into the back and stretched out, tried the radio to see how loud it would go without crackling. The song playing, I remember this, was "Hotel California" so I sat and listened and watched the guy outside just shake his head and go over and jimmy the vending machine outside the shop so it popped out a can of Coke. That song always reminded me of the campground up north, drunken teenagers playing the Eagles on the only rock 'n' roll station, music blasting from our cars, cherry Chapstick, fireworks. Making out with some boy you just met and who would love you until the end of August when he went back to the city while you stayed up north.

Anyway, I bought the car. And that night I drove all the way to the suburbs with the key on a twist tie sticking out from the ignition like a couple of live wires. I even stopped for soft ice cream at the Dairy Treat and sat on the hood while I ate and watched convertibles and screaming kids and laughing girls and bare armed men and for a moment I loved summer. I loved my car. I wished I could think of a name for it, but couldn't.

Mother, of course, said I was crazy, buying that old heap of scrap metal when I could have used the money for a million other things. "Practical things," she said.

I wanted to know what was more practical than a car.

"A pair of pliers? Toilet paper?"

Mother wouldn't answer.

Gloria came with me once, but I guess she thought I drove too fast because her foot kept punching her imaginary brake, and she'd periodically screech, "Slow down, Abby! Jeezus!"

I was telling you how I left. I didn't plan on it, it just happened before I could even think it through. I was out the door in a flurry of half-packed bags. I had to go.

It was just one day before his birthday now, one day, and the letter arrived. Like he knew. I'd just come back from Dolly's and pushed the door to the house open into a landslide of junk mail that had been stuffed through the slot while I was out. I scooped it all up and brought it to the kitchen table to sift through.

That thin white letter. That razor blade of a letter.

It was tucked in there between pizza promotion coupons and a real estate flyer. On the front envelope in tidy blue handwriting was my name in full, but my address had an incorrect street number. It had been corrected in ballpoint pen. It looked like it had travelled to other homes, through other mail slots, rumpled and rerouted into other mailbags.

I flipped it over to tear it open, but stopped when I saw the return address and my throat tightened right up like it was going to close-off completely. I knew his name from the police report, from the officers and the caseworker and the lawyers. They wanted to know if I'd go to court for his arraignment. They'd asked if I'd allow him to speak with me because, apparently, he wanted to. Apparently, he needed to.

"You can tell him I want my son back," I said whenever they asked.

Now he was sending me fucking letters.

I thought about opening it. I did. I looked at his name, his tight little name on the envelope and I hated the curves of his e's and I hated his stupid address and I hated and hated. I especially hated what he might have said in that letter, and when I couldn't stand it one more second, sitting there looking at it on my kitchen table, I left.

It didn't take long at all.

I pulled my clothes from the chest of drawers in my bedroom, dumped them into the middle of my bed and shoved some of them into a knapsack. They either smelled of lemon soap or smoke: clean or dirty. Sweaters and underwear and socks. Three T-shirts I'd bought in the boy's section of the department store. They fit me now. A couple pairs of worn-out jeans. Then the bills from the tip jar under the bed. Those I stuffed into the zippered pocket of Mother's old fringed jacket before I ransacked the bathroom: toothbrush, three bars of soap, the little pills that were supposed to help me relax, a razor, a comb, a miniature pack of wet wipes, a spray bottle of perfume I hadn't worn in ten years, that weird, bright lipstick. I dusted off a pair of aviator sunglasses I found under the sink and propped them on my head.

The packing made me sweaty and Seymour nervous, so he followed me downstairs where I overfilled his bowl with kibble and laid out two bowls of fresh water, spread the classifieds on the floor—just a day or two, I thought. I tossed his squeaky toy across the kitchen and he watched it bounce. I unlocked the back door so it hung open a crack on its chain for Seymour. I remember the soupy summer air blowing in. Before I left, I scratched Seymour behind the ears. Buried my face in the ruff at his neck. Told him to be a good boy. Told him I'd be home tomorrow or the next day or the day after that. I felt like he knew I was lying.

The telephone was ringing as I grabbed Dad's buck knife from the kitchen drawer and the atlas from under the chair, pulled on my boots. Gone, I thought. We'll go everywhere, I thought. I remember looking at that letter on the kitchen table and wondering if I should take it just in case. But I couldn't touch it. It would slice right through my hand.

On my way past the living room and its skeletal Christmas tree and landslide of needles and wrapped gifts I stopped again. It made me anxious to look at that crazy mess. So quickly, and without thinking, I knelt by the tree to shuffle around to find the neatly packaged gift Joseph had brought home from school. I tucked it between two rolled up T-shirts in my knapsack. Put the atlas right on top.

Nothing. There was nothing, no awareness, like I wasn't even awake before I was well past city limits. Then the thought that I'd left my house keys in the door again. I slowed the car when I remembered, but decided not to turn around. Made a phone call to Gloria from a payphone before it was long distance and asked her to go check on Seymour and take the keys out of the door while she was at it. I told her I was taking a little holiday.

"Good for you, honey," Gloria said. She sounded genuinely pleased.

V.

I WANTED TO GO someplace real, someplace weatherworn and bust-ed-up and imperfect. I thought about touring south, maybe heading to Alabama or Georgia. I had all these sleepy childhood memories of driving south to Disneyland, really just glimpses of moss-draped towns with Dad driving the Chevy, Mother endlessly tuning-in the radio. I thought about driving west, about California and tans, girls with hair that looked like spun sugar, and men who kissed their arm muscles. I could never fit in in a place like that. No way.

The highway widened and the city thinned out. I stopped for gas at a huge service station just before the border and loaded a basket with mostly-useless knickknacks from the gift shop. Here's what I bought:

Maple crunch popcorn
A doll dressed in buckskin clothing
A colouring book of Canada
A mug with a cityscape on it
Minty gum
Candy bars (2)
A small bottle of maple syrup
Deodorant
A tiny bottle of mouthwash
Three pairs of sport socks
A fridge magnet saying *What is Home Without a Mother?*
Two packs of cigarettes
Folding manicure scissors

When I stood in front of the clouded mirror of the gas station washroom, my face looked like a balloon hovering on top of my neck, idiotic and pointless, totally blank. I was pale from having lived through half the summer indoors, and my hair fell all raggedy down the middle of my back. I tried to tuck it behind my ears. Part it differently. But I just looked beaten. Dishevelled no matter what I did.

So I rummaged through the plastic shopping bag for those miniature scissors. I was careful about it, unfolding the handles and clicking the two blades into place, and then I began to chew the blades into clumps of my hair, starting right up front. I cut through fistfuls of strands, leaving inch-long tufts. The edges of the blades grabbed and pulled and were just sharp enough to get the job done. It made my eyes water to do it.

A woman wearing enormous sunglasses swung open the door to the bathroom at one point. She was talking into one of those tiny cellular phones. She came over to the bank of sinks where I was standing and I thought about stopping or ducking into one of the stalls, but I just kept slicing into the clumps of hair. The woman sidled up to a sink at the far end, pulled a shimmery colour over her lips and glanced at me by accident. She felt stiff and nervous to be near, made of wire hangers and fabric. Maybe she was worried about the little blades of the scissors or the mess at my feet. I don't know. Maybe she thought I was a criminal. The woman looked down at where my hair had fallen all over the sink, all onto the chrome, all over the tiles at her feet.

The woman stepped over the mess as she left. Very dainty.

Once the last bits of it were off me, I folded the tiny blades back in place, brushed my shoulders clean as best I could, shook out the front of the fringed jacket, and scooped the pile of hair up into the trash. For a second it felt like some kind of dead animal in my hands. I didn't regret doing it, but I did feel a little sentimental at the sleep scent of it. I threw it away anyway.

I had to show identification to a skinny customs official before they allowed me into the United States. The woman wanted to know my citizenship, destination, and purpose of journey, to which I answered without hesitation, "Holiday."

The official's uniform was crisp and pleated and looked almost like a cut-out she was standing behind to get her picture taken. Her head was too big for the uniform, and her messy ponytail was off kilter. I was nervous and not thinking clearly when I handed her my deeply-creased birth certificate and driver's license. The official took a mechanical-bird peek at the photo I.D.

"This all you've got, ma'am?"

I nodded, wondering if she was going to tell me to get out of the car or something.

The official checked the I.D. again, then looked at my face like it was just made up of colours and shapes and parts all stuck together.

"Doesn't look like you," she said.

I didn't know what to say, so I didn't say anything.

"You must have lost some weight." She smiled, suddenly all chummy. She handed the I.D. back to me.

"I cut my hair," I said, and she nodded and let me go.

Like a balloon set loose from the hand of a child. That's what it felt like.

All lost on the wind.

Near Dayton, miles and miles south of the border, it was just the middle of the night, no different from the middle of the night at home, really. I don't know what I wanted it to be like, but it was just like any summer night in Toronto. Even the air-smell was the same while I drove with the window right down. So I decided to just keep going until it felt new. I turned the car radio on and they were playing Bob Dylan and it was making me feel all jangly so I lit a cigarette. The cars moving in the opposite direction seemed too close. They could lose control and hit me head on. Or I could lose control. I could veer off the highway. I didn't want to think like that, but couldn't help imagining fishtailing onto the shoulder, then the car slamming against the trunk of a pine tree on the other side of some ditch. I had to slow down and say relax, relax, relax over and over.

Bob Dylan was saying that I should look out, that the saints were coming through.

I had to turn it down.

Don't think about it, I told myself and tried shaking my head to see if I could shake it all away like sand from my hair. All those luminescent white signs and highway lines and fast food billboards were swishing by too fast. I stretched my fingers out against the steering wheel and they looked so strange, like I'd never seen them before. I wanted to see his hands in mine. Couldn't remember his hands. I thought about him hard, his tanned wrists, the plastic watch I gave him on his eighth birthday, the chewed watch strap the puppy got at, his shoulders, square and small like mine, the blonde fuzz on his shins, his red running shoes stained with grass on the sides, his golden hair shaved at the nape of his neck, the bristle there, his cheeks, eyelashes in a fan, blue-eyed baby, blue like his daddy, and his knees, his scabs, they were deep red, nearly purple, his scabby knees.

I had to pull over to the side of the highway and I got out and just left the motor running. I had to walk around the car breathing deep, like I couldn't get enough air.

It was late, it was dark, so I don't think anyone saw as I vomited into the ditch on the shoulder of the highway. Then I got back in the car to clean my face with a Wet Wipe from the glove box. I wiped all over my face in the rear-view mirror, and it was then that I remembered his freckles because, paler now, they showed right through my own skin.

VI.

THAT NIGHT MY CAR roamed streets and row on row of quiet clapboard houses with private lives moving around inside of them. Families in the amber glow of old lamps, lounging in the blue bath of television light.

There was never anything stopping me from turning around or from getting off at the next exit and taking I-75 back north, not that first night or any other night I drove until I pulled over and passed out.

When I couldn't stay awake any longer, I stopped wherever I could. Rest stops. Beneath vacancy signs in motel parking lots. A mall parking lot with these otherworldly ponds of opalescent light on the black tarmac. I pulled the car to the edge of one of the glowing circles and parked. There were moths around the lamp posts. I watched them with the seat all the way back, their glowing bodies looping round and round. Then drifted.

Morning started with a thud. I woke when a shopping cart with a toddler in the small metal seat rolled flat into the driver's side of the car. A mother shouted, "Goddamnit Steven!" Then the sound of a child being whacked on the bottom and whining "Ow!" She was saying, "What did I say about the cart!" Then there was a woman's face, close up at the window, a woman's knuckle on the glass all polite at first, all squinchy and polite, about to say sorry, then she saw me, and I guess she had second thoughts about it.

"There's no damage or anything," she said. Then: "You can check if you like." After a second: "You okay in there?"

I told her I'm fine.

She rumpled up her mouth and took her kid away, pushing him in the basket of the cart, crouching beside the groceries. She turned back around once when she was leaving, which made me think she might tell security or something. So it was time to go.

When I stretched and looked around, America was everywhere. I'd woken in a sea of it on my little raft.

Popsicles. Shorts. Shoes with pink rubber soles and sandals with daisies between the toes. Plastic bags. Painted nails and clean hair. Skateboards and teenagers. Somebody dragging a child in a tantrum.

Somehow America made me hungry for the first time in six and a half months. Everything about it made me want ice cream and the interior of the car was already hot with morning sunlight so I wanted a cherry cola too, maybe both together. A float. When I started the car, the keys in the ignition were hot and so were the radio dials and I thought I must be getting as south as I could get before hitting the ocean. Then I'd turn around and go home again. I told myself that. I'd go home. And only vaguely and in the farthest corners of my mind did I bother to ask myself: To what? I think it was that far-off, deep-down idea that kept me driving that day and maybe one or two days after that.

On the road looking for the ocean in an uncertain kind of way, there were signs with names of streets I wouldn't mind seeing. And there were bigger green signs with amazing white reflective letters with the names of cities that were just too close not to drive right through. So I kept on. Wandered.

Whenever I'd get scared and wonder what the fuck I was doing I'd just tell myself: I'm on holiday. I'd remind myself that I could do whatever I wanted. That's the prerogative of people on holiday. The idea made me want a straw hat tied to my head with a scarf, a straw hat and red lipstick and cherries on top of the hat, artificial and de-licious looking.

I kept driving and fiddling with the radio until Mick Jagger sang that he wasn't waiting on a lady that he was just waitin' on a friend and for some reason that song warmed me and I accelerated because I wanted to keep the feeling as far down the highway and as deep down into me as I could.

When Cincinnati turned my car around on its over and under-passes and the interstate gave all its split-second options, I just acted on impulse and chose west, because in the moment the word was right, and not far down the road I would go through a town called Seymour and feel guilty for my dog. I wondered if he was howling. But then I thought about how he'd be happier with Gloria anyway. Her apartment was carpeted, comfortable, and she and Mother cooked up something different for dinner every night and you could bet the leftovers would be scraped into Seymour's dish. She'd let him sleep in her bed. Mother would spoil him, comb him, let him up on the sofa during reruns of *The King of Kensington*. Seymour would be fine.

So that afternoon near the town of Seymour I decided to leave the quiet highway I was on and turn off onto a dirt road that was all crazy and alive with cicada song. Some combination of that sound and the hours on the road had made my eyes so heavy the lids felt fat, so I napped there on the edge of a farmer's field with the car radio still on.

When I woke up it was sunset and everything was all golden and easy looking. A whole herd of Jersey cows had come out from some lit-tle shed in the distance and were right there at the fence, nuzzling the dirt and staring at the car. I got out to touch them, the stubbly muzzles and wide foreheads with swirls of fur. Velveteen faces and eyes deep and gentle. If only people could have eyes like that. They were slow and heavy on those little feet, and for the moments when I watched them I completely forgot where I was, and even who I was exactly.

It wasn't all easy like that. Not all of it was so peaceful and pretty, I don't mean to suggest that. There was this one time when some drunk tried to get into my car when I was sleeping and I had to scramble to the front seat and lean on the horn because it was all I could think to do. He was boozy-looking and wavering and he had his pants unzipped, if you can believe it. Son of a bitch. My heart beating out of my chest. And of course, it's only after an incident like that that you remember the buck knife. Like how after the fact, a week later, I always have the perfect comeback. So by the time I had the buck knife out of the glove box, opening it with my fumbling fingers, he'd disappeared. My fear was gone and it just left behind a kind of pulsing anger. I jammed the buck knife blade right into the dash and drove with it like that. So no one else would fuck with me.

But they did. They fucked with me. Of course they did because I'm small and you couldn't see the buck knife I put down my boot to go into that diner with the motorcycles parked outside. What would I do with it anyway? Dump my boot out? Stick someone? Ridiculous. But I was too thirsty not to stop, so despite the motorcycles parked outside, I went in.

Inside, I took the only vacant stool and felt eyes creeping all over the small of my back where my T-shirt pulled up. The men sitting there said dirty things to each other as I waited for my order, watching the waitress like there would be a test later. Then when it got bad, the things they were saying I mean, one of them told his buddies off. "Shut the fuck up, you goof. The lady's trying to have her dinner." I turned and said thank you with my Rueben sandwich in my cheeks. And I guess I smiled too and wiped my mouth with the paper napkin, and when I did he reached for his crotch, adjusted himself, and gave me a wink.

I went back to staring straight ahead as I ate, and I could feel my pulse in my neck and my fingertips. I thought about that knife in my boot. I thought about it. And I balled up the paper napkin and asked Diane's nametag for the bill to which Diane said, "The pardon-what, honey?" and I replied in American, "The check."

The truck stops were the same over and over again. Variations of the same restaurant: a counter with stools upholstered in red or orange or pea green vinyl, checkerboard linoleum floors, a Formica counter with false marble swirls or flecks of fake silver. On the stools were usually three or four men with battered baseball hats or cowboy hats and wide backs. Heavy-looking men. Stern and tired. Their hands held sandwiches that were too big for their mouths. One of them usually stared into his coffee like he was thinking about how to drink it without dipping his moustache into it. Or else he was trying to remember what it was a person did with coffee, the road having made nonsense out of everything.

Driving south, the menus changed: Breakfast combo. Bacon and eggs. Coffee. Toast. Flapjacks. Skillets. Whipped butter. Orange Julius. Grits.

In some places the waitresses looked like they'd been serving tables since the place opened, and some of them moved slow and looked like they were full of sand.

Sandbags in pink uniforms.

The menus told me stories about the people who ate there and most of all about the people who worked there: Chicken bites in the shape of dinosaurs. Chicken and dumplings. Skillet steaks. Mashed potatoes. Homemade rolls. Veal. Rice pudding or Jell-O. Cinnamon ice cream. Country breakfast. Chocolate malts. Pancake sandwiches. Home burgers. Becky's double-decker. Al's chicken. Things charred, double-baked, double-stuffed. Coca Cola and a soda fountain that hadn't worked in fifteen years according to the girl with the bright eyes and a Wal-Mart happy face sticker on her cheek.

"Fifteen years!" the girl said. "That's longer than I been alive! You'd think Lois would get it fixed. Where you from anyhow? You've got an English-sounding accent, you from Europe?"

I told her Canada, and she said, "No kidding, huh. I'd like to go up there."

I told her she should someday. She might like it. And she laughed a laugh of a much older woman. A loud laugh.

"And do what? Work in a diner up in Canada? Yeah. I'd be a great waitress up in Canada. I don't even have a fur coat. And I can't understand what y'all are saying half the time, I'd be all, Do what now?"

The girl wiped a bleach-smelling rag over the counter and then tossed it in the sink, adjusted an earring in the lineup of earrings in her ears.

"Anyways, me and my best friend are getting out of here." She looked back to where the cook was taking an order off the wheel. "We're leaving for Las Vegas in a couple of weeks but don't tell nobody. We're going to get rich playing blackjack and the slots, but you can't tell no one that." The girl went on to say that they had fake I.D. from a boy in school and when they wore makeup and did their hair they looked twenty-one, no problem. She told me that if getting rich didn't work out for them then they could always be showgirls and wear feather hats and sequined bathing suits, because even if her best friend did have big hips, she was still "real pretty in the face."

I couldn't say anything. I just nodded and worried and drank some cherry cola while the girl cocked her head and squinted at me. Finally she said, "You know, you'd be pretty too if you grew your hair out." She smiled and held out a maraschino cherry at the end of its stem. I shook my head no, and the girl popped it into her own mouth. I asked for the check and the girl asked me if I had a boyfriend, the half-chewed cherry in her cheek. I told her no.

In a booth nearby there was this guy sweet-talking his wife and asking his kids end-of-day questions on the booth's built-in telephone. "Put your brother on. Hey, how'd it go, Tiger? You guys win?" That sort of thing. I started listening closer, but the waitress wasn't finished with me.

"No kids or nothing?" she asked. I could feel my face flushing red and I told the girl I had to make a phone call and good luck with everything.

I slid into the only available booth while the seat was still warm and the tip was still on the table. I picked up the phone and contemplated the tone for a moment before hanging it up. When I picked it up again I quickly dialed 0 and made a collect call home. Or north. Or whatever you want to call it.

As it rang through to my number I got all shivery and tense. Pick up, I thought. Pick up, pick up. And I willed the sound of his child's voice on the line, his clumsy hands on the receiver, holding it too close to his mouth. But kept on ringing through. Pick up.

The answering machine clicked on and my own voice apologized for missing my own call. The operator asked if there was another number I'd like to try. Some other time, I told her.

It went on like this: I ate in diners and public parks. I washed in picnic ground restrooms. I slept in fields and parking lots and sometimes felt afraid all at once and for no clear reason, so I'd check into a motel on my Visa card, just to feel the sheets, clean and orderly and correct, folded tightly around me. You can slip right into bed without un-tucking them completely, and there's a feeling like being inside a cocoon or hospital. I liked that feeling.

In those motel rooms the TV was usually bolted in place and the lamps were screwed into the bedside table. Even the binder with hotel information was tethered to the table beside the air conditioning unit. When I went to hang up my fringed jacket I always found the hangers welded around the closet pole. Only the Bible in the bedside drawer was without screws or clamps, I guess because anybody who would want a Bible wouldn't steal it.

I liked the American TV programs. So after a hot shower I'd slip into the clean bed without un-tucking those snug sheets and I'd sleep with re-runs on: *Gilligan's Island, Love Boat, I Dream of Jeannie*, things like that. I'd always wake in the middle of the night to the single, loud tone of the end-of-day signal. That sound can become a million different things in your dreams: a howling dog, a train whistle, a boiling kettle, a heart monitor gone flat.

I was going to end it in Garden City, Kansas. And I was serious about that. All this nonsense, the road, the wandering untethered from everything and everyone, done after Garden City. I'd go back home. But it didn't end there of course, it just took off, spiraling south and getting all out of control. And just before Garden City the car started acting weird and I wondered how I'd gotten so far away and what the fuck I was doing anyway, spending too much money and getting shaky and thinking crazy things about finding Joseph somewhere neither of us had ever been before.

I'd rifled through my wallet and calculated costs in my head. No more holiday. At Garden City, I'd turn around and go straight back north. I smoked and got decisive.

I remember cars passing with that whoosh I love. Tires and air, wind over hoods and through wheel wells. Slipstream. Like they're pulling you along with them, like the little ducklings up north on the lake. When I finished my cigarette, I followed that traffic all the way to the edge of Garden City then stopped for directions back to Canada.

I flipped through the maps lined up in the gas station magazine stand and unfolded one across a freezer full of ice cream bars and Popsicles, tracing my finger across the coloured veins, trying to find the highway. The gas attendant had stopped reading the sports page. He came over and leaned on his elbows beside me.

He said, "You're right here," and plunked a greasy fingerprint onto the map and I got uncomfortable and a little charged-up with him standing so near, breathing smoky breath and smelling of gasoline and sweat. I asked him how to get back on the highway.

And he said, "You taking the Road to Nowhere?" And I didn't know what the hell he meant. He must have figured that out.

"You want to take 83 north or south?" he said. I told him north.

He straightened up and took a pen from his pocket and drew this series of tidy arrows to show me the way. He said I could have the map for free.

"Nobody buys them," he said, half-laughing.

"Why, does everybody just know their way around?"

"I don't think so," he said. He looked straight at me. Not up and down like some men I'd met on the road. I asked him what he'd meant about nowhere.

"That's what they call I-83. Road to Nowhere. I don't know. Sounds romantic, I guess."

I asked him where it ends up.

"Well, you go that way, Canada. And the other way, it'll take you all the way to Mexico."

VII.

BLAME HIM. Blame that service attendant and his grey eyes. (Did I mention his grey eyes?) Blame him for the turn south, my wicked escape, my pilgrimage. For scrapping everything, too. I sat against the back wheel of my car somewhere in Oklahoma, or maybe Texas, cross-legged in the gravel-grime, that gritty spit-out asphalt, and up-ended my knapsack. I dragged handfuls of clothing into a pile and thought about each thing before I threw it into the scrubby field beside me. Socks, pants, shirts, comb, Wet Wipes. All of it. Junk. Excess.

Then I took the bills from my wallet, and took my credit card and shoved them in the back pocket of my jeans, I.D. in the other, and flung the wallet into the field, which felt especially good. I took two plain white T-shirts and stuffed them back into the depths of the bag (one to wear, one to wash). I threw three balls of woolen socks overhand, one by one. Woolen socks in summer. Woolen socks in Oklahoma or wherever the hell I was. Then there were the knickknacks. I decided to keep the doll, settling it on the passenger's seat, I kept the fridge magnet but threw the cityscape mug, the maple crunch popcorn, the tiny bottle of mouthwash over a thin, useless-looking wire fence. Of course, I tucked the atlas and the tightly-wrapped package from Joseph back in the bag, laying Mother's fringed jacket gently across them both for protection.

By the time it was all done, the side of the road was as littered as our street back home after some animal tore through the Thursday night garbage. Maybe traffic would slow at the mess—pickup trucks

47

would stop to pilfer or speculate. Traffic accident. Frenzy. It looked like the lawn of an unfaithful husband. Whatever, let them guess.

Inside the car I stuffed the bills deep inside the plush seat-crack, and removed the Ontario maps from the glove box and dropped them too, one at a time, out my window as I drove away. In my rear-view mirror I watched them flutter across the highway. They looked so funny and foreign flapping around like that, then laying splayed-out on the highway. Think of what they'd look like run over by an eighteen-wheeler. Ontario flattened. I kicked off my boots and drove in bare feet for thirty-eight miles until I stopped to fill up.

Inside the chilly convenience store there were cigarettes, packages of something called burnt peanuts, and Patsy Cline. You couldn't help but like this woman on the cover of the tape. She looked like a no-nonsense kind of girl, someone you could trust. You could see it in her eyes that she knew a thing or two about heartbreak and survival.

It was good to be on the road while Patsy crooned with her sad piano tinkling and her singers singing all those low notes in the background: ooh and ahh they sang as Patsy called herself crazy.

It was good on the road to drive in silence, too, with the air so dry and warm coming in through the window. You could trail your hand out and rake the wind. I'd keep it rolled down even after the sun had set and the highway smudged black, and the sky erupted in stars, and the fields all exhaled.

At sunrise, I was standing on the edge of the highway looking for something to fix my eyes on. I could have killed myself for not stopping thirty-six miles back. I'd wanted to take the car in to the mechanic's shop to have the knockity-knockity sound checked out, but I changed my mind when I saw the mechanic sitting there. Like everybody I'd met on the road, he'd probably want to start up a conversation, ask where I was from, where I was headed. When he looked up, I waved impulsively and accelerated again, out onto the highway toward a stretch of road flanked by wind turbines.

There were still rows of them where the car slowed. But against the arterial rush of their blades and the wind, I couldn't even tell if the engine was running anymore. I hit the brakes and turned down the radio. Still couldn't tell. Accelerated, and nothing happened. The car just rolled forward, disengaged. If I tried the ignition it would catch but only go a few feet before stalling again, even if I hit the accelerator while the engine was running. I was suddenly hot as hell.

The wind field droned on and I didn't want to listen to it anymore so I started banging around the car for my boots and bag and atlas and doll. The windmill sound made me turn the radio way up with just the ignition of the car turned on. Country radio. Only this time the music was older, like I'd tuned-in on some wavelength from a cattle town, nineteen fifty-five. Even the announcer's voice sounded, somehow, as though it had been pulled from a signal sent out long ago into the very high, cloud-strung sky. It made me feel all crawly, so I started the cassette tape. Patsy sang about being blue or loving her man or both those things at once as I shoved the bills from the seat crack into the knapsack, along with the doll, whose head wouldn't fit under the flap and poked out through the opening. After thinking about it for a minute, I stuck the topographical atlas under my arm. Because it covered all of America. Idiotic. But that's what I did.

Before I left, I was sorry I never named that car but I patted the hood and left it there in the field of thrashing giants, belting out Patsy Cline from its crackling, too-small speakers, under the constant drone of hot air turning to energy.

VIII.

SO WHAT DO YOU DO in a situation like that? You walk. You go. When you're lost, people always tell you to stay put, wait for someone to find you, save all your energy and all that kind of stuff. But what's the point in sitting around waiting for the sun to bake you like a potato wrapped in tinfoil? Sit and listen to the radio's God-awful crawly old music and hope to get saved? No. If there's ever one thing Mother taught me, Our Lady of Perpetual Motion, it's to keep moving. So you walk.

When I started, the sun was a thumb's width from the horizon. I followed the line of wind turbines swinging their arms out of sequence, all clean and white against that perfect sky. With the sun in my eyes at first, by noon I was walking on top of the dark embryo of my own shadow and I could feel the sun searing my scalp. Then that shadow stretched out in front, little by little, thinner and longer and maybe it would be all the way to Mexico by sundown with stringy, shadowy arms and legs.

I remember the highway running out forever in both directions, to the left and to the right, like a spool of ribbon. The only difference between what lay behind or in front was the tiny glint of a vehicle approaching way off in the distance.

I walked down the centre line until the approaching glimmer became a pickup truck hauling a horse trailer. I'd been enjoying thinking what it could have been, flashing and flickering. An angel. A man in a mirror suit. A knife salesman. Close one eye then the other and the glint jumped left and right like magic. Then the distance between us shortened in these undulating waves of heat and I stopped walking as it got near. It slowed right there in the middle of the lane, not bothering to pull over. The cab of the truck contained a Border Collie type of farm dog and a boy who looked too young to have a driver's license. He made me smile because he was wearing this oversized felt cowboy hat with little feathers peeking out from the hatband, and a white T-shirt with smudges of dirt all over the shoulder.

He asked, as you would, "You alright?"

I fixed my knapsack on my shoulders and said I was fine. But that boy still looked skeptical.

"You need a ride?"

"Nope. Just heading over there." I gestured vaguely in the direction the boy had just come from. You know, squinted that way, signalled with my chin.

He contemplated and sucked at whatever it was in his cheek.

"Texas?" he asked.

I told him yep. Texas.

And again that boy thought about it for a moment.

"Well, you're a long ways from Texas yet," he said. "Takes a couple hours driving just to get to Perryton."

My eyes were stinging from squinting into the sun. I told him that maybe I'd take a ride with the next car going that way. I didn't want to take him off his route.

"Okay," the boy said, shrugging. "You're sure."

"Yep," I said, and patted the side of his truck, like to signal that he should get going. Bye now.

Oh, God, what scrubby-looking grass there is in that flattened, windy, bare-bones part of the world. What beautiful fields of absolutely nothing except dirt and clouds. While I was walking, I was thinking about some giant herd of cattle that could have passed through, razing the fields and leaving beautiful nothing, just open space behind them, all this earth you've got to touch and when you do, it's warm, maybe from their fleshy muzzles. I could have laid down and died there. I could have covered myself in that warm dirt and slept forever.

By the time I was finally past those endless fields of soil and reached a farmhouse with a tin roof, the sun was only a brilliant red gouge on the edge of the horizon like the whole of the state bled from where its fields had been stripped and scraped raw by relentless sunlight and wind. Reaching that farmhouse with blisters on my heels and a burn across my nose and all my city clothes tied around my waist, I'm sure I looked like I'd been sleeping outdoors, walking for days. There, a farmhand offered to drive me to the Eden bus station.

"You certain you didn't walk all the way from Canada?" Not even taking the time to answer, I smiled and downed the bottle of Dr. Pepper she gave me in record time. Best thing I ever drank. I stifled burps as that farmhand said, "Well, you get some rest and I'll wake you once we're across the state line into Texas." And I just loved the sound of that and closed my eyes, cradled by the seatbelt strap, head against the window, in and out of sleep for miles as she drove perfectly straight in her red flatbed truck, because straight was the only kind of road they seemed to make around there.

By nighttime I was waiting behind a couple that leaned into each other and kissed without speaking every few minutes. Both of them had on beautiful blue jeans and brand new matching sneakers. The lights above two ticket booths lit up at the same time.

The ticket man was a chubby guy, nice face, and had this filmy cloud over one eyeball you couldn't help staring at. Switch to the other eye. It looked as though the whites were glomming onto the iris, overtaking it. He didn't say anything. So I blurted out something stupid like, "When's the next bus leaving?"

He told me, of course, that would depend where I was going. He sucked a tooth, smiling. His egg-white eye looked fixed on the locket around my neck so I tucked it inside my T-shirt, Joseph's tooth rattling inside.

"The one that leaves soonest," I told him, dumb and honest. "Doesn't matter where."

He said, "In a hurry," and typed for a minute. "There's a seven-fifty to Laredo if you want to take that."

And I asked him, "What's after that?" half-hoping there was something north, something home. I fingered the locket through the T-shirt.

"Eight-twenty to Amarillo."

"North?"

"West."

"No. What about Laredo?"

"That's south."

"I know. But is it, like, a good place for a holiday?"

He told me it was nice if you liked Mexico.

And I took it, feeling oddly Texan in my momentary certainty. Then there was the zotting sound of the printer while I rummaged through the knapsack for forty-seven dollars, three cents. My hands shook. Mexico. X in the middle. Exotic Mexico was a place you won a trip to, a game-show place.

"You got some vacation time?" he mumbled.

I didn't know which eye to look at. Left-right.

"Yes."

The printer was still printing out my journey leaving this awkward pause we were supposed to fill up with conversation. I watched him as he organized his desk, shifting pens, piling paperclips back into their little green box. The bad eye was bluish in the way a suffocated fish's eye turns cool and cloudy.

"It's scar tissue," he said out of nowhere. "Chemical burn when I was a kid. I could've had it fixed but didn't want the hassle."

I stammered something, "It looks fine ..." Something foolish. And he told me to have a nice trip and handed me an envelope containing one ticket due south.

IX.

IF YOU'RE SLEEPING on a bus, you want to take whatever jacket you have and turn it inside out so the lining is smooth against your cheek, and you can sleep like that, with the jacket balled-up into a silky pillow. It's not so bad. I loved that bulky, ugly jacket and its satin lining that was coming unstitched and how, if I buried my nose in it, there was the smell of cigarette smoke and Mother's closet. I remember Mother wearing it on autumn mornings at our home up north when I was a little girl. I had to salvage it from one of her Goodwill bags when Mother moved in with Gloria.

Mother had said, "Oh, Abby, give me a break. You don't want to look hippie-dippie." But of course I did. I always wanted to grow my hair long and part it in the middle and wash it infrequently, damn the smell. I wanted small hidden braids and bangles from Marrakesh and old peasant skirts. A wardrobe with stories and scents and spices woven right into the fabric. But that was never me. The fringed jacket was the only bit that suggested I had a life beyond my little street and my little job and my little world.

On the bus, with my head on the jacket, my legs took up the seat next to me and my Kodiaks stuck right out into the aisle when I slept. So anytime anyone made their way to the washroom they knocked by my feet and I'd wake up apologizing. Then I'd retreat into sleep, head vibrating against the Plexiglas window. Look up and you'd see the vibrating Plexiglas moon.

When we rolled up to the San Antonio bus station, the woman in the seat behind me was trying to calm her motion-sick grandchild with an old rhyme about an owl and a pussycat.

The owl brought honey and plenty of money wrapped up in a five-pound note.

I knew it by heart but never once recited it to Joseph. Why.

The woman's voice was low and smooth and soon the child only whined sleepily as he listened to her.

And hand in hand at the edge of the sand they danced by the light of the moon the moon, they danced by the light of the moon ...

We would.

In San Antonio with my tickets crammed into the knapsack, I let the long line of passengers nudge me past the seats and into that hot, rubbery scent of the bus terminal.

There are a few things about a big city bus station. At the station, you can buy a cheap leather flask with a Texas longhorn on it, and fill it with cold beer under the restaurant table, not spilling much. You can brush your teeth with the mineral-tasting water from the faucet in the washroom. In the back booth beside the kitchen door, you can rest your head on a stack of napkins but they'll stick to your face when you sit up as the waitress asks you to please order something or leave the restaurant.

The San Antonio bus station had been waiting for me to come along and lean into its corners. We were meant to meet, that place and me. I liked to sit there listening as numbers were called over the loud speaker in muffled English then in Spanish. I felt closer to Mexico at the bus station and liked how, if I wanted to, I could snake around the building, just following the slow-moving lineups, just merging and moving with all of them, all around and around and right back to a starting point.

Then after a few hours, the southbound bus was ready to take us all away again. On board, I dug around the knapsack for that flask of body-warm beer and I opened the atlas to a page that showed all of southwest Texas, right to the border and down into the northern Mexican states. I ran my finger over the plateau that stood out from the skin of the map like a hive. I traced my finger down to San Antonio, along the flat plains that had been coloured green, even though in reality they're ochre. A couple pages on, Laredo kissed Nuevo Laredo. I loved looking at Mexico: the rumpled ridges of the Sierra Madre range with all its hiding places, craggy terrain, all valleys and plateaus. Where the mountain ranges came together there was a little crescent, a little bay of flatland. It looked like those towns rested in the crook of an arm. I read those city names under my breath, loving the sound of them: Zacatecas, Santa Domingo, San Tirburcio and a very tiny dot delineating San Judas Tadeo. I drew a thumb over that pretty name.

When I tucked away the atlas I took out my plastic I.D. cover to, just for a minute, look at the photo I had tucked inside. Now it was folded and coffee-glued to the inner flap, so I peeled it away with a sticky sound. It was old now. Three years. Taken in the backyard of Gloria's apartment in the summer. Joseph had been swimming in the plastic kiddy pool in fish-like circles, his goggles covering most of his face. He was wrapped in a striped beach towel and was sitting on my lap. He still had the imprint from where the goggles had pressed into his face. I felt bruised all over when I looked at him. In the photo, we were both seated on the folding plastic lounge chair. I could feel the warm, wet weight of him on my lap, I could smell his hair, his sunscreen. I wasn't smiling in the picture and my lips were pressed together in a way that made me look pinched and angry. What stupidity. To worry about crooked teeth. I could have smiled. I should have smiled.

No one took the seat beside me until deep into South Texas. There had been two pit stops along the way; delirious pit stops in the middle of a day's sleep, where the flannel-truckers and leather-bikers did a slow turn to watch the city girl spill sugar into her coffee. You're never fully awake despite the coffee and pure, unfiltered sunshine and you start to forget what time it is, what day. The Texas light persistently told me it was close to noon, just before or just after. I tried to tell with shadows but never knew what direction we were facing. Only the bus knew it was rocketing south.

The bus driver's unlocked hydraulic seat bounced playfully along the highway like a slow-motion pogo stick ride. He glowered at cars that cut him off as he bounced by them, shaking his head. The motion-sick child vomited up his strawberry milkshake and his grandmother stroked his sweaty forehead while he cried. Sometimes, people did beautiful things like that grandmother did. Gentle things. Like an older man sitting near them tried to help by giving his best raspy rendition of *Dock of the Bay* and the child was lulled a little until his voice cracked on the line "watching the ti-ide roll away ..." and the song just faded out into embarrassed humming.

I looked up to see a huge, emaciated man making his way down the aisle, his duffel bag banging into the heads and elbows of sleepy passengers. His arms were so thin the veins looked like tattoos and when he dropped down next to me, the bag released a horrible moldy, wet smell. Trapped. Stretching his feet out under the seat in front and tucking his hands under his armpits, he ground the back of his head into the headrest and fell asleep.

After a few minutes that big scraggly head lolled right over, against my head, and everything inside of me clenched as I sat trying not to think about the smell of the dirty hair that hung in ropes to his neck. I sat thinking about his scalp, wanting my flask but it was just beyond reach. His mouth creaked open at one point and smelled of Doublemint gum. I could see a little wad of it in there. I used my foot to knock the knapsack on its side. One of my socked feet held the bag steady while the other toes clenched and pulled out the under-shirts, the jeans, the underwear. I had to wriggle both my feet into the mouth of the knapsack and toe-scrunch out the flask onto a pile of clothes, which proved pointless. So I rested my palm lightly as I could against the side of his head and tried to ease his head the other way, let his head nod so that his chin rested on his chest where a skinny little paperback book called *Wise Sayings from the East* poked from his shirt pocket. Then I leaned to pick up the flask. I took a few good swigs but it didn't help with sleep.

When he finally did wake up I was lightly pulling at my eyebrows—bored of the landscape—watching the little loose hairs fall onto my T-shirt. He was groaning and stretching. He leaned over me to look out the window and said something like, "Yep. Still Texas. It's always Texas." I didn't want to smile at the guy so I sort of squished my lips together the way you do.

He had these bloodshot blue eyes that looked straight through you, and he said, "You got hairs on you," as he picked them from my shirt and scatted them into the aisle of the bus. I watched the scrub blur by and told him, thanks.

He asked me in a disinterested way where I was headed and I told him South and he said, "Mm-hm. Look at that. South on a south-bound bus." He laughed to himself and nudged me saying, "I'm just fuckin' with you." He scratched his scalp. Eyed my flask.

"Yeah, I'm getting out," he said. "Too hard to live here, man." I supposed he meant America, because then he told me Mexico had everything he needed and it was all "cheaper than dirt." He proceeded to list the market prices of a pound of corn tortillas, three mangoes, two avocadoes, a bag of limes, a 32-ounce *caguamá* of beer, a night on the town, a girl for a night, an endless list as I sat there with my eyebrows half-raised not really taking it all in. As he prattled on, listing the price of a pair of flip-flops, cotton pants, a mini boom box, I unscrewed the cap of my flask and took a swig. Before I realized what I was doing, I'd offered him a drink and he accepted saying, "Salud," before he tilted it back.

He was going to San Judas Tadeo. He told me and tapped a finger on the side of his nose. And when he said that, my heart started thumping in a way that seemed audible. I shifted around in my seat and I'm sure I was flushed at the thought of that town named after my newspaper saint. My weekend edition miracle man. I was short of breath.

I guess he saw something shift in me because he said, "You too?"
I told him yeah. I tried to play it cool.

The guy scratched his head and checked over his shoulder, looked
down the aisle. "Hey, you party?" he asked me. He sniffed a little.
Raised his eyebrows.

I told him no. Not really. And he said, "Hm, too bad." He winked.
That attempt at flirting made me cringe, so I went back to looking
out the window. He shrugged. And then we sat silently until he said,
"Now don't get all uptight, chula. I was just askin'."

"I'm not uptight."

"You from New York?"

When I told him no, he ignored it.

"Everybody's from New York. Fuckin' hate New York. Used to love
it." He spoke in bursts while periodically picking his teeth with a baby
finger. Terrible. But still, he had this unpredictable smile that made
me want to watch him. When he told stories of squatting in the East
Village and Central Park beatings and the things he'd done for dope,
he hollowed right out into bones and wrinkles that made him look
much older than he probably was. He pulled an arm across his chest
and pressed on his elbow like he was stretching. His shoulder popped.

"That's from a cop," he said. He wrinkled up his forehead and
stared at me like he wanted me to ask more, and all I wanted was to
look away from him and that too-naked stare. I passed him the flask.
He passed it back empty.

The bus stopped a couple of hours later in what the guy called The
Badlands. I wasn't sure if it was really called that, and his badly acted
wistfulness made me woozy. The bus stopped not for fuel or food for
the passengers, but because the driver needed a phone in a hurry. She
told us we had ten minutes to get a soda and then after ten minutes
she was leaving with or without us. She threatened us first in English,
then in very rapid Spanish. We'd already stranded a passenger in each
major town we'd stopped in so far, the lure of washrooms and thin,
greasy hamburgers being too much for some people to resist despite

the tight schedule we were on. Just outside San Antonio as we were pulling out of a station stop, a man who'd been sitting at the front of the bus came running from the diner, dropping his paper-bag lunch, waving his arms. I went up and tapped the driver on the shoulder and said, "'Scuse me, we left someone," and the driver just said, "I said five minutes." And that was that. He left his windbreaker all crumpled-up and sad in the empty seat. Somehow that guy managed to catch up with our bus by the time the driver said she needed to make her call. He was boarding again while the skinny guy and I stood at the gravel edge of the parking lot, patting our pockets for a light.

"Your jacket's here," I called to him. "It's on my seat." But he didn't respond.

We lit cigarettes off one of the skinny guy's bendy wax matchsticks and he just dropped the lit match to the dirt at his feet. It was so dry there, so hot, that the match might just burn on and on.

While the guy stomped around in his motorcycle boots, flipping over flat rocks and flicking old bottle caps that had been pressed into the dirt, I took my boots off and peeled my sport socks from my sweaty feet, balled them up and stuffed them in my back pocket. I clenched my toes into the dirt and it made me happy in a small way. Old earth.

The land was stretched out in front of us like some flattened carcass on the side of a highway. There was a scrap wood shack that leaned with the wind and a rusted sign creaking on metal screws, threatening to snap. I watched as a Mexican family with a freshly-napped baby pooled American change to buy an orange soda from the vending machine.

For minutes, the guy and I smoked our bent cigarettes and looked in opposite directions at the same thing—the dry earth bristling with stalks of grass. The land, so anonymous, so ominous, had no imprint. A half-mile away was the dark smudge of a pile of old wood where a house must have stood at one time. One of the boards was jutting skywards against that enormous silky sky and it looked like it might rip right through. Miles to the right and left were post and wire fences claiming identical areas of honey coloured dirt. It made me feel good to think that someone loved this place enough to want to claim it with fences.

A few feet away, two dogs broke from their mating lock and one turned on the other to savage it. The guy whistled and bent to toss a rock to break up the fight. The rock didn't hit the dogs, but they yelped just the same and loped off together toward the leaning shack.

"There snakes out there?" I wanted to know.

"Rattlesnakes," he said, pitching stones. I don't know if it was true. "You probably won't see 'em til dusk. That's when they come out to warm their bellies on the rocks."

I wanted to know what happened if you get bitten.

"Well they say, Once bitten by a snake, she is scared all her life at the sight of a rope." Which told me nothing about whether or not you'd die.

I felt dazed by the heat as we made our way to the bus door. Little bits of broken glass were squelching under foot and even though I walked as carefully as I could, a broken cactus thorn punctured the thick meat of my heel. I must have still been thinking of snakes because I made a noise that was a little too shrill. I pulled out the thorn and tossed it aside as the guy said, "You been bit. You're one of us now, chula."

X.

AND SO THIS WAS MEXICO. There was nothing but a glutinous kind of darkness all around the bus. The sun had gone down behind Nuevo Laredo's corrugated metal rooftops and we pushed into the thick black of desert night, like looking for light—we tunnelled. I was a little sad that there would be no more dead towns and motels with unfamiliar logos glowing and buzzing warm in the middle of the night, motels with names like Hav-a-Nap, E-Z Sleep, and Land of Nod or whatever. For a while, there would be no more rows of gently glowing homes with sleeping children. The desert night came right up and rubbed against the Plexiglas windows of the bus.

That night, except for the oom-pa-pa and looping trumpet of the driver's music, the bus was silent. All the passengers were half-asleep, their heads rocking and drooping in the warmth of our collective breath. Sometime during the night, the guy, Lucky, he called himself, had moved to the back where he stretched out across all the seats beside the washroom, his elbows crossed over his face. I wasn't sure if his name were a joke or a passing whim or what, but I decided I'd call him that anyway, since it was a scrappy dog name that somehow suited him.

I sat up front with the driver so I could watch the road and read the signs.

You could just see a few feet in front, and even less to the side of the highway. The dry, crooked bushes along the roadside were sometimes alive with the mica of flashing eyes.

"What are they, los ojos, the eyes?" I remember asking the bus driver in the first words in Spanish I'd spoken since high school.

And he sort of shrugged and pressed his lips together and said, "Son solo ojos, just eyes."

So when I sat back I imagined that they were the eyes of rattlesnakes, with their black tongues tasting the air, bellies on the slabs of warm rock, or the eyes of children who had been waiting, crouched, to watch the silver bus rocket by.

"Coyote," the driver said, just above a whisper and swerved a little to the left to avoid him. I only caught a glimpse of a man with a bag over his shoulder ducking quickly across the highway and disappearing into the scrub.

Miles then. Dreamless miles.

You do not arrive in Tadeo. You descend into it. And there's trumpet and fanfare on the bus radio, and there's the brushing sound of the feathers of wings from pigeons or angels, and the stars and the streetlights glitter all above you.

Hallelujah. Or something like that.

When the bus rounded the first corner just after five in the morning, Tadeo, below, looked like it had leaked from the cracks in the rounded mountains and pooled around a shadowy-looking cathedral. Past the fence of sharpened cypress trees, the town was moving, breathing. Its hundreds of lights twinkled and coursed.

The driver looped the periphery of the town once, then twice before spiralling down into it. I slipped my fingers out the crack of the window and stroked the face of the air. A draft of spice, cinnamon maybe, blew on my face and I breathed it in and wondered about miracles. Weren't you supposed to smell flowers? Mother always said there was an oratory in Montreal where people left their crutches, hundreds of crutches, and that when they were cured they'd leave the oratory smelling lilacs. She swore up and down it was true.

The bus driver dropped deeper into the valley on the outskirts of town and we bumped by ranches beside dim fields of agave cactus with thick, rubbery skin. Octopuses.

Sometimes there was a single light outside the ranch door or hanging above the chicken coop, but inside the houses were still and dark.

We passed a cantina where some men were singing a drunken, mournful song in unison, and someone was asleep or drunk or dead beneath the barred window. I stared at his body.

I watched as the buildings passed by, squat, like the builders respected all the sky that hung overhead. The walls were all painted or peeling. The bus jounced past torn murals advertising tires, milk, and orange soda.

As we rounded a sharp corner to the terminal, the driver turned on the interior lights and everyone shifted in their seats. Tired and stumbling, they stood up and rustled mesh market bags.

We were here.

All the small blood vessels and thin muscle fibres in my body tightened right up and I thought I'd faint or be sick. This was the bus's final stop. If I wanted to get home again it would be days and I just couldn't stomach the highway anymore. I wanted a bed and narrow streets and a room with a fixed view. No more strangers and drifting cologne and conversations. I wanted the movie to stop.

Before I left, I quickly glanced to the back of the bus to see if Lucky was awake, hoping I could make it out before he saw me. He was stretched out along the back with his shirt up over his eyes to block the bus's grating light. His sunken belly exposed. Look away. Quick.

A man with a chunky silver belt buckle and brown cowboy hat pulled at his guitar case wedged in the luggage compartment above my seat, so I quickly got out of his way into the aisle and he flashed this warm, gold-toothed smile with a gentle, "Gracias" which I stupidly said in return. Sorry, we say in Canada, and in return we say sorry, like we can't think of what else to say.

The passengers filed into the aisle, the old *abuelas* pulling their shawls tightly around their shoulders, one holding a cotton handkerchief over her mouth and nose as she stepped onto the bus platform. Just like Mrs. Commetti, back home. She did the same thing on winter days when she walked to the corner to buy vegetables.

I'd be shovelling snow from the front steps while Joseph's mittens tunnelled into a fort he was building. I'd shout hello to her and ask if she was feeling alright, and Mrs. Commetti would invariably call back through her handkerchief, muffled, her eyes all watery and pink, "The cold air, Abigail. Get inside, your lungs will freeze!" I remember Joseph pausing to look up after she said that the first time. His eyes squinted at me in disbelief and I shook my head to tell him wordlessly that his lungs were fine. He huffed a lung-full of air in front of him. A frozen cloud of it just to be sure.

I took a deep breath and tightened my grip on the knapsack straps and stepped deep into Mexico.

The first thing to do in a new place is look up. It orients you in a way that looking for the exit or the tallest building cannot. I expected those crystalline, cold stars of northern Ontario, but the sky was even blacker here, and the shot-blast of stars seemed stuck and wriggling in it. Around the terminal were trees with feathery leaves, shimmying. Making a hissing kind of noise. And the air was richly scented, hot and dry.

I needed a taxi somewhere, even if I didn't know where that was. Heading to the taxi stand I could hear Lucky just a few paces behind me. He was rambling on in Spanglish to a girl at the concession stand where they seemed to be selling cigarettes, peanuts, and pornographic comics. The girl was laughing, but not too loud. I quickly stepped through the glass doors of the bus terminal.

Inside, there was a small restaurant with a television playing loudly and a mechanical horse for children to ride, and turnstiles to enter the washroom, and a woman sitting on guard to ensure that anyone who entered the washroom had deposited the requisite pesos into the coin slot and had taken a few sheets of toilet paper.

I walked like I knew where I was going and found a line of yellow taxis. My heart felt like it was pumping too much blood, like I was over-oxygenated. I could feel my skin flush as I approached the cabbies who were laughing with their arms folded, leaning against their cars. As I approached, their conversation abruptly ended and the driver popped-open the trunk of his cab. He took my bag from my shoulder, but I wanted to hold onto it.

"It's better," he said in Spanish, with an overly-sympathetic look and he placed my bag gingerly in the middle of the trunk and closed it firmly.

"A centro?" he asked from underneath his neat moustache.

So I told him *si, a centro*, knowing nothing, thinking only of too much air and blood.

A centro. Right in the middle. The perfect place to end up. I'd wander there, *a centro*, until the sun came up and I could go inside a church and say the novena nine times in a row. After that, well fuck, who knew. I didn't know what it was that people did *a centro* during the day anyway, and there was this feeling of panic when I thought about how people filled their empty hours. I patted down my pockets for a light, but realized it was in the trunk. The driver leaned back to help me out. I smoked and figured I would work it all out in the morning. Sleep in the park tonight, under the moon-shadow of a statue of some important person, and he could listen to my sleep talk. He could tell me what to eat for breakfast. What to do all day. Where to find a drink and a payphone. He could be Zapata. He could be San Judas himself.

As the taxi snaked along I quickly realized I could never find my way out. The driver was silent but there was a plaintive love song on his radio and a rosary and a baby's crocheted shoe swung from the mirror, perfectly in time with the music.

Tadeo was a town of walls, a labyrinth cast in adobe and cut from stone. In each block of walls were a few mesquite doors, some nine feet high and studded with metal bolts all in a row, and each door had brass doorknockers in the shapes of cherub faces or a woman's limp hand. I decided then and there that I'd never touch those long brass fingers. I'd knock at doors with my own knuckles, thank you very much. Then the crumbling walls. The bullfight posters all side by side by side, some of them so close to the taxi you could touch them.

I did, scraping my hand and upsetting the driver whose look as he barked "cuidado! cuidado!" told me it wasn't a good idea.

There were hulking statues on the corners of the buildings in the centre of town, I didn't even know what they were, saints or soldiers or gargoyles. There were sleeping dogs on doorsteps, behind fences, and there was a graveyard chained shut with statues of the Virgin of Guadalupe and broken-hearted angels lamenting over tombs. The taxi driver blessed himself whenever we passed a church or graveyard. I chewed at my thumbnail and saw the driver check his mirror to see, maybe, if I'd bless myself too.

We stopped to let a young woman cross in front of us. She was dressed in a simple cotton dress and carried a basket full of white Easter lilies on her back. It was at that moment that I noticed the sun was coming up, because the Easter lilies were faintly glowing orange, and the roosters all over town were crowing to each other from their walled gardens. They sounded like pull-string toys.

"Centro," the driver announced. I didn't want to look at what "here" looked like yet and even thought of telling the driver to forget it. Take me home. But I got out and paid like a normal person, tipped him, and looked up in the orange light to see where it was that the Road to Nowhere had finally dropped me off.

The square was quiet. There was only the shush-shush of a twig broom on the steps of a café, the trill of a few nighttime insects still awake in the trees and my heavy breath.

I'm too alive, I remember thinking.

At the centre of the square was a white gazebo, trees and cobbled pathways with wrought-iron benches spotted with bird droppings. Next was the jail where a young officer stood, one hand casually pulling on a glowing cigarette, the other on a gun hanging from a shoulder strap.

"Pssst" he whispered and when I looked to see what he had to say, he smiled, so I crossed the square past a sleeping dog with raw, hanging nipples, legs jerking from a dream. Asshole, I thought. Let me be a ghost.

Light-headed then, which is better than inertia any day, it felt as if I was wearing clown shoes on huge feet that slapped loudly on the cobblestones. From the cathedral gate, I could see a statue of St. Jude, bearded and messianic, a thorny club at his side. I pushed my face between the bars to get a better look. It wouldn't open for a few hours, so I walked the perimeter looking to slip through a gap. A quick look showed the guard straining to see me. Still, I tried weaseling through a gap where the gate connected to a stone wall. I managed to get a hipbone, a shoulder and an arm through but my skull wouldn't fit. No angle worked. My head even got caught between the bars for one hopeful then panicky moment but it wasn't enough.

With my back to the fence I slid down and had a cigarette, wondering if rolled-up jeans would work as a pillow. Three figures came staggering up the main street to the square. As they got closer you could see two women arm in arm with a man, presumably drunker, trailing behind a little. One of the women was soft and rounded, with white waist-length hair pulled back from her cheeks. When she stumbled, she yanked the arm of her smaller, dark-haired friend, who whooped at each lurch. Then the man jerked to a halt while the women ambled along ahead. He threw his arms up into the air, exposing huge sweat stains on his neat button-down and shouted, "Basta! Good night you ridiculous creatures!" He blew a kiss from his large hand, a gesture the women didn't seem to notice. Smoothing his hair back into a glossy helmet, he turned and disappeared down a one-way street.

Of course they would stop. Of course I was not invisible, though I willed it to be true. The little dark-haired woman asked me in a lilting kind of a voice if I spoke any English, and I don't know why but I just nodded, like speaking to her would somehow draw me in, make me more real, less shadow. Then she asked me if I'd seen two big white poodles around—bushy, she made sure to tell me, no pom-poms, just bushy. The woman was blinking her spiky mascara, waiting for an answer. You could tell she couldn't focus properly and so was opening her eyes extra-wide to compensate.

I just shook my head.

The woman with the white mane began to walk away on her own, wobbly on the cobblestone.

The littler one leaned close to tell me quietly, "Keep an eye out, would you? They're her life. If you see them their names are Cesario and Viola. But call them both 'Vi-vi' otherwise they won't come." She watched her friend's unsteady progress. "We're at the hotel up Golondrinas. No sign, just big red doors." Then she jogged after her friend, everything fluttering and jangling, all batik and cheap silver jewellery.

For some reason I watched them until they turned a corner. I felt a kind of relief when they were out of sight, like I could breathe again.

A newspaper vendor thumped a bound stack of papers onto the curb and counted change from his pockets.

I must have fallen asleep after that, because the last thing I remember seeing was the glossy black birds dive and explode from the sculpted trees, weaving side by side like embroidery thread. Hypnotic and strange. I laid crossways at the foot of the gate so someone would wake me when the church opened. No one did.

When I finally opened my eyes later that morning, I'd slept through the ringing of church bells, the arrival of a draught horse with a cart of ice cream barrels, parishioners as they stepped around me, and the tinny bird-whistles of the balloon salesman.

I awoke that morning to the laughter of a child.

XI.

THE BOY COULDN'T HAVE BEEN more than three years old. He still had all his baby teeth in precise, gleaming little rows, and spit bubbled between them as he stifled his giggles. When I woke up, his little fist was hovering inches from my cheek. The sleeve of his shirt smelled cotton-candy sweet, with that faint underlying scent of sour milk or apple juice—that child smell.

There was a moment before I could get my eyes to focus, before I knew exactly where I was, when I was sure it was Joseph. And it felt like my body was bursting with light. I laughed and sat up quickly from the curl I was in on the church steps and his tiny hand wiggled with a feather-festooned iguana between us. But as quickly as it came the feeling was gone, and I saw that the boy wasn't mine.

"Mira!" Look, he shouted in Spanish, thrusting the iguana close to my nose. "Wake up! "Despiértate!"

He danced the iguana lightly up my arm like a marionette, and onto my shoulder so we were eye to eye. I thought I was about to cry but didn't want to scare the child half to death, so I pretended to rub sleep from my eyes, rub my face into wakefulness. I just smiled and petted the iguana on the nose. That sent the boy into a fit of hysterical laughter, so I did it again, scratching its chin this time too. The little boy laughed and pulled at my sleeve and I wasn't sure where he wanted me to go. He got behind me and pushed my shoulders. As I got to my feet the boy's mother came jogging up the church steps. Her red leather pumps with a rose on each toe clickity-clacking as she approached. She scooped her boy onto a hip, smiling at me, all apologetic, nervous that her boy was bothering me. Her boy pushed the iguana into his mother's face.

"Precioso," I said in my best accent as she gently spoke to her boy under her breath. He's precious, I told her. I felt that my chest was caving in, like before a deep sob that just won't come out. And I stood there probably too long watching them go. They crossed the square to the gazebo where the boy wriggled from her side and ran to a group of little girls in party dresses.

I stare too long. I stand too long. I do not fit.

The square was a new place now in the fierce white mountain-light: there were benches lined with bodies in Sunday clothes, fried tortilla shells glinting with grease piled on newspaper, huge bouquets of coloured balloons that seemed self-propelled until the peddler's head popped into view. A vendor spun through the square on a uni-cycle, forward, backward, whirling foil pinwheels, and his bird whis-tle shrilling from the corner of his mouth. Joseph would like one of those—gold, blue, purple, pink. Which one. He rolled forwards-back-wards-forwards, past a vendor with gourds piled high on his hunched back and they nodded like they knew each other. Another vendor with shoulders slung with thick ropes of garlic and enormous stone rosa-ries settled on a bench with a row of cab drivers. Beside them, a fruit seller filled cups of pineapple wedges, bright mango slices, and husked coconuts lined with fleshy white meat. Wasps swirled and lighted in-side her glass-encased cart and climbed over her hands onto the fruit. She dreamily swatted at them from time to time, her focus somewhere far off in the distance, in the future, or settled into the past.

Everywhere the townspeople sat and chatted on benches, on café steps and low walls, legs swinging, elbows on knees, or legs crossed and tilted, knees politely together. Beneath all the noise of the silver traffic whistle, the tolling bells, the chatter of black birds, there was the ever-present woosh-woosh of the broom from the night before.

The whole thing gave you the feeling that a painted set had been quietly wheeled out while you slept. Like waking up halfway through a ballet.

I'd been sweating in my sleep, overdressed for the morning sun, and I could feel the slow, hot wind cooling my scalp where the tufts of hair lifted up, messy. I could also feel that the button and seams of my jeans had left an impression on the side of my face. I tried to let the air flow under my wet armpits and felt frustrated by my ridiculous body. Small and pale and wet and rumpled.

People leaving the café made me envious. They all had the dozy, satiated look of babies. Like they all needed a nap and it wasn't yet noon. I dug into my knapsack for the flask before remembering that Lucky had emptied it in the Badlands or wherever that scalded place was. We'd passed a cantina on the way into town, but it would be impossible to retrace that route to find a barstool where I could sit and just collect myself a little. Refuel.

Across the square a couple of tourists were building a bouquet of straw flowers from the colourful constellations in the vendor's plastic buckets. The man crouched down and chose a handful of purple blossoms and the vendor helped him release them from the tangle. Then she interspersed them with deep red blossoms and tied their stems together with string, winding them round and round. They paid and looked pleased, then the two of them sat on a bench in the square where the sun filtered through the trees and made lace out of the sunlight and shade. They looked my way, then quickly looked away before I even had a chance to smile at them. For a second I knew exactly what I looked like in my boy-sized T-shirts, my bones and angles. It wasn't what you would want to see on holiday and I didn't blame them for looking away. A holiday was supposed to make you well. On a holiday, you get tan and plump and full, you eat at restaurants and build bouquets and everyone around you should look beautiful. And if not beautiful, at least they should not look so barren.

The gates to the Cathedral had been open for hours, it seemed to me, and the beggar women and the rosary sellers had all sat themselves down along the entrance steps with their wares spread out on scraps of cloth, one of them passing a spit-shine rag over the silver medals she was selling. I watched her rag gobble up the tiny medals and spit them out glinting and polished.

The cathedral bells were tolling a big bronze sound, a warm sound that makes your whole body and the whole atmosphere shudder. I made my way to the statue of St. Jude who, as it turned out, had two deeply drilled holes for pupils that made it look like he was watching you wherever you stood. Even crouching at his feet to look at the little medals pinned there, St. Jude could see you, if only peripherally. I took my time with the little medals held in the dirt with straight pins. Some were tarnished with age and rain. All those separated parts: hearts with veins and ventricles, hundreds of tiny bent limbs, pairs of eyes with eyebrows, silver profiles of cows, chickens, kneeling men, crosses, lungs, angels and children. There were cars, bicycles and hands in prayer. Even a bag of money. As I touched them I wondered if they were things people were waiting for or if they were some kind of thanks for miracles granted. There were dozens on dozens all piled up atop one another with orange and purple strawflowers pinned here and there. I wanted to see if the vendor would sell me a medal to leave there, but she was gone, so I rummaged for my wallet and the photo of Joseph and pulled a silver heart from the hard dirt and skewered the edge of the photo with the pin pushing it, hard and deep, into the soil.

Then the smallest woman with the biggest hump I'd ever seen hobbled up beside me. She wore a belted black dress, her black shawl stretched over her bony shoulders and across her arched spine. She was like standing beside a shadow, a cold draft. I tried not to breathe. The beads of the old woman's wooden rosary stopped moving between her fingers, and slowly she slipped the rosary into the pocket of her dress. Then she leaned to pin a set of small silver lungs into the ground, her hand's blue veins bulging and slipping beneath the skin. Then she sort of stopped and pursed her lips over her gums, staring at the photo of Joseph. From the front of her toothless mouth she asked, "Su hijo?" The words slurped from her lips. I nodded. "My son," I told her. "Yes. Joseph."

The woman smiled and nodded and said something in Spanish that I couldn't understand so I shook my head, confused. "No entiendo. I don't understand" and felt suddenly desperate to know. This shadow-keeper, this spirit woman that somehow, maybe, was bringing me news of Joseph from elsewhere or just around the corner, from her house, some cool bedroom where he lay recuperating, this woman, this shadow, was here to inform me he was coming home.

"With God." Then her hand drifted upwards in explanation, like a dried leaf on the wind. She blessed herself and kissed her thumb. She patted my arm. The woman's lined face creased into a closed-lipped smile. She reached to her collar and tugged at the gold chain that was around her neck. Pulling the chain, she produced a gold locket from the folds of her dress. She pushed the clasp to reveal two photographs that had been cut to fit inside. She held it open for me to see.

"Mi hijo," she said, pointing to the photo of a baby in a lace bonnet, "Y mi esposo," she said, pointing to a photograph of a man in a formal portrait. Half of a wedding photograph.

"Your son and your husband," I said.

"Si." The old woman made the gesture with her hand once again. "With God."

She closed the locket with a click and slipped it back inside her collar. She touched my arm more for balance than out of any kind of tenderness, and she smiled to herself as she turned to amble across the courtyard into some shady spot on a bench under a pepper tree. Once she'd gone, I stooped and took my photo back.

Keep moving.

Weave your way through the mourners on their way into the cathedral. There's quiet there. And cool. When you pass through the brass-studded doors there will be an explosion of grey birds from the building's recesses. At first you will think that there are an infinite number of birds forever exploding in frantic flapping but you'll see, if you pause, if you watch, that the birds only circle and settle. They coo in their hidden nests.

Inside the doors, in the fragrant residue of frankincense and amber, in the woody darkness, I felt hidden. I looked at all the statuettes in glass cases with their doll faces and glass eyes. They bled red paint and wore purple velvet robes. White Jesus wore a razor-sharp crown of real thorns against his plaster forehead, and Mary was chestnut-skinned and held roses in the crook of her arm, her eyes rolled all the way to heaven. Those haunting faces: tiny white teeth exposed, all bleeding and reverent.

Before the mass started I slipped into the confessional booth where I could be alone and it would be muffled and safe. Another hymn. A censer streaming smoke that filtered its way right into the booth. I counted the number of times the congregation sang "Ah-men." Then once it was quiet I sang "Ah-men," to myself in the hush of that confessional, chewing on my thumb. The screen between the confessional booths slid open, and a priest on the other side of the dark muslin said in Spanish, "In the name of the Father, and of the Son, and of the Holy Spirit." So I said it again. Because that's what you do. And I didn't have anything else to say. I sat breathing shallowly through my nose, trying to be silent.

The priest brought his face close to the muslin cloth, so close that it almost grazed the screen between us. He sat back upon his bench and he asked me something, not sure what, calling me "Mi hija," my daughter.

I couldn't reply. That was a strange thing to call me. I listened to the fabric of his frock shift. Maybe he was crossing his knees, getting comfortable. Maybe he would become frustrated with me and kick me out. He waited for an answer and I waited to see what would happen.

"God forgives anyone who asks for His forgiveness." He spoke in English now. In English, his voice seemed softer. "Bueno," he said. "We will pray to Saint Jude for a miracle together, mi hija." I said nothing. So he began this impassioned incantation that unnerved me so much I almost left the confessional. I closed my hand around the wooden seat, held myself fast.

"Oh glorioso Apóstol San Judas Tadeo, discípulo fiel y amigo del Señor de Jesus, te invocamos como Patrono en los casos dificíles y humanamente desesperados. Ruega por mi, pobre picador, a Dios Todopoderoso, pues me allo desesperado por ... su causa?" A question. I was confused.

"What?"

"Your cause, m'hija?"

Of course. "My son."

"El niño de esta mujer, y socórreme, si es para mi provecho, Gloria de Dios y honor tuyo. Te prometo, glorioso San Judas, acordarme siempre de tu protección y hacer lo que pueda para extender to devoción. Amen."

Someone peered through the purple velvet curtain, then apologized. I got to my feet, picked up my knapsack, and held the curtain back for a waddling old woman who sank heavily to the wooden bench, gusting great, exhausted breaths and complaining about the heat.

Outside, bolted to the side of the jailhouse was a pay phone with too many slots and extra buttons. As I fiddled with it, pressing silver keys, listening and hanging up again, a small group of police officers watched from inside the station, laughing and commenting to each other, calling me *flaca*. Skinny. I watched them peripherally.

"Pss-Pss," one of them hissed. "Flaca."

I didn't turn. I wanted to. But I didn't. Three of the guards were standing with gun muzzles pointing at the ground, while two smoked cigarettes on the long wooden bench.

While I dialled, one of the guards flicked the burning butt of his cigarette overhand onto the pants of an officer with a fully automatic rifle. He slapped at the sparks on his pant leg and swore at the others who were laughing.

The telephone hummed in some kind of dial tone. I pressed a sequence of buttons as the diagram indicated. After a moment, a Spanish-speaking operator was on the line trying to connect my collect call to Canada.

Finally, a familiar sound. Dialing in. The sound of the telephone ringing made my heart pump deeper. I lit a cigarette all trembly and clenched while the operator asked me my name.

"Who's calling?"

"Abby."

"Allie?"

"Abby. Abigail."

The phone stopped ringing through.

"Hello."

"You have a collect call from Allie in San Judas Tadeo, do you accept?"

The operator's English was heavily accented and I could tell that it took Mother a moment to understand what the operator had just said.

"Yes, yes." Finally. "Put her through. Oh my God ..."

"Mother, hi."

"Oh thank God. Gloria, it's Abby. Abby, where in the hell are you?" Her voice was hard. There was a long pause before her response, and I could hear two lovers in a crossed connection. The man called the woman *mi amor* and *mi vida*. The woman had a purring kind of voice. The conversation sounded rehearsed.

"I'm on holiday." And I tried to sound all bright and easy. Holiday with a big, cherry-coloured letter H. "Can you hear me alright? Gloria said I should take a holiday. We were talking, so I did. You alright there?"

My mother's voice was ripped tin. "How can you ask that?" It wasn't a question. "I'm out of my mind. More than a week, Abby. I've got no phone call to tell me where you are. I've got no numbers to call. All I know is Gloria gets a call from you to feed the dog and you're on a holiday. So what is all this? You tell me."

Now she sounded so close, so familiar, she could have been talking from the other side of the jailhouse wall.

"Listen." All breezy. "Everything's fine, I'm just ..."

Mother interrupted, which I was glad about because I wasn't sure what to say next.

"Just what. You just decide to disappear?"

Something about that word infuriated me. "No, I did not disappear. I took a necessary trip. It was necessary for me to do this."

"Oh don't bullshit me, Abby."

"This isn't bullshit, Mother. I need to think. And I can't think there. I can't fucking breathe there ..."

She was quiet. I swore and she was quiet. All these years later. I waited for the 'watch your mouth' that didn't come. Silence.

"Mother."

"Where are you?"

"Mexico."

"Mexico? Why Mexico? Who goes to Mexico?"

I told her people like me go to Mexico. Silence. And then: "You know you're not the only one hurting here."

I said I was sorry and a part of me really meant it. Sorry for this, for that, for it, for her, for myself, for everything, everything.

"I know that."

She wasn't finished. "Did it occur to you to call and say: Mother, I'm alive, I'm not in some hotel room cooped up. I'm not in some hospital." Her voice was getting all constricted. "You don't want to know what I've been thinking, Abby."

"I know what you've been thinking," I said before I could stop myself. "What an ugly mess. Look at what an ugly mess she's made and she just up and disappeared."

"You need to get back here and start figuring yourself out."

"Not yet."

"Listen to me. Tell me where you are and I'll come and get you."

"Tell Gloria hello."

"You come back, Abby."

"I can't."

"Abby."

Mother was silent for a moment. You could hear her breathing.

"You would never hurt yourself. You have to promise me that."

"I'm sorry I scared you, Mother. I didn't mean to scare you."

I had to hang up the phone because we just couldn't let it go on like that. Pointless. I just couldn't take any more words and any more worry, and any more talk of the big ugly mess I'd gone and made again.

XII.

I WENT LOOKING FOR a cantina after that. Let's be clear: I needed a place to stay but more immediately I needed something for my nerves and the lightning bolt pills were all gone. So I made turns around buildings that looked like they housed all kinds of stories. You could sense it, like they were whispering to each other. Angels and gargoyles perched everywhere, gazing down with their wings outstretched or folded around themselves. Calico cats sunned their fur on sheets of corrugated metal stacked on the rubble of abandoned homes. Their wild kittens skittered away from under fallen beams as I passed. Sisters, I thought, all of them.

On this street named after swallows, Golondrinas, the rooftop gardens were wild, with small stone icons of saints and birds nesting in the tangles. There, across from a grocery store with a sign painted with ears of corn and eggs in a basket, were the big red double doors the little dark-haired woman had told me about. It was just two storeys high with stone balconies protruding from its façade, balconies crowded with wilting succulents and wild-looking hanging plants. There was a vine of papery bougainvillea up the front doorway and stapled to the double door was a cardboard sign that read Hotel Los Vacios in heavy black print. I think that meant either Hotel Vacancies or Hotel of Gaps. I don't know if there were always vacancies or if that was the name of the hotel: who would call it that? Like everything in this town, utterly confounding. Beside it was a photo of two poodles on which someone had drawn a big black dollar sign and what I assumed was the Spanish word for reward.

I don't know why I did it. I thought maybe it was someplace safe, I guess. It's not that I wanted anything to do with those women. Maybe they'd let me slip into one of their rooms and just disappear and sleep for a while. Maybe they had a glass of gin on the go. Obviously I wasn't thinking clearly and I blame it on everything including the altitude. It fucks with your thinking.

The cherub-face doorknocker made a sharp tac-tac-tac sound resonate from what sounded like an open space behind the door. You could hear the watery sound of birds chirping. No one answered at first, so I pulled the long string that came through a hole in the door and a bright bell sounded.

After a few moments the dark-haired woman unbolted the door and, thank God, she had a punch-pink drink in one hand. She was barefoot with small shells and tarnished bells strung all around her ankles. Her thickly coated eyelashes looked like rubber spider legs.

"Hey ..." she drawled, all dreamy, ushering me into the courtyard and shutting the door behind us. She slammed her rear-end against it with a grunt. "Got to keep the street dogs out," she explained. "You come bringing news?" She took a sip from her cocktail and smacked her lips. She sat the drink down on a stack of birdcages and before I knew what I was doing I told her I might be in town a little while and I was looking for someplace to stay. I didn't even mean to say it.

The woman pursed her lips and made bird noises to the canaries in the cages along the inner walls and the yellow canary in front of her nose made a throaty growling noise.

"I saw the sign outside. Hotel gaps?' I kind of laughed.

The woman stared at the bird and shook her head slowly from side to side.

"Isn't that just about the saddest thing you ever heard in your life? He lived in the market so long he learned how to make traffic noises. I'm trying to teach him to peep or tweet or something."

And then she whistled a delicate little tune and on cue the bird started up his small engine and revved it.

A few moments passed. I stood there wondering about the room. About a drink.

"You want to see him?" she asked me, her eyebrows all arched and excited.

I told her nope. No thanks. Didn't tell her that I don't like birds (they were too frantic) but she was already reaching into the cage and easing her fingers around the canary's wings, shushing it. She had him on her finger, his wrinkled red feet and black claws clenching her skin. All fragile with its thin little bones.

"See now?" the woman said as he bobbed his head from one side to the other. "We're not so bad. No we're not."

Then she handed him to me with her hand over his clipped wings, holding him like an Easter egg. She smiled and something about it reminded me of Joseph's kindergarten teacher.

She made me pet him. She was saying, "Go on, it's alright." And he was delicate. I told her so.

"Yeah!" she said, looking amazed. Widening her eyes she said, "Pet his wings!"

So as lightly as I could, just barely touching him, I stroked the bird's wings. He felt so exposed, like the stalks of his smooth feathers barely concealed his breath and his small red fluttering heart. His wings were folded like a Chinese fan. Like the one I bought for Gloria one Christmas, then kept for myself.

As the woman ushered the bird onto his perch and closed the cage with a twanging sound. The bird mewed. She shrugged her shoulders.

"My friend's always saying—how's it go?—a moment of patience may ward off great disaster, a moment of impatience may ruin a life. Anyway, something like that." And then she blurted: "Hey, sorry. You need a room ..." She squeezed my arm and jangled up the stone steps to the second floor.

Someone was shouting on the second level. It sounded like an argument between two women. As the dark-haired woman entered one of the rooms without knocking, the shouting stopped and some-one came down the stone steps while I lit a cigarette and sat on the edge of the courtyard's splattering fountain. The girl was covered in tattoos, a tapestry, long hair wound in a rat's nest atop her head and the sliced-off sleeves of her Grateful Dead T-shirt revealing the sides of her breasts. Her leather sandals slapped past. Then she turned around to ask if I could spare a smoke, using her hands to mime along with the request. I gave her one, lit it. The girl gave the sign language gesture for thank you.

"You're welcome," I said, trying not to stare at the purple scars on the tender skin of her wrists. Don't look there. Or else you will stare and stare and stare.

"I thought you were German." Her voice was low and distant. "Sue," she said and nodded at me. "You just get here?"

Sue's eyes had the tiniest pupils I had ever seen. A cat in sunlight. Calico sister.

I told her yep. I might stay a day or two.

"Yeah right." She chuckled and coughed wetly into her fist. I must have looked confused because she said, "I came here for a party. That was, like, six months ago." When she laughed she blew out smoke like somebody's grandmother, like the ladies at Dolly's diner who seemed always to have lungs full of smoke no matter how long their sentences ambled on. She dragged on her cigarette. More rings than fingers. She was looking up at the balustrade.

Another young woman had appeared at the top of the staircase, looking like she might belong with Sue. Unlike Sue she looked somehow translucent. Everything about her played with the light. She even wore a long skirt with tiny mirrors sewn all over it. The young Mexican man behind her was all hipbones. Bare chest and leather pants. I felt awkward, looking. Shoeless and thin and watching the girl, he stood there grinning as she hopped onto the ledge of the balustrade and stood, wavering, arms outstretched like a circus tightrope walker. She walked from one end of the balustrade to the other as Sue looked on, indifferently.

"She's going to fall." Again, I had not meant to say anything.

"Naw, she's got angels holding her up."

Sue ground her half-finished cigarette into the grout of the floor and told me she'd see me around. Then the girl hopped down with a ta-da gesture and the young man grabbed her by the waist, swinging her around. She laughed and the two disappeared behind their hotel room door.

I figured I'd leave. This was all a bit too much. Maybe they'd forgotten about me and I could slip out. Just as I hooked my knapsack over my shoulders to leave, they descended the staircase, the little dark-haired woman jingling along beside her friend like a companion dog.

The hotel owner said nothing, wearing a dreamy movie star expression, her chin lifted. As she descended the stairs with her floor length muumuu drifting, she gave the illusion that she was hovering an inch or two above the ground. Her long white hair had been parted in the middle and braided which made me wonder, for some reason, whether she sang opera. I pictured her in a horned helmet.

She gazed too deeply as she introduced herself, this Delilah Bell, seeing too much, peering at me like some kind of fortune teller. I wanted my sunglasses. She said, "I have the honour and, on occasion, the very grave misfortune of calling myself the proprietor of this hotel." She smiled all easy and slow, a little lipstick on her teeth. "Since nineteen seventy-one, which likely reveals all too much about my advanced age." Again she grinned her lipsticked, tea-stained grin. I imagine she'd said the same thing to each of her guests, week in, week out. I wondered if she'd been getting in costume all that time, if the little dark-haired lady had been helping her, misting her throat for her aria, powdering her nose.

"We have one little apartment suite left, small but charming like you. Gas, electricity, hot water when we've got it. Two twenty-five monthly."

"Monthly, no. I'm here a couple days." I got ready to retreat.

"Of course there's week by week and day by day if you prefer to fly by the seat of your underthings." Her laugh was deep and closed-lipped.

I told her it would be just for today, maybe tomorrow, at most the day after that.

And she said, "Let me show you."

Except for the shaft of light shining through the glass balcony door, it was a dim and airless little place. There was a carved mesquite headboard and yellowing mosquito netting pulled to one side of the bed. There was a padded wooden armchair, a gas burner stove, a 1950s-style fridge, and a stainless steel sink with circles rusted into the basin. The putty marks on the wall suggested that there had once been a rectangular mirror there. Smashed, all that remained of it was a shard in the shape of a crescent moon. That was fine.

Down the corridor was a bathroom shared by all the tenants in the rooms along the balustrade. It consisted of a showerhead that drizzled lukewarm water in a thick stream onto the tiled floor and a toilet that looked like an afterthought. When Delilah cranked the taps of the sink, the faucet begrudgingly gave up a few drops.

The little dark-haired woman, Mojo, opened the shutters of a small window behind the toilet, then shut them quickly when they saw a syringe inside an empty bottle of tequila.

"Oops!" she said. "Never mind that."

Delilah grunted as though the whole scene wearied her and she waved it away with her hand.

When I threw my knapsack down on the bed I told her I didn't have pesos but could give her six bucks cash. American. She accepted and I expected her to tuck it between her enormous breasts. But she produced a worn leather wallet and smoothed the money into the billfold.

Alone, finally, I glanced around the room and the first thing I noticed was the dried exoskeleton of a scorpion frozen on the night table. Ridiculously, it made me thirsty just looking at it. I wondered if Mojo and Delilah were drinkers. I took one of the pain pills I brought because the ones to help me sleep were all gone. Only took one-and-a-half pills and thirty minutes or so later, I sank deep into that foreign dust scent of the soft bed. Shrouded by mosquito netting, lying backwards on the bed in bare feet and underwear, I watched as images of mustachioed faces, little boys, and girls with surprised mouths emerged from the grain of the headboard.

The afternoon slipped away in bells ringing and traffic sounds and I dreamed of home. I dreamed of the half-frozen rivers where the missing always surface in the spring. I dreamed that I was waist-deep in water, trying to break ice with my elbow and all around were Joseph's things: his clothes, his books, his toys, all trapped under just an inch of impenetrable ice.

XIII.

YOU KNOW THE FEELING. Everyone knows it. You wake up and you could be anywhere, or anyone. Your whole identity, your whole past and all you've ever been and known and needed is just gone and there's this kind of itchy panic as your mind stumbles around in the dark like a drunk feeling the walls for a light switch. Anything to illuminate the room in which you've found yourself.

I'd kicked and tossed my way around the bed somehow so I was lying crossways on the mattress, feet hanging off. Then the apartment kind of shape-shifted through all the bedrooms I'd ever slept in over the years and I strained to make sense of any of it: the position of the bed, the swinging street lamp outside the balcony door, the furniture. For seconds there, my eyes blurred then refocused on the wooden armchair facing the bed and I swear to God that for several seconds that chair was occupied, taken over by the form of a man. The figure was stiff and still. His body sat sideways but his face, at a sharp angle, was looking directly at mine.

His focus was so fierce that I thought for a minute we were both dead.

He wore white. Of course he did. More a blur than a man. The opposite of shadow.

I tried to rationalize that it could all have been the residue of a dream or a pill, or travel, but I knew better. And once my eyes sorted through the grey static of the room, the armchair was empty.

I clambered from the bed, inhaled and stood motionless, trying to detect the scent of flowers, but no. Dust. Wood. I sat on the crude fabric of the chair and waited for any sensation at all, for the backs of my legs to burn or whatever, eyes rolling back in my head, chattering teeth. Then I just kind of slid onto my knees and put my palms together anyway. I don't know why. Maybe in moments like that you become the child you once were, and I was a child who prayed on my knees and meant it. I whispered: "Go on." I whispered: "show me." I don't know what I expected: the marble face of Jude to emerge from the chasm to envelop me in his mouth, or the enormous thumb of Jesus to press firmly on my head, grinding me into ash.

Instead, the shadow of a moth on the street lantern outside meandered across the slash of light on the wall. And that was it.

Feeling like an idiot, I sat back on my heels and ran my hands over the gooseflesh on my arms, all the little alert hairs. Chewed my thumb. What the fuck. What the fuck was that.

There was a series of knuckle raps at the apartment door. I'd left the deadbolt unlocked and as the door opened a crack I pulled on my dirty jeans from the heap on the floor. That kitteny voice said, cooing, "You alive in there?"

"Just a minute."

"I'm not going to bother you," she said. And I didn't believe her, not a bit. "I just brought you something."

I saw her arm stretch through the door, stack of bangles, as she slid a plate along the tile.

"Fruit plate," she said, like it was what one expected on a holiday. Fruit plate. "I was going to leave you alone." She said this with her mouth at the crack of the door. "But I know what it's like when you first get here. It's all a little bewildering. I don't know if that's the right word."

I smiled but she didn't see it. And I wanted her to go.

She told me she "had to split" and I was glad. So I thanked her and she quietly closed the door and after she'd gone I slid under the wool of the blankets and slept.

A day passed.

Time went something like this: I'd take the plate of green and yellow and orange fruit from the floor and think about eating it. Those overripe mangoes, peeled and slippery and naked, they turned out to be so punishingly sweet. I'd eat stubby plantains cross-legged on the kitchenette floor in my underwear and socks and T-shirt. The sun would move over the tops of the buildings and make these different, beautiful shadows on the apartment floor. I'd sleep and wake. Ignore noises in the corridor. What was left of the fruit on the plate drew a fly and dried out, puckered a little. I watched the fly rub its hands together and eat.

Knuckle-raps at the door. Bangles-and-eyelashes kept turning up there clacking and blinking through the peephole, wanting one thing or another: did I have bottled water, her pen's out of ink, could I button the top button on the back of her jumpsuit. Then my raggedy thumbs on that tiny batik loop and her holding up all her curls. God, it was all so awkward.

"I'm going out." Triumphant, bathed in perfume.

"Oh yeah?" It felt rude not to ask where.

"Thing is, you always just dress up in the same outfit for the same people so we can tell each other the same stories. Anyways, beats being alone." She dropped her curls.

"Hey, come with." She shook my wrist.

"I'm so tired," I said, lying. And I think she knew it.

"One drink," she said. My magic words, my charm. "Don't make me listen to Delilah tell me one more story I've heard a million times."

"Okay," I said.

Bangles-and-eyelashes clapped her hands together.

After I turned off the light and pulled the door almost closed, I quickly peeked through the crack toward the vacant chair by the bed. Nothing. The streetlight swung a diagonal pattern across the empty seat.

We walked for six or seven blocks, past the cathedral where Jude guarded his tiny miracles into a part of town I hadn't seen yet, turning onto a narrow street where the cobblestone just ended like they'd run out of them and the road became hard-packed dirt. She told me her real name was Marjorie but that no one had called her that since high school. Everyone called her "Mojo" so I could too. I didn't want to tell her my name but I did. I did because I couldn't come up with another name on the spot, like with the car. My imagination for that sort of thing had just disappeared.

"Buddy came up with it. I was just a kid and he was introducing me all around saying this is my girl Mojo and I thought I'd just about die. Like, swoon."

"Who's Buddy?"

"My old man."

As we came up to the swinging half-doors of the Toro Rojo a young man splashed yellow vomit into the gutter. One of his friends clapped him on the back and laughed at his misfortune. There was the sound of ranchero music blaring from a jukebox, the sound of people shouting and whistling and the clattering of bottles on full trays. A not wholly unfamiliar sound but a little more silvery, a little more decked-out, like with more *conchos* and leather. I felt my salivary glands twinge as I thought about having a shot of tequila, the taste of lime and salt if they even did it that way here.

Mojo ushered me past the vomiting man, yelling, "Híjole, Carlos! Get a bucket, man!" The light in the cantina was so glaringly bright, so fluorescent, that it revealed pock marks on faces, the oily lines of sparkly eye-shadow caked in eye creases and the sweaty pores of drunks.

Most of the men wore plaid shirts tucked evenly into their ironed blue jeans. Some of them wore oversized silver belt buckles embossed with spurs and cow skulls and old pesos. Desert hippies, with their wild hair wound up in coloured string and snake spine necklaces around their thin throats, stood out in the crowd. They slouched and drank with each other, casting dubious glances around the room. One, who must have been six or seven months pregnant, awkwardly got up from where she'd been sitting cross-legged on that sticky floor, her friend pushing on her butt to help her stand. She took a drag off a cigarette, and went over to the jukebox where she languorously swayed back and forth, one hand under her belly. When the Eagles song *Hotel California* crackled over the speakers and a couple of them looked to the jukebox nodding in approval.

Mojo took me by the arm and dragged me deeper into the humid room. At the centre of the commotion, a man was aboard a red vinyl mechanical bull. Just the beast's back and shoulders. It looked like the head had been lopped off. No tail. And his legs had been replaced with one thick, greasy looking hydraulic shaft. Mojo brought me in closer to watch the rider. He seemed stuck to the bull, like he'd been sewn on. No amount of jerking and twisting would dislodge this guy.

A table of people waved Mojo over. As she manoeuvred through the crowd she would pat her hand on the backs of most of the patrons who stood waiting for a drink. When she did, they'd turn around, kiss her cheek or embrace her, muss her hair, squeeze her shoulders or whatever. Even the bartender gave her a wink and a nod.

The group was seated at a folding card table with a scattering of dominoes and empty shot glasses with sucked and pitted limes stuffed inside. Lucky was there but didn't seem to notice me, as he was carefully constructing a multi-tiered pyramid of sticky shot glasses. Delilah was seated off to one side with her thick legs propped up on a folding metal chair. She gave me a vague look of recognition when she nodded hello. She looked droopy, and her braids were coming unraveled. To her right was a boxy man with sweating underarms and gold rings on his fingers. He was absentmindedly tracing the ear of the young man sitting next to him. While Mojo introduced the rest of the group, I kept looking back to that young man. So beautiful. His was the only name I heard in the introductions. This was Ilario Tristán from Tlacotalpan. All almond eyes and soft, wavy black hair. I found myself saying his name over and over in my mind, Ilario, Ilario. Eel-arr-eeyo. A gentle cleft in his chin, lightly bristled. The feminine lines of his facial bones, the subtle sulk of his mouth and dark arch of eyebrows. He was so small against the man who fawned over him, touching the edges of his curls, passing him a cigarette for a drag. He seemed to live more slowly than the others. While everyone around him fiddled and itched and swigged, he lived in the still moments between their frantic movements. When he heard my name, which was suddenly a stubborn, ugly name, his eyes crinkled at the edges and he smiled at me. I wanted to sit by him.

Ilario. Name like a sailboat. Name like a single cloud drifting.

Mojo wiggled a folding chair in between Delilah and the sweating man called Luis Reynosa. I found that out quickly because he often spoke about himself in third person.

"Come on, Luis, get it together," he'd say, rubbing his hands together. Or, "Okay, believe me, Luis Reynosa is a man of his word." Mojo gave the man a bear hug, her arms barely fitting around his large shoulders, and when they parted, Luis looked ruffled and red-faced and he smoothed his thinning silver hair back in place. A moment later, still using his wet palm on his skull, he left for the bathroom.

I sat in the open space between Ilario and the two very young, very stoned hippie girls from the hotel. Mojo introduced them as "Vula 'n' Sue," and even though Sue's eyes were closed, she bobbed her head at the mention of her name. We'd met but she wouldn't know that. Vula made a sipping sound on the smoke she was pulling from the joint between her fingers. She offered it to me under the ledge of the table, croaking out the word "hash" as she did. Right there with two *federales* on barstools not five feet away. No fucking way. I shook my head. Vula just grinned big and shrugged her shoulders. Lucky had finished his pyramid of shot glasses and told me I was on the "right tour" to find myself at the Toro on my second day in town. He called me *chula* again, and I wasn't sure what that meant and wasn't sure I wanted to know. It sounded sticky and sweet. He kept unfolding his pretty smile under those sun-parched lips and poured the two of us something that looked like it had come from the stomach of a cat.

"You tried pulque?" he asked me, holding it loosely between his thumb and his index finger.

I told him no.

He handed me the shot. "Well, chula, here's to lost causes."

I put the thick glass to my mouth and threw my head back, the thick shot splashing against my palate and sliding in that familiar hot way down my throat. For a moment, eyes closed, I was deep inside that sensation of warm fingers rubbing spirals all the way down my throat to my ribs. God, I needed it.

"Thank you," I said, more to the drink than to Lucky.

"Well alright." Lucky looked on in approval as I downed another one from the half-empty bottle in front of him. He had the expectant look of a child at the petting zoo, wondering how many handfuls of corn the billy goat would eat. Again, I briefly rested the smudgy glass against my lip and tilted back with a tip of the wrist and the shot was gone.

I should have known it was going to be one of those nights.

They looked like the kind of people who wouldn't mind. Delilah was so drunk that both her eyes were settling in ever so slightly different directions so it was unclear who she was talking to.

I poured myself two shots. By this point Luis had returned from the bathroom with his hair looking like it had been freshly raked with a comb and tap water.

"Have you ever tried that before?" he said, wrinkling his brow up. I just shook my head because I was afraid that if I opened my mouth to speak I might gag.

"The ancients used to give it to their sacrificial victims. They thought it would ease the transition into the next life." Luis smiled cheekily. "So welcome to San Judas Tadeo," he said. "And watch your neck." He mimed slitting his throat, with a loud "zzzzzzziip!" and laughed.

The night slid along. Luis didn't seem to mind Lucky running up his bar tab. I drank straight tequila Lucky brought me from the bar, gold and lukewarm, and then a cheap mescal that burned my throat as I swallowed it. You could feel it in your stomach for minutes afterwards, like it was churning with burrs. Each time, Lucky would hand me the shot with a boisterous "Salud!" before lurching once more through the crowd to feed the jukebox and flirt with underage

Chilean girls backpacking through the high desert on their way back to Mexico City.

I felt my focus loosen. Scanned the bar for something plain and bland enough to tamp down nausea. Sweating faces made my stomach roll.

Ilario. I watched him sip a beer, stub out a cigarette. A guitarist's hands. Then he got up and I lost sight of him. I tried desperately not to look at the mechanical bull, the violent swinging of its riders, but I couldn't help myself. How could you not when every ten minutes or so one drunk or another would mount the bull to all that jeering and laughter and shouts. The man at the controls, the boy, really, with that thin pubescent moustache, rocked the bull slowly at first, then he started the gyrations, the twisting, the bucking. As the rider's floppy body gave in to the movement of the bull, it would speed up until finally the machine was heaving and jerking in spasms. The body on its back would snap at the neck and turn around and around. I thought about how it would feel to be whipping past those grinning faces and finally falling to the ground, outside the padded ring. Hoisted up at the armpits, dusted off, brought by the crook of an elbow around the neck to a shot of tequila, on the house. Grins. Eye-wiping laughter. Back slapping.

When a woman boarded the bull the crowd whooped and whistled and brought their drinks ringside for the show. There, with legs wrapped around the barrel of it, one hand slipped firmly under the frayed rope at the neck, she waited to prove herself to the men in the cantina. But each time, the operator would alternate between slow, dipping movements and a steady bounce that would make her breasts and belly jiggle and her face flush red. Some riders would shout angrily at the guy running the machine, violently motioning for him to speed up the ride, but others just endured the humiliation only to slip off the bull when the ride was over and retreat to their table of friends.

I watched, staying as still as I could, avoiding conversation. I closed my eyes to block out the swinging of the bull then opened them out of curiosity when the crowd whistled. My elbow met Ilario's on the tabletop. He leaned in close and took a sniff of my empty shot glass.

"Smells poisonous," he said and smiled. He wrapped his lips around a clear beer bottle and drank, his eyes flitting away. Luis slid a hand down Ilario's thigh and stared deeply at me in drunken assessment.

"You're pretty," Luis said glumly.

"I'm going to get some water," I said, more to myself than him. As I got up from the table I heard Luis call after me, "Careful! There's sharks in the water."

I took a barstool beside a woman who was sitting alone. She looked comfortable there. Happy in her stupor. I stared at the woman's long, false fingernails. They had miniature designs on them. Stars. She fanned herself with a pleated napkin and I wondered if it really cooled her or if she was just showing off. Like a peacock.

When I ordered a bottle of water the woman sighed, expelling a gust of wine. Her mouth had lines that turned down at the corners, like she'd frowned for a year straight. All rubbery. When I learned, while drinking my water, that her name was Rubia, I was glad. I'd be able to remember that. Rubbery Rubia. Everything about her was rubbery: she moved without bones, her pushed-up wrinkly breasts, her elastic mouth.

Rubia folded her fingernails into a fist and leaned onto it sighing, "I'm so bored." She sat staring straight ahead into the mirror behind the bottles. I said nothing.

"Tell me something new," the woman said after a moment. She looked at me from underneath a peeling false lash.

"I just got here," I said. Like nothing had happened yet.

Rubia just stared at me, expressionless. "So what. So did everybody. Just get here." And she took a rubbery sip from her drink leaving a fuchsia stain on the glass.

"Make up something. Make it interesting."

What do you say? I thought I could tell her about how the car had died in a field of wind turbines, but she probably wouldn't care. She'd probably say 'so what, so does everybody's car. Die in a field of wind turbines.'

"I'm waiting," she said, chin still on fist. Her eyes were droopy, sad with boredom.

"I think I saw a saint in my hotel room," I said because I was drunk and she was staring and maybe I did see a saint and who would I tell but Rubia. I could tell Rubia.

Her face was long and limp. Then she laughed. A hearty back-clapping kind of a laugh.

"Yeah?" she said.

"Mm-hm," I said and couldn't help but smile along with her.

Rubia laughed hard and when she finally stopped she proclaimed, "I like you. You're crazy." And she asked me, "So what about your saint. Did he say anything to you? Did he make love to you in your hotel room?"

"No."

"Oh." Rubia seemed disappointed. She pulled a Chiclet from the cellophane packet on the bar and chewed it slowly, cow-like. Offered me one.

"You have a boyfriend?"

"No."

"Girlfriend?" She smiled playfully, showing a gold tooth.

"No."

Rubia squinted, thinking. "I have so many. So many boyfriends." She held up a finger. "I have hundreds of boyfriends but I love one."

I asked her what he was like. "Famous! Like an American movie star."

"An American?"

"Yes. Like James Dean."

I leaned on my elbows and asked her if she wanted to marry him.

"Like Richard Burton," she said. She chewed her Chiclet then removed it from her mouth and stuck it under the bar. "No, I don't marry him because he dies."

"No."

"Yes. My parents don't like him. They think ..." She grimaced to illustrate what they thought of him. "But he decides he is going to marry me. To take me away. So he takes a bottle of mescal, for fuerza, to be strong, and he starts walking to my hometown along the tracks. But he dies on the way."

I needed to know. "Was he hit?"

"No. There is no train anymore. Not since the silver mines close. He just falls asleep in the rain and he drowns."

"He drowned?"

"Yes, drowned. Drinking and he falls asleep. Maybe his mouth is open."

So we finished our drinks silently, mostly, maybe exchanging little comments as we slouched side by side. Telling stories without endings until I felt a little less dizzy and ready to go. Mojo and Lucky were ready to leave, so Mojo linked her arm in mine while Lucky and the bull operator tried to convince me to ride the bull before we left. I shook my head at them both and left the table without saying goodnight to the others.

Outside on the corner was a teenager with what looked like a car battery on a black strap around his neck. He held the battery's two cables, one in each hand, and called out to every man leaving through the swinging doors "Toques! Diez pesos, diez pesos," and something about testing their strength and impressing the ladies. I stopped to watch him hook up a group of young Mexican tourists, hand in hand, on the deserted street. A jolt of electricity passed between them. Their eyes went wide almost in unison, quick as dominoes toppling. Laughter. Shouts.

Lucky, Mojo and I made our way up the incline toward the cathedral, Lucky barking at the guard dogs that lunged at him from the flat rooftops overhead. Where were these dogs by day?

"Bow wow wow!" he shouted back, in a not-so-bad imitation.

A red pickup truck with iridescent tinting on the back window passed by and Lucky sprinted to catch up with it. Mojo took my hand and we stumbled after him while she explained, panting, that we were going to hitch a ride.

"You just jump on the back," she said all breathlessly as the truck slowed a little. "The kids do it all the time. Nobody minds."

Lucky was already on the back-bumper climbing over the mesh tailgate into the truck's flatbed. He shouted for us to hurry it up as the driver punched playfully, rhythmically, on his horn.

Mojo clamped her hands onto the back of the truck and bounced up on one foot and onto the back bumper, so that's what I did too. Just like her, even though my head was spinning, and I could barely feel my feet beneath me, and it felt so good and free to be like that. The night air and buildings rushing by. I felt like I no longer existed. Cathedral steeples whizzed past, the palms and the stars and the cypress trees all swimming together as I leaned back beside Mojo. That crystal studded sky. I didn't care where the truck was taking us, didn't care that my eyes made all the starlight bleed together. We vibrated and we jostled up against shovels, spades, and suddenly Lucky got up and stepped over the tailgate and let go, running for a moment then slowing to his long-legged stroll. He saluted the truck, then waved it off like he was telling it to go to hell.

"Ready, Abby?" Mojo positioned herself on the back bumper, hands clenched around the edge of the truck. So I mimicked her as best I could and Mojo said, no pause in between the words, "Ready go!" And I flipped my feet from the bumper but held on just a moment, just one single moment too long.

From the placement and thickness of my scabs I later determined that I landed on my palms, elbows, knees, chin, likely all at once, maybe a kind of belly flop, and must have skidded a foot or so, ending with my cheek on the ground. The scabs were thick and meaty for the next few weeks, and although the wounds were cleaned, they still became slightly infected. When they softened in the shower they oozed this stringy yellow pus.

There's no memory of hitting the ground. No memory of the truck taking off or Mojo hoisting me up or the neighbour-nurse across the street swabbing my cuts with iodine in the vague cat piss smell of

Mojo's apartment. I don't remember dreaming that night or asking Mojo if she'd hold my hand or telling her I was scared. I don't remember any of that crazy shit. All I know is that when I woke up the next morning Mojo's tabby cat was licking at splashes of vomit on the soft skin between my bare toes.

XIV.

I AM NOT A blackout drinker. My nights do not disappear. They are sometimes patchy and missing bits, but not often, not so often that I should worry. So there is the smell of iodine, a crocheted throw, and a cat with a sandpaper tongue. Then the clear morning hours, dipped in gold light, a stick of cedar incense clouding the room with smoke, the smell of it lingering in the folds of the throw. Shadows of Mojo coming in and out of focus. I knew I'd really fucked myself up bad this time, is all. I gave my brain a good rattle.

Noon came closer, all bright-faced and gleaming through the balcony doors and I tried hard to stay lucid, but was too tired to put up a good fight against sleep. I'd wake for bits of conversation I forced myself to have out of, what, politeness or duty or something. I'd rest my eyes. Just for a moment. And when I'd open them again Mojo would be telling me to try some water, have some soup. So embarrassing to be that out of it. I rearranged myself on my elbows on the sofa and told myself to stay awake. I fell asleep one time just after I heard Mojo ask, "What you been through, Abby?"

I must have been crying in my sleep, because the sofa pillow was wet and it wasn't blood. It was like time was hiccupping and burping, giving glimpses of the next few days and hours and then dragging me back to Toronto where it was always mid-winter and Joseph's bedroom was always empty.

Sometimes there was this buzzing sound blazing through my head like a supersonic bumblebee. Like something charged and electric was navigating the contours of my brain. Then it would hum all the way through me and let everything just drift away again, slow and soothing. I was worried that the pills were doing it. Thought about flushing them down the toilet.

In the early afternoon, sick to my stomach, my scrapes tightening as they dried, I fully came to. Propped on elbows with the throw bundled under my knees, I squinted around the too-bright apartment and I saw Mojo's feet first. She was on her back on the floor with her splayed, unshaven legs pressed into a V against the wall. A long rope of sandalwood beads was wrapped several times around her neck and fell beside her shoulder onto the floor.

"Mmm, nothing like a good stretch in the morning, right Nefertiti?"

Mojo's cat was licking the yellow vomit that had dried in splotches on my bare feet. The cat's ears were half-folded, her eyes were slitted, and she purred. I leaned down to pick her up but she scrambled away and leapt onto the coffee table.

"I'm so sorry I made such a mess of your place."

There were yellow stains all over the crocheted throw she'd put over me. One of the pillows was streaked with browning blood.

Mojo kind of rolled over. "Hey listen, as far as houseguests go, you're one of my better ones. You kidding me? I had this guy named Don, Don Juan we called him, anyway he left a tooth in my sink and his dirty underwear in the refrigerator."

"Thank you for helping me." I meant it and she didn't have to. "I'm so sorry."

Mojo was up and thudding on her heels around the kitchenette.

"Oh man, you went right out for a minute. Scared the shit out of us! And then when you came around you kept upchucking, sitting down, you took off your shoes ..."

I repeated my apology and pressed my fingers into the corners of my eyes because it felt good.

Mojo brought over some leafy concoction that we had to strain with spoons into these hand-thrown coffee mugs. Nerve tea she called it. Catnip and hibiscus flower or some shit like that. She said it was restorative, which is a touchy-feely word that made me queasy all over

again so I tried not to think about where she procured the tea, some
stinking apothecary with glass jars and roots like shrunken limbs.

Canned Heat was on the record player. Mojo asked if I minded.
I didn't.

I pressed the corners of the surgical tape onto my skin.

"Ines did that." Mojo sipped from her mug. "The gauze and everything. She's across the street. She came right outside with her iodine
and her kit. She knows, she's a nurse. Plus she's got a bunch of little
kids."

I vaguely recalled a woman's voice speaking in Spanish, calm
and hoarse with sleep, and the sight of an official-looking black bag.
Someone, must have been Ines, gave me a kind of exam, bending my
joints, pressing beside swellings.

Mojo slung the tabby cat over her shoulder and sat on the hammock swing that hung from the middle of her ceiling, facing the balcony doors. Her bottom pushed through the heavy mesh in diamond
shapes. She swung back and forth lightly, talking quietly to the cat,
her dirty feet brushing against the tiled floor. She looked over her
shoulder and smiled at me once, then just kept swinging. It was like
I was hers now. Another potted plant, another cat, another friend.

"You know, you've been so great, I should go," I said, trying to fold
up the throw.

She turned to me like she didn't even hear me and asked, "So why
you here, Abby?" And I asked her what she meant.

"Why'd you come all this way on your own?" She was shifting her
feet around so that the hammock twisted to face me. "I mean, let's
be honest. Everyone around here is either running to something or
running from something. Everybody's got an idea about you already.
Luis says you're a lesbian and don't know it yet, and Ilario says you're
leaving a bad marriage, Delilah thinks you've got a gambling problem
but I think they're all wrong."

I didn't know what to say. I searched my pockets for cigarettes
and they weren't there so I sat back down, struck mute for a moment.

"What do you think?" I asked, shrugging, feeling more injured by their gossip than maybe I should have.

"Grief." Mojo wasn't smiling anymore. That greasy, flat, flapping word.

I picked up a butt from the overflowing ashtray and lit it. "I just needed a holiday."

Mojo nodded. "Oh." I could tell she didn't believe me.

My joints were aching as I gathered myself up from the couch saying I'd like to go lie down awhile and I'd see Mojo later and thank you and sorry and all of that. "Don't sweat it." She started to prune the dried leaves of her potted plants as I pulled on my boots. Scooping two handfuls of them, yellowed and crumpled, and threw them from her balcony. The wind caught them and they flew from her hands like moths. Mojo peered over the railing and shouted a greeting in Spanish. She waved her hand hello, bracelets clinking. I could hear the woman down below on the street, faintly. She was calling up to see if everything was alright with the *flaca*, the skinny girl. Mojo laughed and shouted back that everything was fine and Abby was just *crudo* and pretty sore.

She waved again and pulled the balcony doors closed behind her. Still laughing a little to herself. "Does crudo mean rude?" I asked then regretted asking.

Mojo laughed. "No hung-over, wiped out." Of course it did.

So she sent me on my way without a hug, just a soft palm on my good cheek and a loosely rolled joint and a book about plants indigenous to Mexico's high desert.

I lay propped up in bed smoking the joint and flipping through the colour photos of cacti and jacaranda trees, ludicrously purple in their Easter blooms. I decided I should stay just one more night here at the *posada*. I would leave just as soon as the swelling went down.

That evening, I heard pistols and a parade of horses coming down the street and at first I thought it was a revolution so I pulled on my boots and tucked my buck knife into my back pocket, shaking with adrenaline.

Out on the balcony, with the sun in a crook between the cobble-stone and the cornerstone of the old monastery, the street glowed orange and the horses were all snorting and spirited. I had my back against the building, like to be safe. One of the horses was skittish and raised its whinnying muzzle, opening its mouth against the bit as he passed. Its rider wheeled him around in a tight circle and proceeded past the hotel, past the parked cars.

Ines and her children squeezed in behind the barred window of their house across the street, and in minutes the three youngest were there sitting on the sidewalk as the cavalcade went by and fear flooded my limbs. Those kids. Ines stood calmly by as they chattered and waved enthusiastically at the riders.

I guess Mojo wanted in on the action because there she was on her balcony, too.

"What's going on?"

Mojo whistled with her fingers. "A cavalcade! It's for Pancho Villa!"

The horses seemed to feel the elation, the spirit of pride and rev-elry in the air. Somebody threw a handful of miniature firecrackers on a side street from an upstairs window and several of the horses bolted at once. The men shouted and laughed at each other. Sweat lathered out from under the saddles and the bridles. "¡Viva la revolución!"

Soon, you could hear the faint clopping of the hundreds of hooves way off down the road. I closed the balcony doors and waited for the prickly adrenaline to leave my blood so I could try to fall asleep on top of the covers, bloody bandages and all.

I was sleeping more and more, it seemed. Maybe to make up for all those lost nights in the winter. Maybe just for glimpses of Joseph.

This time, Joseph was on the telephone but he wasn't speaking. I could hear him breathing. I could feel him. I said his name again and again, begging him to speak.

Please say something baby, please.

I was saying I was so sorry, so sorry for everything I'd done, for failing him, for losing him. And finally he spoke to me. "Come get me, Mom. I'm waiting." But I had no idea where to find him.

XV.

THERE COMES A POINT when you've got to call home. You're kidding yourself if you think they're not wondering about you, worrying about you. Sick with worry is what Mother would say, after all the time that's passed. Sick with worry. So you aim to make it brief and not let on where you are, hoping the church bells won't ring or there won't be any mayoral candidates rolling by in those vans with the speaker system bellowing—as if these things might magically reveal your exact whereabouts in a country as vast as Mexico.

I waited there for the phone outside the jailhouse with its cigarette-smoking guards and its tourist in the Panama hat going on angrily about a late money order. Just over there was a cowboy with crooked legs. He was selling sunflower seeds in little bags in a basket, right outside the cathedral gates where townspeople passed and they would drop a few pesos into his hand and he'd pat a pack of seeds into theirs.

The tourist on the telephone said that yes, he would hold, and he inserted a new fifty-peso phone card into the telephone. So I crossed the square to where that leathery cowboy stood and bought myself a pack of seeds he said were *muy sabroso*, very tasty, very good. He had a gold tooth that glinted in the dark cavern of his mouth when he spoke and he had deep-set eyes just like Jude.

They were good, those little seeds. I ate them while I waited, watching the group of schoolgirls in green tartan skirts and knee socks sitting around on benches while boys with poor adolescent posture chatted with them. I sat in the churchyard with them and no one noticed or cared. I ate my seeds on the edge of Jude's sculpture and I tried to pray the novena but couldn't remember it right. So I thought this instead: bring him home. I don't know how else to say it. And I promised all kinds of crazy shit in return. I promised Jude or God or the saints of scrawny suicides or all of them together that there would be no more drunken nights, no more tobacco, no pills. Done. I was done, and I meant it. I would be healthy and normal. I would get real. A ready mother. A better mother. I would be careful. Sleep early. Rise early. Spend the days walking, praying, looking, listening, learning from the routines of the graceful old women in their grieving clothes and the beggars with thin, chalky legs, and the devout who blessed themselves every time they passed a cross.

It would start with a responsible phone call.

The phone was finally free. The tourist left a pencil sketch on a wall of the metal booth, a woman's lips. When I dialed the operator, I was struggling to remember Gloria's number. I don't know, maybe the fall from the truck had scrambled all my digits. My head, I remember, was aching in the resolute afternoon sunlight but if you stood tight against the jailhouse there were cool shadows, so I pressed up against the wall.

The conversation wasn't as brief as I thought it would be and mainly consisted of Gloria asking me questions and after each question saying 'Jesus Christ, Abby!' I tried to get her to talk about the tavern, like who was being rowdy, who'd been kicked out for the last time. I asked about Mother, about Seymour since she had him now.

"Listen to me, this is nutso! This doesn't feel safe. Jesus Christ, Abby! You're in Mexico? Why wouldn't you fly?"

I told her I couldn't help it. I had to keep going and that's where I ended up. It's something she does to me—I'm suddenly eight years old and spilling my guts to my big sister.

"You were the one always telling me to get away and do what I need to do and all that shit, Gloria. So what I needed to do was leave. And that's what I've done. And I really don't know how long I'm going to be here or if I'm going to stay here or keep going or what, but my car's dead, so I guess I'll have to take the bus home eventually."

"Eventually?"

"I don't know. Soon."

"Did you even pay rent?"

"No. I will. I'll mail it."

I could hear Gloria covering the mouthpiece of the telephone. She was talking to Mother. So obvious. Then she passed the phone to her just as I was saying "don't."

Mother's voice was fast and firm. "I'm coming down there." Like Mexico was some basement TV room I was holed-up in.

I could have sworn I heard her closing the clasp of her purse and putting her arms through the sleeves of her spring jacket.

"Don't you go anywhere," she said. "I'm coming. What's the name of the city, Judas something?"

"Mother, that's ridiculous. I'm hanging up."

"Don't you hang up on me. Don't you dare hang up on me."

"Fine," I said. "What."

"I'm not going to live like this."

"You're making this into a crisis, Mother, and it's not."

"Prove it. Come home."

"Not yet."

"Then I'll bring you home."

By that point I was quiet and had started to shake. I could hear Gloria going on saying Ma, you can't do that, with what money, Ma?

"I'm hanging up." And I meant it. I heard Gloria say my name.

"Don't do that again! Don't put Mother on. Fuck, Gloria!"

"She's giving you a week," Gloria said. "She's serious, Abby."

"Well then she's crazier than I am. I'm hanging up. I just called to let you know what was happening, that's all, alright?"

Gloria was quiet. "Don't be crazy."

"I'll see you soon, Gloria, okay? You keep good." And I hung up the phone and could imagine their voices still dangling along those wires, strung up over Texas. I thought of all the things Mother and Gloria would say to each other once they'd hung up. Gloria would pick up the phone again to make sure I wasn't still there and she'd say something like She doesn't sound good and Mother would say I'm giving her a week. They'd be shaking their heads at each other. Taking big, deep breaths. Sighing. It made me crawl all over to think about it.

I suddenly felt the need for either a shot of vodka or to walk until my feet were blistered raw. Feet in heavy boots, abraded knees bending, a head-pounding kind of penance nobody else gets to see. Nothing showy: something secret like a hair-shirt. That's what you do when you can't have vodka for whatever reason.

My bandages stuck and lifted as I walked, making sticky sounds, which no doubt would be disgusting to be around. I walked until the shadows widened. And each time I rounded a corner and paused to feel a pull in one direction or another there was a new scent of smoke, like a whole town of separate little fires.

Here are some of them: on a turn past a white chapel with swinging paper banner there was a sweet leaf-smoke smell, autumn when you're young; then from the open door of a one-room house where a baby played with an empty water bottle there was the bad-breath smoke that wisped from the corn on the cob burning over the family's grill; then down by the bridge that crossed over sulfurous-smelling water drifted the black plastic-scented smoke that seemed to contaminate even the waters of your eyes. Down into the heart of the valley there was a weird and pervasive smoke that smelled like the burning of hair or bones; the drilling of teeth in the dentist's chair, or a strand of hair lighting over birthday candles. You know, human interference with fire.

A few miles past the slaughter yard where the animals screeched like metal on metal, where you walk fast and try to swallow but can't, and just before the train tracks, I stopped to remove this bit of gravel from my boot. I took off the boot and shook it just outside the wall where the grade school met the cemetery. You could hear the loud voices of children inside their classrooms. I stopped there to listen and separate the voices. But two little boys in uniforms came running by, sneakers slapping the stone road. They stopped in front of the scrolled gates of the cemetery, hands on the bars, and shouted into the stillness there: "Despierta y juega!" Wake up and play. They were laughing hysterically as they ducked into the front doors of the school.

The gate was open which was reason enough to go in. A brand-new padlock was hung, half-cocked, from the handle, and the gate was propped open by a wheelbarrow packed with soil, and a trowel and a pair of dusty gloves lying beside it. I touched where the wooden handles of the wheelbarrow had been worn smooth by the worker's hands. Then I inched the gate open and slid through like a spirit.

First there were the ash-white tombs with their bouquets of bright flowers: phlox and marigolds catching fire against all that white. I figured the rich folks would be buried here, kept from desert light and scorpions and light-footed geckos by slabs of bleached stone. Graveyard of fresh flowers and old photos. I wound my way in deeper.

The faces of women looked solemn and drawn as they crouched and fussed with flowers, used rags and water to wipe caked dust from the epitaphs. Their children with those intent brown eyes, they all watched me. I didn't anticipate the gaze of so many children.

Then there was the graveyard of iron crosses and frayed silk flowers. There were handmade things there, beautiful things like foil hearts and hand-painted Rest-in-Peace signs that made me think of rounded scissors and paste bottles, the Christmas present tucked in the bottom of the knapsack.

Then there were the babies.

So many babies buried at the back of the cemetery. So many nearly-loved and deeply-loved babies with their tiny crosses, dust-smudged and sinking into the ground at all angles. You could tell where their small caskets ended by the shape of the sunken rectangle of earth. In one tiny grave, the recessed imprint was barely the size of a carton of milk. On one newborn's grave, with its fallen cross and blanket of dried pine needles, was etched, in Spanish *Remembered by parents and family with profound pain*. I crouched there to straighten the cross, pushing it into the earth and then scooping up and discarding the pine needles. Then grave by grave I was moving along the row, squatting to tidy other tiny graves, pushing their stakes hard into the ground, uprooting half-buried cherubs and placing them gently over the buried caskets. I thumbed away the dirt from cheeks of capsized statuettes. I shook dust from the cheap fabric flowers and laid them atop the graves as mourners passed.

Crazy foreigner.

Ruined mother.

I don't know how long that went on.

When I came to the boundaries of the yard, where coffee and black bean and hot pepper cans were piled in a pyramid against the low brick wall for makeshift vases, the scent changed. It smelled of death there. Not the smell of a dead mouse in the garage but something like the smell of decades-old clothes. Maybe I was imagining it. Nopal cacti grew from the barren graves, sometimes as the only markers. There, women cleared their throats of dust and pulled black shawls over their thinning hair.

These were the humble graves, the poor graves, sometimes marked by a wooden slat or a chipped red brick or two, twisted metal scraps or a tangle of rusted wire. I just couldn't salvage all those graves. Couldn't make them beautiful if I was there all day, and I felt helpless and useless and small and I kept on going because what else can you do.

Then to the burning yard.

Hard at work with his spade and wheelbarrow was a middle-aged man with thin, muscular arms and a filthy white undershirt. He had the face of a convict, someone you'd see in the news back home, with a drooping handlebar moustache and wild hair, long and grey, a silver earring in one ear, cheap homemade tattoos on his biceps.

Sweat beaded at the end of his nose as he struck the earth with his spade, and a bead fell rhythmically with every fourth or fifth strike at the ground. Behind him lay the charred remains of several dozen metal coffins, semi-crushed, and piled high like a car scrap-yard. The wind was up, swirling a heap of ash beneath the most recently burned casket. I went over to the burning mound as quietly as I could, not wanting the gravedigger to say anything.

All around the burn heap were remains of the last burning: rubber gloves and metal crosses with seared angel faces and what must have been wire and wooden rosaries. And I could feel them, the dead, all around me, whispering among themselves, resenting my presence, my prying. The hairs on my arms stood alert despite the searing heat thrown from the burning mound. They were daring me, tempting me to touch.

The toe of my boot nudged something soft and I slowly moved around the pyre and looking down I saw it was a snarl of human hair. I must have made a noise because the gravedigger said more to himself than me, "You never get used to that."

I looked up to see him resting on the end of his spade, chest heaving, underarms soaking his shirt. He wiped his forehead against his arm. I could smell him, salty and pungent. He peeled off a pair of latex gloves and threw them to the ground, his hands floured with latex powder.

"Nasty fuckin' work." You could tell his throat was tight but his voice loud and gruff. "Makes me sick for the poor sonsabitches. Your family don't pay, your family dies off and you get dug up and burned. Not enough room, the mayor says. Tough shit, he says."

I couldn't believe it. "You dig them up?"

"Rotten fuckin' business. I'm trained, not a ... I don't do this kind of rotten shit. But the regular guy's sick so am I going to turn down paying work?" He smeared the sweat across his nose and mouth. I thought he was actually waiting for an answer as he stared at me, blue-eyed, bug-eyed.

"No."

He ignored that. "You breathing through your nose?" Before I could think of whether I was, or not, he said, "Breathe through your fuckin' nose when you're back here, Jack. Don't get this shit in your mouth. Tourists are always walking around with their fuckin' mouths hanging open then they wonder why they get fuckin' typhoid. Well, why the fuck do you think, Jack? Know what you're breathing in all day long? Dust? No! That's dried-up shit and piss, pardon my language. Probably fuckin' smallpox in one of these caskets. It'll get us … it will. Who the fuck are you anyways?" he asked me, suddenly looking directly at me with those wild eyes.

I told him my real name because I couldn't think of another one. "Yeah yeah, I seen you around the posada." He began shovelling again. "Happy fuckin' holidays and all that good shit."

The weird thing is, I stayed there with him a little while longer. Watching him shovel and listening to him curse. I liked the way his eyes darted around and how sometimes he'd stop like he was watching clouds of imaginary insects, then keep shovelling. I liked all of it. He told me he lived across from the *posada*. That all of those little kids were his, why wouldn't he take a paying gig?

"If you're going to be here longer than a week there's certain things you got to know." He pointed at me. Accusatory finger. "Now I'm a married man. Happily, you understand." He paused looking me straight in the eye, then he continued using the spade to pry a rock from the soil. "But if one afternoon you could use some insights into life here I could buy you a beer, Jack."

"I don't drink," I told him quickly because, as of that morning, I didn't.

"Alright, fine. I could buy you a malt. A good malt. You drink malts, don't you?"

I just nodded and felt unsure, heat in my cheeks.

He stopped prying at the rock and with those wild eyes pointing right at me, looking me up and down he asked, "You nuts or something?"

I laughed a little. "I don't know. No."

"Too bad." He cackled this big boisterous laugh that wound down into giggles and he shook his head a little, sweat sprinkling from his hair.

I wanted to watch him longer but he was suddenly irritated and told me so. He told me to take a hike and let him work. His eyes were kind though, even when he was being rude. I was more relieved than offended, anyway.

On the way out, there was a stern-looking old woman in the midst of all the rubble, dressed in black. With her daughter crouched beside her, she was flinging stones from the grave. As the mother stood, her eyes snatched at me and I had to stare a moment before I realized that she was not really seeing me. It was just the way I'd looked at every stranger since Joseph died. Not seeing, just waiting for some stranger to approach me in the street and say, No, it's not really happening. You'll wake up soon and he'll be back. The woman looked at me that way, and I wanted to say those words to her even if they weren't true.

XVI.

IT WAS ON MY WAY BACK to the *posada*, walking down along the train tracks, that I found the dead dog, seeming more silent, more still, for the buzzing of the flies crawling all over the corpse. Its tongue lolled out the side of its mouth. Fur all matted with blood. Old blood. Seeing something you can't unsee. You can't keep walking like you didn't see it, either, though I tried to for a minute. Tried to imagine it as something other than what it was. From a distance, you would think maybe it was sheep that had strayed from one of the nearby ranches, all curly haired and muddy, but then the collar around its neck, then you know.

I covered my mouth and nose with the collar of my T-shirt as I got close to it—the smell of decay so thick and yellow all around that animal I could barely stand it. I was retching. God only knows what happened to it. Maybe it had gotten sick somehow, eaten something it shouldn't have, and had managed to drag itself to the tracks on the side of the road, I don't know, looking for shade or for what? For home. Mad with pain. The tracks hadn't been used for years, so it couldn't have been that, a train, the tracks were littered with wood and scrap metal.

A bird descended and perched close-by on the rails, and I flagged my arms and lunged towards the nasty thing, frightening it off, but it just barely circled before it descended again, this time even closer to the dog. So I pitched a handful of gravel at it, and managed to hit the bird as it took flight. It made a sound and I instantly felt guilty in a way, and it flew to the roof of the boarded-up train station to wait for me to leave.

And over there, not twenty feet away, under the shade of the ticket window, an identical dog lay on its side.

Twin dog. Hallucination dog.

I tried to figure out from a distance whether it too was dead. Its side was moving quickly. So I bent right down as best I could with knees throbbing and put my hand out to it but it didn't even react. I stood and got closer to it, crouched, whistled softly, called it like you do. The dog lifted an ear, then its head. Slowly it dragged its body to stand, but could only put weight on three of its legs. The dog just suspended the fourth in midair and kind of hopped my way, mouth open and jaws all slimy with saliva. I tried to remember the names of Delilah's dogs, but couldn't. Fifi, Bobo, or some damn thing.

Anyway, when I reached out to touch it, unsure whether it would snap or not, the dog lowered its head and came closer. After a moment of scratching behind his ears, I carefully, carefully took a look at the leg. It was hanging there at a bad angle, broken for sure, infected maybe, swollen. I thought of having him follow me back to the *posada*. I walked a few feet away and called him.

"C'mon," I said, and whistled, slapped my leg. But the dog wouldn't leave the tracks. He sat awkwardly, trying to stay off that back leg. I called him again, but he just sat there panting.

So what are you going to do, leave him there?

I decided to try to lift him up into my arms, and he yelped and snapped at me and I hushed him and wrapped a hand tightly around his muzzle so he couldn't bite.

"I'm helping you, asshole!"

We stopped twice. Once to rest in the shade, and the second time to give him a bowl of water at a mechanic's shop. The men there were sympathetic and kind and probably thought I was crazy, too. They offered to drive us wherever we needed to go. Then they asked about my bandages, and I just told them, "I fell." Mimed it. They nodded, totally unconvinced. I told them I'd take the ride and what I could really use was a bottle of beer. They obliged, and I finished the bottle fast, careful not to belch until the dog and I were bumping along in between two men in the flatbed of their pickup truck.

I wondered then what the hell I'd say about the other one.

By the time we got to the *posada* I was cool again from the airy ride, and the dog had settled down across our laps. He rested his chin on me. The driver helped us out and took the dog into the lobby where I extended my arms and took him, step by step, up the stairs to Delilah.

When Delilah finally opened the door to see me standing there with the dog in my arms she leaned into the doorframe.

"Oh my," she said a couple of times, gathering the glass beads in a fist atop her robe. "Oh my baby." She ushered me in to lay the dog on the velvet upholstered fainting-couch.

"Where were you?" she said, kissing the dog, kissing the bloody fur at its neck. "Oh, my baby where were you?" I was getting choked-up just seeing here there on her knees beside him, burying her face like that, her wet cheeks. And the dog licking her hands tenderly, gently.

"Where was he?" she asked me, and then the dog, "You missed your mama?" And I lied to her. I did, before I even knew what I was saying I said, "I found him in the cemetery."

"The cemetery?" She asked the dog, "How'd you get in there?" And then me, "Alone?" Delilah's hand scrunched into the fur of her dog's back, over and over, distractedly. "He's never alone. Never ever would those two leave each other. I'm going down there after the veterinarian comes and we'll find our Vi-vi, won't we, baby?" Her chin quivered and she pressed her face again against the side of the filthy dog. Unmade-up, and with her hair tucked inside a terrycloth turban she looked plain and old, not mystical in the least, but lovely and real.

She would never find Vi-vi, of course. And I knew that. She could keep hoping that the dog was out there somewhere finding shade and chasing birds. It's better that way.

Delilah later wrote up her version of a voucher slip, an I.O.U. on the back of a telephone message pad, signing it with a flourish, her signature running off the page. It stated that I would owe no rent until August first of that year, should the tenant, Abigail Walsh, wish to stay at the *posada* in suite 2B. She presented the slip to me the next morning when I answered the door with my bed sheet as a makeshift toga. She extended the slip to me, all ceremonious, with her dog, its leg in a splint and a cone around its head, sitting at her heel. She placed one hand on her chest.

"For you, angel-baby," she said.

I wanted to tell her I wasn't staying. This was just a stopover and I'd be out before the week's end, but I've learned when to shut up, so I shut up and said thank you.

On the way back to her suite, Delilah called an invitation to me, her voice echoing vaguely along the corridor, making it a little unclear just who she was addressing.

"Come by at seven. We'll go celebrate with Luis and Ilario. You like stuffed chiles, don't you honey?" The question trailed behind her and she didn't wait for me to answer as the door to her suite clicked shut. I remember wondering how I would ever know when seven o'clock had arrived.

That afternoon I came back from town with my knapsack full of mangoes, sugar cereal, tortillas, guava juice and a couple of bottles of beer too. I'd been all over town that afternoon, up and down the aisles of the open-air market where the birds were stacked in bamboo cages, then to the café with the painted tables and strong *café de olla* blended with cinnamon and piloncillo sugar, then to the monastery where the devout old men sat in drab robes with drab faces and stared out over their bellies at nothing.

With my boots scuffing along the cobblestone and my bandages and a bird in a rickety cage in the crook of my arm, I knew I looked like some kind of a crazy *gringa*. I could feel the amusement of my neighbours, the kids across the street giggling to each other, and I didn't care. I don't know why I did it, buying that bird. But there you go. Blame it on my rattled head or the damn dog or maybe it was the fact that they'd terrified me since I'd tried to save one as a kid, and failed. I remember its scratchy feet inside the cardboard box on the way to the Humane Society, Dad driving, telling me to "sing to it, Sweet Pea." And me, "sing what?" And he'd said, "something cheerful." So I sang the song *Alouette* because it sounded happy and I didn't know the words were about plucking feathers. I peeped in through the box where the bird sat quietly, eyes nearly closed, like it was happy to be out of the backyard where I'd found it. Then the vet's assistant checked its wings and it fluttered. Spatters of deep red blood from its beak onto the countertop. She smeared them away hastily. "Sorry," she said, "didn't expect that." And I wept and wept all the way home in the car while Dad kept telling me I'd done the right thing. It wouldn't suffer.

The bird I'd brought home from the market made these quiet noises to itself as I took the stairs to my hotel room, careful, careful not to jostle the cage. Frightened, but hopeful. But then once I had the cage inside I sat there with it on the bed, not knowing what to do with it. It was a pretty bird. Not unlike a morning dove, with these tapered wings and a kind of elegant head. I wasn't sure why they were selling them in the market, whether it was to eat them or keep them or what, so when I asked the vendor, he just smiled and shrugged and said, "como quieras," as you wish.

Its two dark eyes blinked with a retracting membrane. I was kneeling down beside the bed with my face close to the cage, watching it. I thought it must have hated the dark of the hotel room, sensing that brilliant light outside. So carefully I lifted the cage by its little handle on top and brought it to the balcony wall, settling it down so the bird could see the street. It didn't move at all on its perch, like the change meant nothing to it. So I tapped the cage a little. Then I pulled the bamboo pin from the latch holding the door shut, and I flicked the door right open so the bird could escape, and I stood back. All it did was scuttle along its perch. I tapped behind the cage so it would fly out, but it wouldn't. I tilted the cage toward its open door and just very slightly, I shook it. Very slightly.

"Go."

The bird was still there inside its bamboo cage when I went to the door to see Delilah standing there, her head in a turban, long earrings dangling beside her rouged face, and her dog combed to resemble a whipped cumulous cloud.

The bird was still there when I rummaged through the pile of clothes at the foot of my bed for something fancy to wear to the party, and decided that, even with the heat, I'd wear my fringed jacket. Its embroidery making it the only thing I had even resembling fancy.

And the bird was still there as I peeked in through the hotel room door before I closed it, locked it, and pocketed the key.

XVII.

ME AND DELILAH and the dog with a splinted leg. What a sight, the three of us making our way from the hotel to the quiet street where Luis and Ilario lived. Delilah taking those tiny, shackled little footsteps, stopping to ensure her limping dog could keep up, then prattling on about the cobblestones, about the *posada* falling apart, about how Vula and Sue were going to give her an aneurysm if they didn't check out soon.

I was trailing a hand along the chalky painted walls as Delilah told me about the worst guest she'd ever had at the *posada*.

"A convict," she said. "These itty-bitty tears tattooed right there under his eye like he was always crying. And the boys at the cantina told me that means he's killed somebody, so it was fine by me he never left his room. But he never paid either, so finally when he owed me three-and-a-half weeks' rent, I convinced the boys at the station to come and persuade him to pay. Well, when they broke down his door they found he'd made a bull's eye right there on the back of it, and was sitting there with his revolver, waiting to shoot."

Delilah pointed to the door we would enter.

"Did he?"

"He used it on himself. We're here."

I wanted to ask why, what'd she know about him, what'd she do, but Delilah lifted the oversized bronze knocker and rapped it several times with force enough that it startled me.

After a few moments, Ilario answered, sweet-faced and barefoot.

"Our guest of honour." He smiled at me but petted the dog's whipped curls. Then he took us through the entranceway to a massive court-yard that seemed like a different atmosphere from the world on the other side of its walls. It smelled rich and earthy, with good black soil and potted plants and well-hydrated leaves. It was easier to breathe in there, warmer, wetter. A stone fountain plashed away in the mid-dle, surrounded by mature potted trees. Lime, lemon, mango. Some of the fruit had fallen to the ground and been left there, so that Luis and Ilario didn't have to boast out loud about their gardening skills. Blooms climbed the walls. Swags of cotton were strung overhead between them.

Rich people can make Eden, I thought, even in a desert. Breathing in the jungle-atmosphere, you could completely forget you were in a high desert town in the middle of a drought.

Ilario had padded away for a moment, and when he returned he brought with him two fragile-looking flutes of champagne, each adorned with a sliced strawberry.

"To happy homecomings," he said, and Delilah grinned and downed half her champagne leaving behind a thick smudge of bright lipstick. She handed it to me saying, "Thank you, baby-doll." And began speaking in Spanish with the group seated around the fountain.

I decided not to drink that night. Even though I'd been able to take the gauze off, I still felt like an asshole and didn't want them to see me mess up again. Anyway, I ditched the glasses on the edge of a potted palm and took the jacket off. Folded it and tucked it away, too.

Someone was playing the accordion in a room somewhere, and someone else was kind of melodically sighing, like a warm-up vocal exercise, in time with the wheezy breath of the instrument. I found myself moving toward the sound and watched as Ilario went about lighting the lanterns strung up in the fruit trees. They were shaped like stars and made of punctured tin, and once the candle inside was lit, they flickered in tiny points of light.

The accordion breathed, and the singer sighed. I moved closer to the strange sounds and imagined it was someone giving birth to an angel.

A guest knocked her purse into the burbling fountain and, hiking up her skirt, stepped in to retrieve it while Ilario finished the last of the lanterns.

Not meaning to say anything, I blurted "beautiful!" as he came off the stepladder. I think I was just dazzled by all those wavering pinpricks of light.

"Everything has to be beautiful in the kingdom of Luis." He smiled. "Didn't you know?"

The singer was now making these breathy hooting sounds to the quick squeezes of the accordion. I saw through a wide arch that the singer and accordion player were on the floor in a study, the singer on her back, her green dress crumpled-up under her so her garter belt hooks were showing. She held a champagne flute on her diaphragm and each time she hooted out, the champagne jumped in the glass. Laughing, she propped herself up to take it sip. The accordion player had his eyes shut and was now squeezing the bellows in and out, swaying to his own non-melodious tune. The woman shouted to him in Spanish.

"Play something sad!" Rubia. I knew her voice.

So he changed the rhythm of his playing, but not the notes and Rubia nodded agreement. "Si, si. That's a sad one. I know that one."

I wandered back to the courtyard, leaving the wistful, tuneless music behind me.

The guests, sitting around the fountain, were chatting and laughing and someone was strumming a guitar while a man with a beautiful voice serenaded a shy little girl who was clutching her mother's blouse.

"Hey, the lady of the hour!" Mojo said to me from a door that presumably led to the kitchen. She was licking her fingers. "Come and taste," she said, gesturing with her head.

The rich smells would make your mouth water, make you feel hungrier than you already were. There, over the blue gas flames, heavy pots bubbled and simmered. There were near-empty bowls of walnuts in milk, tiny glass bowls of thyme, clove, cinnamon, and a bottle of sherry on the counter. He was cooking *chiles en nogada*, Mojo explained, a family recipe he demanded from Ines after trying it one night. Delilah mouthed the words "so rude." Ines had written the recipe out for him on the back of a typhoid pamphlet that now sat open on the countertop, rings of oil all over it.

I watched Luis pour the sweet-cream sauce over the stuffed *chiles*, the sauce steaming and pooling. Then he pinched bright red pomegranate seeds from an earthen bowl and scattered them on the white sauce of each *chile*.

A smattering of red kisses.

Without even looking over his shoulder he said to me, "Nobody stands around in my kitchen, nena. Take a spoon and stir something." Then he turned and gave me a disarming laugh and a wet, swollen wooden spoon.

"Sopa Azteca." He nodded at a big cast iron pot.

"Luis is a very famous chef," Mojo said, smoothing a circle over his broad back.

"Was a very famous chef. Now a much happier nobody."

The broth smelled rich with tomato and onion. The yellowing oil sat on the surface of the brew in puddles, so I ladled the soup over onto itself, breaking the oil into tiny drops. The kitchen was noisy but calm as I stirred: sounds of Mojo cracking walnuts, the soup quietly burbling to itself, Luis soaping and scouring a saucepan under a stream of hot water and Delilah, giving directions into her glass of sangria.

"You know," Delilah said to no one, to everyone, "they say that every *chile* has its own soul. No two are alike."

"Who says that?" Luis asked as he ladled soup into a tureen. Slopping noises.

"You Mexicans do," she said.

Luis straightened up. "I never say that. Who told you that? A gringo?"

And Delilah said, "Honey, I can't remember every person who ever told me something."

"I think that's lovely, Delilah," Mojo said, feeding her mouth with pomegranate seeds from one of the plates of *chiles*. "I'll bet this big ol' chile's got a wicked soul. Look at her, nasty thing!" She laughed as Luis took the plate from her hand and told her to leave something for the guests. Then he stood in the doorway of the kitchen and called everyone to dinner with the clanging of a fork against his dripping pan.

After dinner, the kitchen table looked ravaged. The plates were all smeared with sauce and the linens were littered with crumbs and bleeding wine stains everywhere. All the red wine and the peppers and the heat of the night had left every one of the guests glowing like they stayed too long at the beach. Luis was preparing his bananas *flambé*, lights out, sprinkling cinnamon into the blue flame as we watched it sparkle and ascend like magic in the dark. But the heat had taken what was left of my appetite. I sat rolling my perspiring water glass over my cheeks, while the accordion sigher-singer beside me aired herself with a sandalwood fan.

We all moved out to the courtyard with our plates, into that oasis of cool, that illusion of cool, with the plants and the cotton swags and the water-sounds. Some of the children were falling asleep so Ilario pushed chairs together for them to drowse on. One of Ines' boys, the eldest, had been flitting from guest to guest all night, stealing sips from the tops of their glasses and now he was asleep on a sofa in the study. His father, the gravedigger, Jimmy his name was, sat nearby in an armchair smoking a big cigar and clearly eavesdropping on conversations while pretending not to.

Ines stroked her youngest child's fine hair as the baby slept against her. When she looked at me I smiled quickly then turned to watch Rubia.

Look away.

Rubia and the accordion player were arguing in Spanish, too fast for me to understand.

When I went back inside the kitchen to refill my stubby glass of water, I found that the dog had somehow, even with a splinted leg, climbed up on the table and was there in between the piles of plates and spilled glasses, licking cream from one of the serving platters. I watched him for a while, then went back outside to the sound of breaking glass.

Rubia had thrown down her glass in a rage, and to punctuate her point she was grinding the sole of her leather mule into the shattered bits on the ground. She spoke through her teeth, her hair all over her face and sticking to her lipstick. I was entranced. Yes, I thought. That's it. Goddamn, that would feel good.

I saw that Ines had quietly laid a palm over her sleeping baby's ear. Her mouth played in a slight smile and she raised her eyebrows at me. Rubia then took the glasses from the face of the accordion player and tossed them into the fountain. She turned and very formally thanked Luis and Ilario for their hospitality and Ilario saw her to the door.

After she left, the group just fell apart in laughter. The accordion player retrieved his glasses and was wiping his lenses on his shirt, shaking his head. Delilah scolded the dog in the kitchen, and the guitarist fingered the strings of his guitar. The baby girl's arm dangled from her mother's side as Ines slowly rocked her to the music. I watched her little hand. I touched her little hand and stroked her fingers and the baby's hand instinctively closed around my finger, so I stayed as still as I could, feeling, in that moment, held by the song and the stone walls and the child's small fingers. And for the first time since I could remember, I felt as if I might not drift away.

XVIII.

AS MUCH AS LIFE IN TADEO carried on, pretending it was just the continuation of one long day, you couldn't ignore time passing. A bell tolls and you know it's Sunday, high mass. A whole week has gone by. The clean white bar of soap you brought from home has worn thin, cracked from morning showers and afternoon heat. Your hair has gotten longer. Ragged toenails and fingernails need cutting. The deep maroon scab has begun to lift. The days dry out the earth more and more, and the nights grow unbearably warm, a long hot breath of night. Time to go, these things say. Go back home. And you think, What's that? Genuinely unable to remember.

Then there's the routine and all that you've come to rely on to tell you it's alright to stay. It's just another day that'll bleed into a night nearly indistinguishable from the one that came before it and that's alright. Patterns start to bring you a kind of security. Comfort, maybe. Like the noises from next door. I liked knowing I was waking up at the same time as someone else in the world.

Sometimes I would imagine that Joseph was waking somewhere and I'd try to invent what he was seeing—squeeze my eyes so tight that spots and splotches of light would show up all over the inner screens of my eyelids. Turn the splotches into a window, a clothes-line blowing with bright T-shirts, the sun over a spiky row of pine trees—always a better home, sometimes with a new mother. Him, with rumpled hair and sleep scent, waking up.

Then those other images would barge in before I could stop them. The balsam wood plane turning on its fishing line, the cruiser outside our house, the skeleton of the Christmas tree in the corner of the living room. And before I could get clear of them, there were others. The grave with its cheap headstone, his name his perfect name, the freshly-laid dirt frosted over. I'd jerk my head from this half-sleep and he was gone and Mojo's kettle was shrieking.

New day.

Mojo's day would begin like this: the taps running, the teakettle, the Spanish lesson on her portable record player with those terrible recordings, like the speaker held a cardboard tube to his mouth and told you things you'd never say in town to anybody, ever. But Mojo would practice anyway, repeating each word, each phrase twice after he said it, like she was hoping for the occasion to use one of those phrases in some breezier, jet-set life. Travel words, hotel, airport customs, immigration, phrases for restaurants, for the beach.

Would you care to share a taxi?

This soup lacks flavour.

What is the catch of the day?

Sometimes after the Spanish lesson there was *Canned Heat* and I'd hear Mojo clapping and dancing while I was brushing my teeth or fishing out something to wear from the pile of clothes at the foot of my bed.

By noon I'd have accomplished exactly nothing.

The water truck would pass by with its little brass bell and I'd be sitting on the balcony with my cigarettes to watch the children come home for their lunch and siesta.

On the first day I saw them, they'd caught me by surprise as I sat there in the sun doing something disgusting like picking at the scabs on my knees. I heard their leather-soled shoes tapping along the cobblestone, their high voices echoing across the square. They stopped in a circle right below my balcony and squabbled over who would pick from the bag of candy. I was peering over the ledge, looking, I guess, for a pale boy among them, when they saw me and froze then all four of them lunged through the front door across the street. They must have told Ines something, because she came out to peer up at the balcony and wave. I waved back, of course, quickly stubbing out a cigarette into the potted aloe plant.

Curious strangers.

Then I got to watching them every day. I don't know why. To see they made it home safely, maybe. To hear their voices. I'd count them under my breath, worry when one stayed home sick with a stomach bug or fever. I'd watch them straggle back to school after siesta, walking slowly always, stopping to look at some little trinket produced from one of their pockets. I watched like some kind of gargoyle, meant to protect, but so horrible to catch in the corner of your eye. I felt I must have scared the children with my bony shoulders and hollow face, these shadowy eyes. Must have looked insane.

But slowly they made a game of it. Shouting up to the skinny woman living in the hotel. Whoever was loudest would win the praise of the others. One day they threw the shoe of the little one onto the balcony. I held it in my hand for a moment as they howled with laughter. It was warm and smooth, still sweaty from his small foot. Before throwing it down to the little boy, I untied the laces. It bounced and landed, and he sat on the road in his grey tartan school pants and once he tired of his attempts at a bow, he took it off and carried it with him, wiping his nose, shoulders shuddering with humiliated sobs.

It's just when you get into a pattern, when you get to depend on things being the same, that everything changes. You can count on it. So when Mojo's day began with the kettle and the music, pretty soon everything went sideways. The phone was for her and Marcella called out to her. I heard Mojo reply, "Ya voy! I'm coming!" And then her flappy sandals on the stone steps.

The record skipped and the kettle screeched, on and on.

I was still lying on top of the bedsheets, with the itchy wool blanket on the floor, counting seconds until Mojo took the kettle from the element. Then cursing, I pulled on some clothes and went out to call downstairs, "Kettle's ready!"

No response. But I could hear her on the telephone in the office and the little television beside the office sofa playing Telenovelas—always somebody on the screen reprimanding her lover. You would always see Marcella in there, entranced, amused, polishing wood in slow, distracted circles. Mojo had dragged the phone into the courtyard for privacy.

I hate the ugly siren noise a kettle makes. And my head was bound up tight in pre-rain knots, so I stomped over and took care of it myself. The kettle was whooping and spewing a torrent of steam. I turned off the gas and the rattling kettle slowed to a choked squeak. The record's repetitions were getting to me too: click whirr click whirr click. Too much. So I pulled the needle off the vinyl and it made that horrible zipping sound. The cat pounced down from a high bookshelf, startled, and slipped through the balcony door up onto the roof.

Then Mojo was sliding her bare feet into a pair of worn-out cowboy boots.

I said, "Sorry, the kettle ..."

And she said, "Ilario got beat up bad." Just like that. She stood there with this look on her face like I knew why. She used her sleeve to squeeze at her nostrils. "Luis's running around like a lunatic over there." From a bag of weed on the coffee table, she took out a half-smoked joint and lit it up.

"You're coming, right?"

In her weatherworn cowboy boots, Mojo leapt onto curbs and over gutters. She barely spoke as we hustled from one side of the street to the other, past a sleeping white dog with its tail over its nose, past the man who sold avocados on a blanket.

As we hustled onto side streets I asked if he was okay, did they know who did it, did he need a doctor, was he at the hospital. Mojo just said things like "come on" and "let's go," but not much else.

At the hacienda, there was no response when Mojo rapped the cherub doorknocker, just the vague sound of voices shouting inside the walls of the old building. Opinions. Directions. Something fast happening inside.

I pressed my ear to the crack where the double-doors met. I could hear my own heartbeat and made out Luis saying something in quick Spanish then adding in English, "I don't want to hear it. Don't tell me another thing, entiendes?" I tried to see in. A thin strip of garden.

Mojo pounded with the flesh of her fist.

"Open," she shouted through the crack.

After a minute, the deadbolt scraped and the door fell open and then Delilah was walking away with those careful little steps, talking to everyone and to no one in particular. Her single dog was at her heel, looking guilty. Mojo trotted up the cement staircase and disappeared so I followed Delilah, not knowing what else to do.

There she was in the kitchen, getting down on her knees to stick her head under the kitchen sink. She saying things about vengeance and it all sounded very biblical and frightening to me. She was addressing the plunger, the dish soap, the red onions under there. She pulled them out one by one as she spoke.

I crouched down, closer.

She pulled three cotton dishrags out and laid them on the kitchen tile and continued whatever diatribe she'd been on. "It is mine to avenge, he says." She loaded the cupboard back up with its contents and stood stiffly. She started in on the cutlery drawers, searching.

Then she told me this: "When I was a little child, I was different. Everybody knew it. Everybody knows a different child. Of course, all the boys called me sissy, that's what they'd say, li'l sissy. And one of those little boys made my school days a living hell any way he could. Day after day. Pushed me right down, to the gravel. And all the teachers turned away and Mama and Daddy turned away, ashamed. Bloodied knees and bloody noses. He knocked my tooth right through my lip once. And nobody did a damn thing but say, Daniel, you need to fight back. But I wouldn't. Oh I was big, but I was soft inside."

At that moment, she unearthed a bottle of bourbon from beneath a pile of placemats.

"Ah." She unscrewed the cap. "There's a pretty boy."

After a quick swig she closed her eyes and clasped the bottle to her.

"Not mine to avenge," she said. "Anyway, that little boy made me know myself. He showed me who I was. I was kind, and he was cruel. And baby-doll, it took me a long time to realize I'd rather be me any day."

Then she nodded at me. "Now why don't you run upstairs and see if you can be useful."

Nobody wanted me in there. Least of all Luis. I hovered, quivery and breathless and useless, just getting in people's way: Ines leaving in her hospital whites with that black bag, Mojo trailing her, nodding at her directions. "Every half hour. And someone is to stay with him for 72 hours." I waited on the terrace outside the room, and through the crack in the door I could almost see Ilario. His tanned legs on top of the sheets, mosquito netting pulled halfway around the bed, and Luis on the phone, sitting there rubbing the cuff of his shirt over some nonexistent watermark or smudge on the night table. The windows seemed to squint, the whole room unaccustomed to daylight. Luis put a hand over the receiver and stretched the phone cord to the door, shouting down to Delilah, "Bring up the bourbon!" Then he was back yammering into the phone, then slamming it down and disappearing into the bathroom where you could hear him retching into the toilet. Delilah slipped past me in a waft of jasmine, bottle in hand and when she opened the door, I could see him there, Ilario, propped up like a tattered doll.

He was still wearing his clothes from the night before but the white T-shirt he was wearing was torn along a shoulder seam and there was blood, blood all over it, like he'd been holding it to his face. A swollen eye, a gash, a pummeled face. His forehead crusted. God, all those little dried cuts, like he'd flown through a windshield. I lost my breath. I stared and stared and tried to will him well again.

Luis came out of the bathroom with red cheeks and water-raked hair and a pistol in the waist of his pants. He told us all to leave, all of us, to give him a moment with Ilario. He drank straight from the bourbon bottle. "Nobody will ever hurt you again, mi vida." He spoke softly into the perfect seashell of Ilario's ear.

When he blew past Mojo at the bottom of the stairs, she looked up at Delilah, incredulous. "He has a gun, doesn't he?" Delilah said nothing.

I wanted to know if the police had been called and both of them sputtered with laughter. Delilah said, "You think those boys down at the station are armed to protect people like us? Baby, they'd be in stitches the minute we left the station."

Flare of a tiny wax matchstick.

Lighting of two cigarettes. One for me, one for Mojo.

We were quiet and waiting but I'm not sure what for.

Delilah left shortly after Luis blustered by, pulling his cotton shirt over his waistband. She said she had responsibilities to attend to. That is was "unprofessional to leave one's guests in need of a bar of soap or an extra pillow, never mind if there was some kind of real emergency." So she left in a swirl of fabric and that was that. We were left to wake Ilario from fitful sleep.

Left to watch him swell in the night.

As we smoked on the terrace I thought of phoning home and wasn't sure why. My mouth felt all tingly and dry. I could wind my way back north, away from this madness. But what about the things I had here—what to do with them? I loved the heavy woolen blanket and would steal it, I think, and some jasmine tea to remember how the air tasted, and Faro cigarettes, you couldn't get those back home, the bird in the cage, what to do with him. My head was sweating. I could be unlocking my front door in four days. My empty fucking house and everything in it all dried out or rotten. My stinking home. My home with the blinking answering machine and the bills jammed under the door. Toronto swimming with humidity, trees heavy with green, parks bright with children. Mother would be silent and scornful for days, then irate and argumentative for weeks. We'd sit at the kitchen table with Tang and Vodka and I'd tell her about the town with its mechanical bull and market doves, its fireworks and saints. Gloria would shake her head and Mother would say I needed a shrink.

When we stubbed out our smokes Mojo just looked at me with her sea anemone eyelashes. "Drink?"

It was three in the morning and we'd been at the hacienda since noon. Little sips and tips from the bottle. There was the sound of a couple of crickets winding down their song and everything was as heavy as warm, wet wool. The air through the open bedroom window playing against my lips. I set the bottle down and watched Ilario sleep. Mojo and I had been taking turns with the clock, waking him from his dreams every half hour. Now she was curled in the armchair in the corner, her legs all tucked up under her, her head on her arm. Her cowboy boots had fallen sideways on the floor in front of her like they'd given up.

I whispered to him, "Ilario," secretly loving his name in my mouth.

He opened his eyes, the look in his wide eyes of someone who's been staring at the ocean for a long time.

"How do you feel?" I put a cool hand on his forehead. He closed his eyes without speaking. "Ilario ..."

He swallowed hard. "Afraid."

So I took his hand. His cool, smooth hand. And he opened his eyes to look at me. And I don't know why I did it, but I bent to kiss his forehead where the blood had been wiped away.

"Do I look ugly?" He tried to smile but his swollen cheek only stirred a little.

I shook my head.

"He broke my nose." A hand hovering near his face.

"I think so," I said.

"He hit me in the face. His stupid rings cut my face."

He ran his fingers lightly over the braille of bristly stitches. Over his nose, the tape. I had to tell myself to get a fucking grip and not cry.

"I didn't think he would stop," he said just above a whisper. "First he kissed me. I still had his taste in my mouth and he hit me. Why did he do that?"

I stroked the back of his hand. Mojo made a sleep sound from her chair.

"He said I'm going to kill you. That's what he said to me after he kissed me."

Ilario rolled onto his side, his body shivering. I pulled the thick burgundy comforter up to his shoulder and pressed it tight around him. I sat closer to him. I lay beside him.

"You got away. And you're here."

"I didn't think he would stop."

"But he did. He stopped. And you're here now."

"I want to go home." Just like a child. I never imagined him anywhere but here, with Luis. Before he fell asleep beside me, he said quietly, "I want to see my mother."

XIX.

WE NEARLY MADE IT through the night, all of us. An hour before sunrise at the hacienda, and the roosters outside the walls had already begun the day. Mojo took a long sip of her tea, making a shallow slurping sound and humming into her cup afterward. That cool, cloudless gaze of hers. Even without sleep.

Since midnight we'd been speaking in a kind of shorthand.

She said. "Long night."

"Heartbreaking."

My eyelids felt thick. Interstate highway eyes. I got up to stand in the doorway and listen to the night insects quieting. Still dark and cool with night. The fountain quiet.

Still some part of my mother's mind was tuned-in to Ilario. Would he need something. Would he wake afraid. Then out of nowhere I had to rush out to the courtyard to vomit in one of the potted palm trees. Horrible, rice-water bile, drowning the biting red ants in the soil. And Mojo was there with a cold, wet tea towel at the back of my neck like she'd been ready all along.

"I knew this was coming. Your eyes were rheumy."

"I shouldn't have drank."

"That wouldn't have changed a thing. You're getting the fever."

So she hustled me upstairs to one of the rooms with a ceiling fan and stiff white sheets. She didn't say much, just told me to rest, as if all other remedies eluded her and it was the only option now, and I felt like an idiot. Another patient when Ilario needed us. I was someone who could hold my drink. You never had to take care of me after a bad night at the bar, or a fight with a boyfriend, nobody had to take care of me. Not ever. And now here I was with Mojo the nursemaid and it was all too much to lay on one person. But she was so right. I was sick in my marrow and in my blood, a deep, frightening kind of sick.

And after an hour of lying there in that dim bedroom it started to feel alright to be there just listening for Ilario. It was our make-shift hospital, wedged tight in the bed, mosquito netting draped all around. I only wished we could share a room. In my fever brain this felt like a different ward. I felt pinned, strapped in, lunatic. And that, strangely, was fine.

Before sleep, there were the noises of the hacienda: Luis' voice returning, the fountain beginning to patter, someone moving pots in the kitchen, Ilario speaking low and slow somewhere far off. And then I was in and out, watching the room come into focus in fragments. On the bedside table was a wooden burl bowl cut straight from the trunk of a tree. Mangoes inside it. Beside, a blown glass pitcher of purified water, a water glass, a small plate with triangles of toast, and a porcelain washbasin. "In case you need to upchuck," Mojo had said.

I didn't. But there was something strange prickling under my skin and smoldering in my joints. Maybe I hadn't been careful and had caught something. Fool. I breathed through my mouth in the dusty streets, ate market sunflower seeds from my dirty palm, let the shower water run all over my upturned face, and there were the succulent red berries, strawberries the man with the wicker basket had given me to taste. "Eat," he'd said, motioning to his mouth with fingers. "Prueba uno, it's free to try. Muy sabroso."

The hot and cold came then. And the shakes like after you've lifted something unusually heavy. I'd throw a leg outside the sheets and the swirling fan would cool it. Once, exposed like that, Mojo's thin bejewelled hand slid in through the crack in the door and clicked the light switch to the off position. She said, "Rest."

In the dark, the smells of the bedroom were more pronounced. I strained to identify the objects around me: in the corner, on a dresser that smelled strongly of cedar wood, was a large contemplative bodhisattva. His almond eyes were closed, and a loose ribbon of a smile played on his young, full lips. He sat upon a fully opened lotus blossom.

There was murmuring on the patio. Luis and Mojo. I moved the mosquito netting to one side and stared blankly at the bodhisattva as I strained to listen to them.

His face soothed me and after a moment I forgot all about eavesdropping and found that if I stared long enough, trying not to blink, trying to be calm, his face would transform itself into a simpler version of Ilario's. After a while, staring, watching, the lips began to move. At first they smiled wider and I willed him to show a row of small white teeth. He wouldn't. But the lips began to chatter, mouthing unintelligible messages. Maybe he was chanting to himself, or trying to converse. I didn't know. So I asked. I said, "Did you want to say something out loud?" The lips moved on, murmuring, mouthing shapes of words. The silence and the movements were maddening. It made my neck throb, straining to hear. But each time I got out of the bed to get closer to the bodhisattva, his face would freeze. So I would stay very still.

"Go on," I said quietly. "Say something." But he wouldn't. I must have fallen asleep at some point, but I was afraid I'd miss the moment when he spoke, like how Mother used to say that animals spoke at midnight on Christmas Eve, always while I was sleeping.

There was something wrong. Clearly. Each time I awoke that day there was someone new in the room with their cool hands and the excruciating cold sponging of my limbs and abdomen. I'd begun to choke out these dry coughs that woke me at first, but I quickly found this kind of limbo state where I could continually hack and never quite wake. There were sips of water tilted down my throat with the help of Mojo, first, then surprisingly, later in the afternoon, by Luis. They cut like fiberglass.

"I'm sick," I told Luis, whose wrist reeked of spicy cologne as he helped with the glass. I know it made him uncomfortable. He handed it to me to do myself.

"I know you're sick, nena. And you're going to stay here for the night, entiendes?" I nodded and swallowed the water. "That shithole posada you girls are living in should be burned to the ground. I'll bet you a million bucks that's what made you sick. You're going to stay right here." He awkwardly patted my blanketed knee, like he was confounded by his tenderness towards me. He rearranged his clothes and hair as he stood from the bed, smoothing the temples, straightening the robe, retying its silken cord. "Well, anyway, it's probably la tifoidea but you need to get your blood tested to know for sure. I had it about three years ago and I thought I was going to die." He stopped himself. Then adding very quietly, "But you'll be fine."

At the door he turned. "Aha!" He marched across the room to take a small bronze hand bell from the shrine where the bodhisattva sat smirking at us. He gave it a single ring, like he was testing it, and put it on the bedside table.

"Just ring if you need anything. We will come."

I felt flushed with heat as he turned to the door. I didn't want him to go. There was something so coolly tranquilizing about the way he spoke to me. I knew he didn't want to nurture me but he did want me to survive. And that was enough.

"What about Ilario?" I asked, my voice all disconnected, like it was on a string swinging around the room.

His answer was swift. "He'll be okay."

"He told me he was scared." I didn't mean to say that aloud.

"He doesn't need to be scared. I made him a promise that nothing bad was ever going to happen to him ever again. And it won't. I made him that promise."

"How? How can you be sure?"

"He's my life. Right at the centre. And I'm going to keep him right there where he's safe and nobody and nothing can harm him."

This was Luis' crazy lullaby. I could imagine him saying those words to Ilario. Beautiful, empty lullaby words.

Before my eyes closed and before he closed the bedroom door I asked him, "Did you find him?"

Luis answered. "I will."

During the night I woke to a pillowcase soaked with saliva that had been leaking from the corner of my open mouth and God, I was cold. I was tugging at the sheets, pulling them up over my chest, and tugging some more as if all the tugging would miraculously produce more layers, a hidden blanket or something. I thought about scarves from the sleeve of a magician. The bed was like that.

Bundled up, I sipped cool broth in a bowl that had somehow appeared on the night table. Churning it with a spoon, I saw cauliflower, rice, carrots, cilantro, shredded chicken. The more you stirred the more ingredients would emerge from the silt. If I kept stirring I might see something in there that I didn't like: a moth, maybe. A fingernail. All of it made me shivery: the moth-thought, the desk fan sending air in rotating waves over my gooseflesh, the biting smell of cologne, the chill of the soup spoon. I shuffled over to unplug the fan and bundled up in bed again. The bodhisattva was expressionless. Unimpressed.

Luis had provided me with a pair of Ilario's never-used pajamas, blue striped silk-satin that flopped around my ankles. I pulled my feet inside the pant legs for warmth. Pulled up the collar. With everything feeling so smooth and shivery, all I wanted was the musty skin smell of the fringed jacket and its worn suede. I remember how Joseph loved to sit on my lap and have me wrap the jacket around him as I sat chatting with Gloria and Mother. As a baby, he pulled the fringes and the suede wound around his tiny fingers as he sucked his pacifier.

I took a throw from the foot of the bed and put it over my shoulders like a cape, determined to make my way out of the house and back to the apartment for that jacket. My muscles were sore and wobbly, and the house was sleeping as I made my way, silently as I could, into the courtyard. I don't know why, but before I left I crept up to where Ilario was sleeping and pushed the door open just a crack to see the bulk of two sleeping bodies intertwined. I listened for a moment to the throaty sounds of Luis' rattling out-breath. When I pulled the door shut I could hear the shift of their bodies on the creaking wooden bed.

The courtyard was so silent: the insects were quiet, the geckos hadn't chirped or clucked for days, as though they too had given up on the promise of rainfall and now sat there quietly dehydrating. No sound from the kitchen, the study, and the bands of cotton strung across the courtyard were slack in the stillness of the heat wave. Even the street outside Luis' gate was unusually hushed. There was only the distant clamor of a brass band in the town square's bandstand.

Outside the hacienda gate I folded the throw so it resembled a kind of scarf, but I thought too late about changing into my jeans and T-shirt. The gate lock had already clicked into place. So I moved on toward that din of the brass band in borrowed satin pajamas and a membrane of sweat.

Throngs of people milled around the town square and the band hammered on and on, maniacal. Too jovial. The thud of the bass drum, the splashy bright trumpet, the constant smash of the cymbals between the nodding conductor's hands. It was all like you were participating in some kind of jumbled parade. Moving around the *zócalo*, walking in step with the offbeat, my body felt foreign and broken, wood hinged with old wire. I felt like one of the grinning Catrina skeletons, like the one in Luis' dining room, all jaw and long, dangling femurs swinging in a macabre hat dance. I couldn't be sure if I was grinning as I knocked around the crowd.

It was warmer amongst the people. Some of the townspeople snickered at my pajamas, and at some point the edge of my dragging scarf caught the stiletto heel of a young woman, so I let it drop to the ground and left it there.

Deeper into the crowd, closer to the bandstand, my ears were filled more completely with the blood-thumping of the big drum, the blasts of trumpet. Children were out late with their parents and two lunged out of the crowd, dashing in front as they chased after the balloon vendor and his foil pinwheels. The band hammered on a never-ending song, the tuba blurting out its lines like an amateur actor. As I gazed around my eyes fell upon this crumpled-looking *abuela* sitting alone on the stone steps of the gazebo. As our eyes met, the woman crossed herself and mouthed, I think, I thought, the word *demonia*. I could hear the words just behind my ear, whispered there. I jerked around to see if there was someone from town playing a trick on me. I thought that maybe Mojo was imitating the crackle of an old woman's voice, but nothing. Then a man edging through the crowd met my eyes for a moment, just a split second, and I heard in Spanish, *she's always late.* I stared too long at his face. His lips weren't moving. He wetted his lips under his thick black moustache and whistled in tune with the band. He glanced down at me as he passed by and I heard, again, just behind my ear *sonámbula*, sleepwalker.

By then I'd forgotten why I'd left my bed in the first place.

The fever was making it all unclear. I couldn't remember where the bed had been.

Bare arms and a floral dress, shaved napes of necks, soapy smells.

One loud, long trumpet note. A shriek. A siren. And there was more whispering until it all overlapped in fragments of puzzled-to-gether thought. I tried to stay calm, not to panic, to push through.

On the edge of the jostling crowd where a thin wind blew down the street and up my wet back, a hand clutched my elbow. Eye sockets and grinning jaw. Then I was twirled around in a kind of violent dance and spun under an extended arm and pulled in fast and hard to Lucky's chest. He reeked of pot smoke and patchouli oil. But it was familiar somehow. It was okay. At least he was warm. He didn't say anything about me being red-eyed or sweaty or barefoot in ill-fitting pajamas in the middle of the town square. He just started to serenade me in that odd, pretty voice of his, with the words all wrong.

"Stranger in the night, exchanging faces, wandering in the night ... da-da-da-dee-dum ..."

He interrupted himself to ask, "Do you want to get a cold beer, chula?" He smacked his lips, telling me he had "cottonmouth" and was feeling "pasty as hell."

"No. I'm sick, Lucky, can we stop dancing?"

But he didn't pay attention and he kept two-stepping me around, listening to something in the distance, it seemed. "I need to rest!" But he shushed me with a hand, saying "Listen, listen!"

At the far end of the town-square, from some upstairs shuttered window, a trumpeter trilled and then played a plaintive single note, then a mournful line from his trumpet. It was a single streamer dropped from a great height. Lucky nodded slowly and smiled.

"Listen-listen," he said again, smiling. A trumpeter behind us trilled the same melody, so close that we both jumped and Lucky spun around quickly, laughing a little.

The trumpeters continued to call to one another; the first a distant, sinewy cry, the second, strong and close.

"El Niño Perdido," he said.

I asked him, "What's perdido?"

"Lost. The Lost Child."

I felt a wave of nausea as the band struck up between refrains and once again Lucky spun me in these wild circles past dresses, shoulders, moustaches, cologne, my bare feet scuffing on the cobblestone. Near tears, I begged him to stop.

All I could say was, "Please, please ..."

He slowed and stopped.

"Please, I have a fever. I need to get out of here, back to the posada. I've got to get my jacket. I got locked out and I need to get to the hotel. I need to get out of here it's making me crazy." I said all kinds of shit to him in hopes that some of it would stick. And it worked. Something in the rambling must have made sense to him because suddenly he was all solemn and nodding.

"Sure sure. Alright, chula. I'll get you home." He took my hand and we walked. "You got a cold beer at your apartment?"

"Nothing cold," I said, shivering.

"Well, I'll take what I can get. You know how it is, chula." He laughed and bumped me with his shoulder.

XX.

IF I'M HONEST ABOUT IT, I can say I didn't mind holding his hand, his long hand, his skeleton hand, because it was warm and I needed to be led somewhere, anywhere, and he was going that way. I couldn't remember the last time I'd held any man's hand, other than Ilario's, which was different, like holding the soft hand of a child. Lucky's was warm with sweat, especially in the palm. So I held onto him because it felt good, and peculiar, and somehow safe to be walking alongside the strangest-looking gringo in town.

He stumbled and staggered and tripped off curbs, taking me with him. His ragged blue jeans with patches up and down the legs were too short for him and exposed his scrawny ankles, long leather sandals slapping along, his toenails painted an electric blue colour you could find at the open-air market beside glittery barrettes, Ponds cold cream and metal gears, all laid out on a blanket. He wore a policeman's shirt from Long Beach, or so said the patch. The shirt was unbuttoned and you could see his tattoos.

No one would bother us.

Under strings of coloured lights that drooped over the main street, we heard the sound of a tower of fireworks igniting, spinning, and crackling. It sprayed sparks into the crowd below, the entire scaffold whistling from the whirl of flaming pinwheels. Madness. And the crowd roared, Lucky joining in, shouting "Corran cobardes!" as one of the pinwheels spun off its nail and whizzed in mad circles at the feet of the spectators. Spraying silver sparks, the entire flaming wreath ricocheted across the cobblestones and spun out of control. Everyone leapt back from it, laughing. Young boys tried to get as close as they dared, then fled shrieking as sparks began to char their shoelaces. The air was tangy with the smell of sulfur and gunpowder. Like on Canada Day as a teenager, at the lake. Fireworks cinders falling into the dark water, the taste of beer from a can, cherry lip balm.

As a new pinwheel erupted, a bare-chested guy in a straw hat and striped pants came sauntering past us. He stopped when he saw Lucky, trying to remember his name, trying to recognize the face.

"Hey man," he said, punching Lucky in the side. "I heard you was dead."

I stared at his mouth. There were only a few teeth left in it, like they'd been knocked out in a fight or accident.

"Where'd you hear that, brother?" Lucky let go of my hand. He sounded tense, ready to fight. I wondered if he let go of my hand to dig around in his pocket for a roll of pesos to hold in his closed fist.

"Some dude in Celaya told me. You know Mikey? Methadone Mike? I was staying at his place and he said you O.D.'d there. He said they sent your body back to the States and everything. Guess he was lyin' though, huh." He stood mashing his lips together like he was thinking it over or suddenly wondering about the whereabouts of his missing teeth. "Guess he coulda been talkin' 'bout someone else too, huh."

"Nah. Probably me. People are always hopin' I'm dead." He laced his fingers on top of his head.

The guy thumped a fist into Lucky's side again saying, "Glad you're not, man. Listen, I gotta meet somebody, this guy from D.F." Then he said all low, "He's got crank, you want in?"

Lucky declined, patting the guy in the straw hat overly-hard on his back. He got the point. He said he'd see us around, and once the guy'd hopped on the back bumper of a passing truck, Lucky said, "Dickhead."

I waited. "I let that guy stay at my place for a week while I was back in Cali and the fuckin' guy robbed me. He stole my stash, ate all my fuckin' food, and he even left with my girlfriend. Only good one I had. Dickhead."

We turned down my street with its pretty paper banners all fluttering overhead. Lucky amused himself by running ahead down the street,
trying to catch the paper banners well beyond his reach. I knew he was
high, and from the way his tongue roamed around his mouth, I knew
it was probably cocaine and I didn't mind. At the bar I'd served stoners
and junkies, drunks and the occasional speed freak. I'd watch them all
as they tied coffee sticks into knots, or rolled wet napkins into tight
little cigarette shapes between their fingers. And sometimes they had
tics and excess energy and just wanted to talk and talk and talk. So I'd
let them. And sometimes their tongues had explored their mouths, too.

When we came to the *posada*, Lucky stood back studying it.

"Haven't been here in a while," he said.

Then he stooped in the street to pick up a good-sized loose rock
from the cobblestone, and before I could say anything he whipped it
into one of the cactus pots on the edge of the rooftop garden. From
the dark up top was the sound of an animal's claws scuffling, then the
dog lunged forward to the edge of the roof.

"That's the sonofabitch that bit me!" Lucky smiled wide. "He gave
me this." Lucky hauled up his pant leg and showed me a long, meaty
scar along the back of his leg. "I was dating this messed-up Scan-
dinavian chick that was staying here with her sister—I think it was
her sister—and that fuckin' dog didn't like us screwin' around on the
roof, I guess."

"Guess not," I said, just wanting to get inside, wanting warmth,
the jacket, my bed. I slid my hand through the mail slot to jimmy the
lock like Mojo did. Shouldered the door and the lock popped.

The birds in the cages were silent, and only one windowpane along
the colonnade was glowing. Lucky was too loud for the courtyard
when he'd hiss, "Puta!" every time he'd scrape his toes on the stone
steps going upstairs.

In the dark of the hotel room, I rummaged for the fringed jacket
under the bedding without even turning on the lights. I pulled it on
over my pajamas while Lucky knocked his way over to the balcony
door to wrench it open. It screeched against the tile.

"Phew! No offense or nothin' but it stinks in here."

I pulled the fringed jacket to my face and breathed deeply into it. I was feeling better already and had broken a real sweat on the walk through town. My eyes felt too large for their sockets and as I perched on the bed I put my cold hands to them to ease the ache.

I pulled the beaded chain on the night table lamp and it dimly illuminated Lucky, standing in the balcony doorway with his arms outstretched, like he was just hanging there. His armpits were sweating through his shirt.

"How 'bout that beer, chula?"

I didn't say anything. I just got up to get him a beer from the wire shelf in the fridge, popped the cap, took a small swig, then gave it to him. "Salud," He drank deep and long from it, then wiped his mouth on his arm. He leaned against the doorframe while I lay in bed in a cocoon of borrowed silk and hand-me-down suede.

He was quiet when he said this to me: "You get me back here 'cause you wanted to fuck, chula? I'm game. I like you. I like those sexy crooked teeth and your fucked up hair and that skinny little body of yours. The whole bit. I like it." And then he took a drink and he looked like he was all angles and lean muscles and I thought of a praying mantis.

I rambled, totally thrown.

"No. I mean, you're an interesting guy. No, I mean just have a beer and it's fine. I'm fine." The fever made it seem like everything was in a kind of strobe light. Slow and fractured.

"You want to just fool around then?" he said.

I thought he had to be joking but he just waited there, his forehead a tangle of wrinkles, leaning with his beer and that look on his face. I guess it just felt easier to say yes than to explain why not. It felt easier to give in.

He came up and took the cigarette from me. Licked a circle around the end and put it between his lips. Then he flopped down beside me on the bed, leaning on his elbows.

There was breath and wisps of smoke between us. We shared the cigarette, almost shyly, if either of us could be shy. Then he came close and kissed the corner of my mouth, just barely touching. Then he kissed me again and I don't know why I did it, impulse or reflex, I kissed him back. He smoothed the scruff of my hair that fell on my forehead to one side and kissed the place his touch revealed. I touched the blonde down on the bottom of his earlobe.

His mouth. His chin. His cheek. His neck where his pulse beat. He could be anyone at all or no one at all. I watched his pulse pump in his neck then I kissed it, right where the flesh flickered. And then I searched for warmth, sliding hands underneath his shirt and onto his bare back. My fingers nudged and dragged along his skin and my body remembered what muscle felt like. I remembered touch, and gripping with fingers that wanted more. I slid my thumbs into the waist of his jeans. Dizzy when we kissed. Soft. Wet. And I was somehow set free for a moment by the angles of cheekbones and jaw, the light tug of teeth on parted lips, the strain of muscles, the kind of honey taste of him, the smell of smoke, the feeling of sliding away. We were skeletons with plumed hats pairing off for a dance. Our empty eye sockets sometimes peering at each other, neither one of our gazes conveying much more than absence.

He slipped the large mother-of-pearl buttons of the pajama top through their buttonholes, kissing the flesh between my ribs. Slipped the silk pants from my ridiculous hipbones and kissed and nipped and licked at parts of me where bones protruded, where I caved in. Somehow my body came alive under his fingers, the little hairs on my arms alert, my whole body in feverish chills, his hands almost painful as they moved all over me.

He came up to hold my wrists against the pillow as he kissed me. Thinking of my body as something to be wanted, held fast, pinned down and loved was so stupid, so impossible, I felt laughter coming up in me and tried to will it away. But couldn't.

"What?" he said. "I hope you're not laughing at my moves, chula. What the fuck."

"No, no," I said. "You move fine, it's not that." I breathed deep to calm myself out of what was about to be a laughing fit. "It's the fever. I'm sorry."

And we kissed and kind of rolled around for a bit before I said, with him hovering over me, shirt off, jeans unbuttoned, "Stop."

And he did.

He nipped the end of my nose, bit the underside of my cheek. "Why?" he said, and smiled. His hands on me, his fingers in me. "Why stop now." And I couldn't think of a good enough reason so we kept on for a while until we were both sweaty and spent and he was satisfied. I should have been smarter about the whole thing. God knows if I was giving him the fever, if he even cared, or what he was passing on to me that itched or dripped. I didn't even want to think about it. I wiped my stomach off with a sock. Romantic stuff.

He smoked a joint then settled into the pillow, closed his eyes and draped an arm over me. The tattoo on his forearm was blue-black with the name Lorraine. There were others to look at: one just below his belt line was a Chinese character, meaning snake, he explained. A swallow at his heart, a panther in a love-lock with a naked redhead on his bicep, a horseshoe and a pair of dice that dealt, of course, snake-eyes.

"Am I going to crash here?" he asked without opening his eyes.

I told him yes, and he rolled onto his back and laced his hands behind his head.

"Perfect."

So I watched him drift. And I wondered about his age and his skin. His skin wasn't smooth, it was sturdy: it looked like it could take thorns and the tattoo gun, the teeth of a street dog. The twist in his forearm made the blue initials warp and lengthen.

I drew a fingernail over it. You can be rough with tattoos.

Lucky opened one eye to look at me. "Don't be jealous now, chula."

"I'm really not," I said, a little more forcefully than I meant to.

"My kid's mom."

"You have a kid?" I tried not to sound shocked. Failed.

"Mm." Lucky's eyes were closed again.

"Where? Here?"

Lucky breathed deep and sort of grunted. Annoyed with me. I didn't care.

"I don't know, last I seen her she was a baby and her mom and I weren't working out." He stretched and yawned. "Just before I came down here. So she'd be, shit, I guess she's gotta be fourteen by now. Jesus." He propped up the pillows and lit another cigarette.

"You don't see her?"

He exhaled hard.

"Naw," he said. "Better that way. She's doing alright. Her mom's doing better, too, husband and all. I don't need to complicate things."

"Don't you miss her?" I asked, while he threw his long leg over my hip and rolled over so he was hovering above me, cigarette between his teeth. The smoke drifted into my eyes, stinging.

"Don't I miss who?" he asked, taking another drag and flicking the ash onto the floor beside the bed.

"Your daughter." I wrestled out from under him.

He just stared at me. Then he butted the cigarette out on the night table mumbling, "Man, you're too fuckin' much." And he lay back and crossed his arms over his eyes like he did on the bus ride to Tadeo.

My stomach tightened and there was a pulse in my cheeks. I said something about needing some air and pulled the sweaty pajamas around my chest like a robe.

I sat along the length of the balcony wall, toes playing with the bamboo bars of the empty birdcage there. I wondered what other roost the bird had found, if it had made a nest in the cathedral beams or between the spines of some desert cactus. I imagined flying low over the streets too, over hats and Volkswagens, up onto rooftops with billowing white laundry, settling where there was a better view, where the horizon stretched out longer and longer.

XXI.

AS THE SUN ROSE, I closed my eyes and pulled the sheet to my chin.
I dreamed.

A coyote crossed my path. A shoe in its mouth.

Then Joseph. Barefoot across the desert like Saint-Exupéry's little prince.

He called to me.

In the dream, he was standing in mud. I leaned down to pick him up. His feet were stuck and I couldn't lift him out no matter how hard I tried, no matter what I did. So I went to my knees and held him. My hand on his head pulling him close.

"I've missed you, baby. I've missed you. I've missed you." I held him. Kneeling beside him in the mud.

When I awoke, it was still dawn. It had only been minutes, seconds. I cried, lying on my side, careful not to let the sounds awaken the man who was still fast asleep on the far side of my bed.

Just after the noon bells rang, I was standing at the foot of the bed contemplating that long sweating body sprawled out in front of me. He'd left his pants crumpled on the floor beside my feet. He was just in his underwear. The tight kind. His face slick with sweat. His nose shone with oil and he stank. He rubbed his face into the pillow. My pillow. His big hand rubbed at his nose. Those hands let you know he worked for a living, always healing or just torn open from some nail or something. Blisters. I'd seen him working down the road on the way to the market, tossing a shovel up to a man standing on a scaffold, and I remember thinking how it was amazing that, even as he worked and sweated, he could still manage to look lazy.

I grabbed one of his toes and wiggled it.

"Hey, wake up," I said softly.

He looked irritated and blindly kicked at my hand and rolled over.

"Come on," I said.

He didn't respond.

The fever was lifting a little but my eyes still felt all gluey and looking around made them ache. I tired easily, too, and figured if I couldn't get him out, I might as well sleep there beside him as long as I could. So when I crawled back in bed he threw a leg over me.

Jesus, I thought. Trapped.

I lay there like that as long as I could, then I told him I needed some water, but the truth was that my gut was in spasm and I needed the washroom. Almost immediately. I was almost to the door when he said, "Get over here," motioning with his hand. So I humoured him, but I'd already begun to sweat. I was thinking hurry. He took my hand in his.

"Sit down," he said. His eyes looked sort of gentle and puffy with sleep.

"You know," I said, "I'm glad you came over, that we hung out, but you really got to go. I've got, I've got, plans for the afternoon."

I perched on the edge of the bed, patting his hand twice. Go. Take a hint. I cleared my throat and my stomach tightened.

He smiled at me. That pretty smile that softened his face. "Listen," he said, all quiet. "I told you I like you and that's the truth, Abby."

I tried not to wince as the cramps came in waves.

"You and me are the same. You know why?" I shook my head. "Because we're both free, man. You get it. I know you do."

Free, I was thinking. Free spirits. Are you kidding me? But go on. Hurry. I was breathing deep and clutching my knees by that point.

"I just don't want you to get all uptight about this." He gestured at us, the bed. "We could have a lot of fun together but I'm not looking for anything, and I don't think you were looking for me."

I could breathe out a little and smile at him. He was as good as gone. That was what I needed. And I very nearly loved him for that.

"Well," I said, "I don't want to tie you down."

He looked happy. He looked relieved. But then when he got up to pull on his crumpled jeans he shouted "motherfuck!" as a scorpion stung the delicate skin where his leg met his genitals. Right in the groin. Lucky ripped the pants from his body, tossing them toward the balcony. The scorpion fell from him and made an odd little crackle when it hit the tiles, its tail convulsing. When I looked closely I could see it had snapped a leg in the fall. I had to quickly put the scorpion outside into a potted palm, using a glass cup and a cigarette pack. I couldn't bear the thought of it crushed on the tiles by his shoe.

Lucky didn't want to show me the sting and he didn't want ice. He got dressed quickly while I watched the scorpion kind of unwind and die. Devilish thing.

"Do you need a doctor?" I asked, still squatting beside the plant.

"No, I don't need a fuckin' doctor! I need a beer."

Anyway, the injury put him in a miserable mood and we were out of cigarettes, so he left unceremoniously, mumbling something about the Toro Rojo as the door closed behind him.

It was noon already when I rolled up the sleeves of the satin pajamas and shuffled out into the courtyard to fill a jug with water.

It was a hard day.

A hustled trip down the colonnade every half hour to that God-awful shared washroom. Dripping sweat from your forehead and falling right to the dirty tile floor as you sat there. And then Sue perpetually at the door, wanting in, and not seeming to understand that she couldn't come in to take a shower.

"I don't care if you see me, man!" she'd say.

"That's not the problem!"

My seizing gut.

"Come on, man, it's too hot. I need some water on me!"

I just stopped responding.

"You know, you've been monopolizing the bathroom, like, all day and it's not cool, you know. Not cool at all." Then she banged a fist on the door before pacing the colonnade again, I guess. Doing her laps. It might have been the first day that girl ever wanted a shower. So it was her own bad timing.

Feeling momentarily better, I flushed and the toilet water only swirled. I looked around for a plunger. Finding there wasn't one, of course, I thought the next best thing, the merciful thing, would be to crank open the frosted glass slats of the bathroom window. Sue's bottle and kit were in there. I brought them out between the slats and turned the bottle over in my hands, looking between the bottle labels at the needle inside. It made me sad. An ugly tool like a razorblade or a burnt spoon or a bag of glue. That was the stuff of alleyways, not holidays.

On the way back to the hotel room I sat it down outside her door. And as I was walking away I heard the door open, the scape of the bottle, the door shut, quickly.

The room was a mess, sheets still tangled, and the whole place felt oddly masculine. Lucky's cigarette butts were on the floor, on the night table, and the smell of him was clinging to things.

I scraped open the balcony doors to let some fresh air into the room, then lay across the bed in my underwear and pajama top and was pulled into a real deep satiny kind of sleep: the only way to find relief from the heat, the sweat, the twisting of the gut.

Mojo's face peering over me. Ines beside her, looking calm as a plaster saint. Mojo pressed a hand to my cheek.

"Hey sickie," she said.

I stretched, and told her I was sorry, and I was. Sorry to be such a pain in the ass.

"We went up to our room, and there were your clothes, but no Abby! Thought maybe you vaporized."

"I know, it was like I was dreaming. I just started walking."

"In your pajamas?" Ines laughed as she prepared my arm for a needle.

"Ilario's," I said.

When she finished, she put a cotton ball over the needle mark and taped over it quickly. A good mother, I thought. She made you feel all swabbed, bandaged, and tucked-in.

"Listo, all finished." She placed the vials of blood into a special compartment of a padded bag. The blood looked dark and too thick. Couldn't be healthy.

I asked how her little one was doing.

"She's fine, thank you. Teething." She gestured to the centre teeth on her bottom jaw.

"Oh, so hard." I said. "I remember those days. Or nights."

"Si," Ines said, nodding.

She looked at the ground.

"Bueno," she said after a quiet moment passed. "We'll wait for the results and then we will see what we need to do."

I thanked her, and hoped Mojo would follow her out the door, but she'd found the open cage on the balcony railing and produced the bird from behind its bamboo bars. She took it in her hands and brought it into the room, thumb stroking the bird's white head.

I sat up. Couldn't believe it. "Oh my God! Is that my bird? Oh my God, was he back in his cage?"

"Well of course he was! He's a homing pigeon!" Mojo kissed his head. "Aren't you?" She kissed him again and grinned.

The results for both strains of typhoid came back positive from the lab and I was given a shot deep in the muscle of my buttocks to stop the nausea and the rice-water vomiting. There were also large pills for the pains in my temples. They made everything hum. Refrigerator noise. The feeling was good and freeing.

Mojo came by from time to time with bits of news or pungent tea and tidbits she picked up from the open-air market: a honey comb in a jar, dripping; a pair of coconut earrings; a tooled-leather knife sheath.

One afternoon she brought news that Ilario was out of bed even though he was having dizzy spells. Mostly he'd been spending time with Luis in the dark, thick-walled library, where Delilah came daily to practice her piano scales.

But Luis was not improving.

"He's developed muina," Mojo explained.

I asked what that was.

She had to think about it a moment and finally shook her head saying, "Doesn't translate. It's the kind of sick you get when you stuff your feelings down, especially anger. You know, you lose your appetite, you upchuck, you don't sleep right. It mostly happens when something real bad's gone down and there's nothing you can do about it."

I made her repeat the name. I wasn't sure if she'd made it up, or maybe she'd just mistranslated the Spanish.

"Muina," Mojo said, slow and loud like she was practicing her lessons, her mouth elastic. "Muina. It's real common around here."

XXII.

DURING THE HOTTEST week in Tadeo, we were all sick. Nearly all of us. The cloud cover had settled above the valley and kept the heat under it like sweat under blankets. Ines came by with news that an epidemic had broken out in town, the doctor's office overrun by people with glossy eyes and abdominal rashes and that hacking cough. She told me the cafés around the *zócalo* were shut down while the cooks recuperated and were tested and retested until the infection had left their blood altogether.

Around that time Vula and Sue holed themselves up in the hotel so they'd be close to the bathroom while they waited for the fever to empty them. Sue came by in her bra and a pair of bellbottoms, wanting some Pepto-Bismol, her hands rubbing circles on her bare, distended belly.

I shook my head. Told her I didn't have any but she could have one of my bananas.

She broke it from the bunch on the kitchenette counter and peeled it right there, stuffing it in her mouth. She spoke as she ate. "You going somewhere?" Her cheek full. She gestured with her chin toward my pile of clothes beside the knapsack on the floor.

"No, well, yeah. Back home. Canada. I just never unpacked."

"Huh."

She continued eating the banana. She stank of sweat, so bad you couldn't breathe through your nose around her.

Sue scanned the room.

"Can I get your pillows when you leave?" She pointed to the head of the bed.

"Sure, I guess so."

Sue nodded and cleared her mouth of banana filaments with her tongue.

"It's hard to get pillows around here. Hard to get comfortable." She burped and excused herself, thanked me for the banana and left with her slow feet shuffling down the corridor.

Later that day, we had to compete for the facilities. Sometimes Vula would race by me down the colonnade, slamming and locking the bathroom door behind her. Then I'd rush downstairs to the hotel lobby washroom, Marcella shooting me a sympathetic smile as she handed me the key on its oversized wooden keychain.

There comes a point when you think it can't possibly go on much longer. You drink water and smoke cigarettes and watch the bird on its roost. The bird will take flight in the afternoon when your neighbour comes by to settle herself down, quite naturally, like she belongs there, beside you in bed. And you'll try to act natural. Because on the days when she doesn't come by, when nobody comes by and the bird on its roost is restless now that the clouds are dropping lower, rain getting closer, a weird kind of feeling will come over you, and you might wish you'd been a better neighbour, because you just can't stand the hotel room and being alone any longer, and then you'll make your way back out into the world.

Like on this one day, an empty, long day, the street below the balcony was unusually still, nothing to see, so I threw water on my face, brushed my teeth, patted down my scarecrow hair and made my way into town.

I stopped by the smallest café on the *zócalo* for some spiced coffee and found it open, but the usual waiter was away with the fever. I nodded knowingly, nobody had to say typhoid, and ordered a *café de olla*, finished it quickly, left a good tip. I made my way past the restaurant with its tin stars hanging over the tables, where a few people sat having a long lunch over a pitcher of sangria. I thought I'd see how Ilario was doing.

No straight lines in that town. So the first turn was a wrong turn and I ended up on a road that would have led uphill toward the lookout. Retracing my steps, I stopped to ask a man sharpening knives whether he knew of the hacienda of Luis Reynosa.

He considered the name for a moment, repeating it, his forehead wrinkled. The knives stopped spraying sparks against the grinding stone.

"La mariposa?" Squinting, his feet paused on the bicycle-wheeled contraption he sat upon. It caught me. The use of that word, butterfly, and I didn't know what he meant at first. Then I didn't know how to respond.

"Si," I said finally. "Yes, Señor Reynosa de Ciudad de México." Like that would straighten him out.

"Oh," the man said, then in Spanish, "just ahead, not much further. The next block to the right."

I thanked him and he nodded politely and smiled.

When Luis, the king, the *mariposa*, answered the door, I was running a thumb over the lips of the little cherub doorknocker. The door swung open under my hand, and Luis stood there, fat and flushed and handsome as always, in a linen shirt streaked with sweat. At first he looked fierce, like he might charge, but his face quickly loosened.

"Ay dios mío, it's just you." He attempted a smile. "Come in, come in, don't stand around in the street."

He double-locked the door behind us and marched through the courtyard, beckoning me with his finger, "Come on, come."

Ilario leaned against the doorway to the library. He looked thin and vulnerable. His cheekbone was still so swollen that one eye opened only slightly, like a new bud. I stood with him. Hovering just outside the hive.

Inside, Delilah was planted on the piano bench alternately study-ing her rings and shaking her head at Luis and Mojo, who were hav-ing at it. Mojo looked a little relieved to see me but only for a second. Then she sat forward on the sofa saying, "The point is that violence begets violence. That's all I'm saying."

Ilario shot me a look.

"You're getting better," I whispered.

He smiled. "Poco a poco."

Luis stroked his hair back. "What is that, Mojo. You're quoting the bible now?"

"It's not the bible, it's natural law."

Delilah murmured to her turquoise ring, "Martin Luther King Jr."

Luis sat back in the sofa facing her. He crossed his legs. Hands behind his head.

"You're right. I should do nothing. I should just sit back and let the police do their job and laugh at us, and laugh at Ilario, and clap on the back the hijo de puta that nearly killed him."

"I'm not saying that. You're twisting my words."

Delilah chimed in. "You are lucky you didn't kill him, Luis. I thought you were just going to wave that gun around and frighten him."

"Pues mira." Luis was exasperated like I'd never seen him. "It was just the leg."

"He still could have died from it."

"There's no vital organ in the leg. There's nothing in the leg."

"There are arteries. There are big veins, Luis," she said.

"Not here," Luis shouted, leaning over and pointing to a place on his own shin. "Not aquí en la espinilla."

He stretched his arms out across the back of the sofa and checked to see if Ilario was still there. He half-heartedly winked at him and Ilario half-smiled. Mojo was all folded up on the sofa across from him—cross-legged and cross-armed like a little genie or something. She might nod and disappear.

"Bueno, when you two are finished scolding me ..."

"I'm not scolding you."

"As I was saying, when you are finished castigarme, you can maybe help me figure out what the fuck we're going to do."

Nobody spoke for an extra-long minute. Then Mojo finally said, "I'm sorry," and Luis said nothing. Then she said, "I'm scared too. I'm sorry."

Ilario lightly touched my arm. "There's talk that the guy's looking for Luis. That he's sending people. There's talk about that."

"You both need to get out of here," Delilah said.

Ilario's voice was firm. "I still want to see my mother, Luis."

"Well we can't. How do we leave? Everybody knows my car."

Delilah nodded and mouthed the word Mercedes to me. Then she went back to contemplating her rings, turning them one by one.

"I haven't seen my mother in half a year," Ilario said.

"I'm not taking the fucking bus. So forget that."

"I didn't say bus."

"You're right, we've got to go," Luis said, smoothing his hair.

Mojo said, "Okay so you go visit her," Mojo said. "Keep it low-key."

"We'll get you out of here," Delilah said. "Take my car to his mother's."

"Today," Luis said.

"We can go to Tlacotalpan."

Luis wasn't listening. "They're probably here in town already."

"You know what?" Mojo said. "We'll take you out of town. We'll take you to Lágrimas, you drop us there and you take the car the rest of the way to Tlacotalpan. And just lay low. Your Mercedes is here. No one is home. No one answers the door."

"And what are you going to do for the rest of your lives in Lágrimas while we take the car half way across the country?" Luis asked.

"Easy. Trambilla."

I quickly looked to Delilah for translation and she mouthed the word bus, then nodded.

Mojo said we'd go get the car and would be back in half an hour. She wanted to know if they could be packed and ready to go. They said they could.

En route to get the car, Delilah let us know that she had "things to attend to" at the *posada* and we should go without her, that it would be unprofessional to leave her guests without "a matron." She retrieved the car key from the hotel office and Mojo dangled it in front of me on its souvenir keychain from Hawaii.

"You can drive, right?"

XXIII.

SO THERE WE WERE. Driving out to some God-awful joyless place named after tears of all things, in a ramshackle car with Mojo giving wrong-turn directions and Luis and Ilario jamming themselves below window level in the back seat. And I'm driving. I'm driving because Mojo didn't mention that she doesn't anymore and never really cares to say why. She's just happy I can. So I'm silent. Sometimes you just have to do what you're asked to do.

"I got the call," Luis was saying, "My uncle tracked the guy down. Found out where he was and the guy answers the door and ..."

"And you shot him."

"No. My nerve is just gone. Like that. So the guy says 'What the fuck is this?' And then, then it's back. My nerve."

"And then you shot him," Mojo said again.

"Then I shot him. Two times. One hit him in the leg. And now all this."

The car was bumping over the cobblestone and Mojo told me I'd have to hold the side mirror until we were on the highway, otherwise the duct tape wouldn't hold. So I had my hand out the open window, holding the shimmying mirror. The whole car was cockeyed. A patchwork of borrowed parts. It was impossible to tell what colour it had started out—pea green, metallic silver, rust red. When Luis had swung their two matching bags into the trunk of the car he'd asked in earnest, "These aren't going to fall through, are they?" Mojo already had her bare feet up on the dash, her boots thrown somewhere in the back. She just told him to get in and get low.

Once we were well outside of town, Ilario and Luis sat up, then Ilario—even with Luis turning every five minutes to see if we were being followed—eventually fell asleep against his shoulder. At one point the *Policía* truck came close behind us and used their traffic-horn before passing us and turning at the fork. Luis pulled his handgun from his belt—I guess Mojo caught him doing it—Hey-hey!—and before I even knew what was going on she was very calmly, very crisply telling me to pull over.

She turned in her seat and slapped his arm. "What are you doing?" Then slapping it again she said, "What were you going to do, shoot the police too?"

There was no resistance as Ilario took the gun, swung open his car door and threw the gun into the dry scrub where it landed, not far off, with a shot blast, sending my shoulders to my ears, too late.

Mojo nodded. Mouth tight. "Loaded," she said in that calm, flat voice again. "You brought a loaded gun in the car."

"He had a loaded gun down his shorts," Ilario said.

I laughed into my thumbnail.

"You know you're not an outlaw," Mojo said as we pulled back out on the highway.

"I'm a fugitive," Luis said, stroking his hair back in place.

In just over an hour we had to pull over two more times. First for Ilario who announced from a dead sleep that he had to urinate, then ended up walking an inordinate distance to relieve himself behind just the right shrub it seemed, not that one, not that one. Then half an hour later, when I'd had to put the gas pedal to the floor to pass a smog-farting commuter bus, he very quietly asked if I could please pull over. When I did, he got out of the car once again, and stood by the roadside without explanation. First I looked to Mojo, then to Luis in the backseat. Luis rolled down his window and leaned out.

"What are you doing, mi amor?" he asked gently.

"She's driving too fast," I could hear Ilario say.

Then Luis in Spanish. He said something like, "She had to pass a bus, she needed to speed up."

"Not that much," Ilario said. "Not that fast."

Ilario would only get back in the car if I promised Luis I would slow down.

"He's touchy," Luis said. "Everything upsets him right now."

I told him I understood. And I did. And I promised to drive slowly. "Tell him I promise."

Ilario thanked me quietly once he was back in the car.

There, outside of town, the landscape seemed somehow older: all craggy and tough-looking. The edge of the highway was dotted with shrines for cars that had presumably crashed into each other, since there were no flimsy guardrails to barrel through, no cliffs to topple over. On the two-lane highway, a sleepy driver might have drifted across into oncoming traffic, then someone would build a shrine out of white painted bricks and a pretty plastic wreath. But so many. I dragged my fingers through the dry, whistling air, past shrine after shrine. I guess all the tension of having to get out of town was starting to leave me by that time because I was talking again and it didn't seem so bad to have to drive all the way to the place called Lágrimas. But then I said something stupid. I think I was trying to lighten the mood or break the silence or something but it was just stupid.

"It's like driving through a cemetery."

And nobody said a thing.

And I thought, shit. You know that silence. It holds everyone in its warm jelly.

Luis tried to get us onto some other track. "Not much longer now to Lágrimas."

Mojo was wiggling her toes on the dash. Her dirty, painted toes.

"Keep slow, please," Ilario said, reminding me.

I let up a little.

Then Mojo asked me if I'd ever been to Arizona. I told her no.

"Mojo ..." Luis said.

"In Bisbee, where me and Buddy lived, the roads are wild. Turns that bank hard and rock face on one side, canyon on the other. Even the straight lines got curves in 'em." Mojo smiled at me.

Ilario rolled down his window a little more and closed his eyes into the wind that was rushing in.

"Only about fifteen more minutes," Luis said. "No time at all."

Mojo turned back to Luis and smiled. Then to me. "He's trying to protect me. Which is very sweet. But I'm okay, Luis. She can know."

I said nothing.

"Buddy died on the highway." And I thought or said, Jesus.

"He'd just come back from Vietnam. Anyway, he'd *just* gotten back so we went south to celebrate. I had gotten these palazzo pants to wear, I remember. All bright swirls, pink and yellow and blue. Anyway our plan was to go to this place called Agua Prieta across the border. You know, to celebrate. And Buddy just got out of his mind. I was in better shape to drive, anyway we didn't much think about things like that back then. Guys didn't wear seatbelts, I almost never did, and everybody was fine. You know when you're young. And we almost made it back to Bisbee but there was just the littlest bit of snow and I didn't count on that and I guess I took a turn too hard and um, I didn't count on that little bit of snow. Nobody predicted snow."

Mojo had her knees bent. Feet on the seat. She was holding her toes.

"And it was bad. It was really bad. Our car turned over a couple times. God, I went out on the highway, crazy, bleeding and screaming and a man from Sonora stopped his truck and tried to help, tried to help Buddy, but he couldn't get him out either so you know what he did? He just knelt down with me right there beside Buddy. He knelt down in that little bit of snow and he held my hand and he told me to pray. I never prayed before in my life but that's what we did. We prayed together until the ambulance came. But by then he was gone."

I could see her: tattered butterfly on the white highway, snow landing lightly on her hair. Buddy crumpled. Buddy gone. The Mexican man who prayed with her in the blood and the snow.

"Jesus, Mojo," I said.

"That's all the time we had. Bunch of good years, some time apart, then one day and one night in Sonora."

We slowed down a little later in this tiny town of three, four hundred people. Children playing a game of soccer in the street paused to watch our rusted-out car roll by. They had serious faces, like little men. The men smearing cement on a wall, they looked up from their work. A little girl in a doorframe was eating roasted corn with chili. Women were watching their kids. We'd invaded their lives with our presence, disrupted patterns, and I felt apologetic the whole way through town, first past the cemetery, then the grocery store, the mechanic's shop, a *taquería*, a chicken rotisserie, a coffin store, a pharmacy. Everything seemed closed—either for siesta or for good—and I wondered if something terrible had happened there. Something that kept people indoors and close to their television sets.

Near the plaza stood the town's heavy church, where an ancient-looking woman was moving toward its flight of stone steps on her knees. We all watched her as we passed.

"I hear they sometimes wear crowns of thorns," Mojo said when she saw me watching her in the rear-view mirror.

"Who told you that?" Luis suddenly asked from the back seat.

"Well, don't they?"

"Sometimes. Not everyone."

The woman inched along, barely making any progress. The church's opening was dark as a mouth.

"They—sometimes, some of them—whip themselves until they bleed. Can you feel it?"

"Feel what?" I asked her even though my arms were raised in gooseflesh.

"The energy."

A pig trotted across the road on its small cloven feet and I had to stamp down on the brakes. I swore and the pig trotted off.

Otherwise the street was deserted. Fit for ghosts and goodbyes.

"End of the road, kids!" Mojo declared out of nowhere, startling us all.

"Right here?"

"Yeah. Pull over, Abby. There'll be a bus through the square eventually."

I nodded. Glad at the idea of hitching a ride out of that place.

Mojo was already out. Stretching her arms and scratching her curls while Luis and Ilario waited to say goodbye.

She looped her hands over Luis' neck. "Take care of each other," she said, and kissed his cheek. Ilario was already sitting in the passenger's seat. I squatted and he smiled and put his hand on mine.

"In another lifetime, let's be in love," he said.

"Alright."

"Vamos, mi amor!" Luis said.

I wished I had something meaningful to say to him, some little words to protect him like a charm, but the moment came and went.

"Bye." And they drove down the deserted street. We watched until Luis flashed his blinker and turned right at a crossroads.

After an hour, under storm clouds and spindly trees, we determined that soon was a relative term. "Soon," a passerby had told us when we asked about the next bus to Tadeo. So we moved to shadier spaces ever so often, finally settling on the steps of the church door. The church breathed cool air on our backs.

After a while we were thirsty enough to drink the holy water but didn't—all those fingers. The incense and the heat were making me feel high and you could feel the storm coming. The charge in the atmosphere felt so intense I expected sparks to ignite mid-air. The *trambilla* that was to come soon kept us waiting until we both stretched our legs out on the cool of the church tile. Nobody seemed to mind. A couple of old women prayed silently inside, so we spoke soft and low.

"Do you think Ilario loves him?" I was thinking of his dove-wing eyebrows, the way he smelled like cedar after it rains.

"Oh sure, I think so. In his way. Hell, even if he doesn't, Luis has got enough love for the both of them. You ever been in love like that? Can't-sleep can't-eat love?"

"Yeah."

"Oh yeah? Who was it?"

"My son's father," I said. "He said he wanted to marry me but I was only nineteen and he didn't really mean it. But for a while I loved him like crazy and then I think all that love just moved over onto Joseph."

Then, of course she said, "You have a kid?"

XXIV.

I WOULD SAY IT ONCE and that would be it. Never again, I thought. Not to Luis or Lucky or to pious cab drivers who didn't speak my language or drunk hookers who did. I would say it once, the way it happened, and it would all run away from me like the spilling of blood. A story like that cannot live on in Mexico, I thought. Once it's said, the ice of it will melt and the rest will evaporate. I had watched clouds burn off in noonday sun over the mountains there. It would be the same way with this.

So I told her about the slicing sleet and how when you pushed down your foot on the accelerator the car wouldn't move and its tires would spin in slush-ruts. I told her about the steering wheel lurching under your mittens until you straighten it out. Being too hot, clothes all bunched and rumpled, pulling off mittens with your teeth, hat into the passenger's seat of your sister's car, hair all static electric.

I remember running twenty minutes late.

I blamed the grocery girl, the barflies, the puppy, idiot drivers, street ploughs, shots of booze, the doom-and-gloom weatherman, the pervert at the bar. He'd said, "Get us a couple slippery nipples," his fingers waggling at my chest and Lenore, a regular, she laughed along with him and played with his earlobe. And I was red, I could feel it, but it was anger. So when I came back to the table I put those little shots of liquor down hard in front of Lenore and her new friend and waited there until they tilted them back.

Shift over. And his lips looked sticky, not slippery.

I handed them the bill.

"Come on, sit down with us," he said. "We'll buy you a shot, it's the end of your shift, isn't it?"

That was at three-ten. I took a shot. I leaned against the booth.

"Let me ask you something," Lenore said. "If you had twenty-four hours to live, what would you do?" Raised an eyebrow at her friend and he laughed to himself. His neck went all red and blotchy.

"Take my son on a holiday," I said. And neither of them were listening.

"You know what I'd do if I had twenty-four hours to live?" Lenore said. And she smiled and leaned in to the ear of the man beside her and whispered sloppily. He laughed to himself. Then he leaned in and bit her neck and Lenore grinned and mouthed the word, Bingo to me. Then she said, "We'll take the cheque, hon."

Three-fifteen.

The checkout girl with silver braces on her teeth. She clicked her tongue at the plunger in two separate parts and wobbled the rubbery mouth of it around in her hands, looking for a price. She called over the loud speaker and I told her, "It's fine, don't worry about it." There was a plastic clock behind the cash.

"It'll just be a minute," she said. Her mouth close up to the microphone: "Cash three. Price check. Sometime today Carol."

A woman with a fur hat like a raccoon curled around her head. She arrived at the intersection at the exact moment I did. I waved her ahead. "Go go *go!*" And she smiled and waved back for me to go, and the tires of my sister's car just spun uselessly beneath me. Maybe she started forward, maybe the tires caught, we connected fender to fender and had to step out into the ankle-deep slush to frown at the damage together. The woman gave me her business card and I gave her my phone number written in pen on an Italian takeout menu from Gloria's glove box. The last two digits competed with a stain of red sauce.

Then home, to grab his hockey gear. Friday. Hockey day.

The puppy had climbed halfway up to the second floor again and was gripped with vertigo. His paws hung off the stair and he was yowling. He wouldn't let me pick him up. He stiffened and scrambled. So I had to ease him down the stairs, hand on his rump, stair after stair, first front feet, then back.

Three-thirty.

The toilet upstairs was full to the brim with soggy, soiled toilet paper Joe had left behind. It had been running all day and had spilled onto the bathroom tile. I thought Jesus what else and threw towels onto the floor, kicked them around the base of the toilet. Used the new plunger to clear it with that hollow sucking sound. I just nudged the soiled towels into the corner for later. Grabbed the hockey bag from his bedroom, granola bar from the kitchen cupboard, then out the door.

Three-forty.

My head was everywhere but there. The front bumper and what I'd tell Gloria, like she'd never been in an accident before, probably wouldn't notice. Three forty-five. He'd probably started to walk home already. I'd probably just missed him. Drove right past him. I always said, If I'm not there, walk home. And walk fast like you know where you're going. Don't hang around and wait for some weirdo to grab you. I'd feel sick whenever I'd think of him once again opening the front door with his own key, still around his neck on a shoelace from my ice skates. It's weird what you remember and where there are blank spots.

Like how I remember that the sleet had turned to granules of ice on the way to the school, and as I came to the side of the school there were all these dozens and dozens of little boot treads quickly filling up with ice pellets.

I tried the side door, but it was locked. Circled the building and knocked on a glass window where there were paper snowflakes taped up. The janitor was inside using paper towels on the desk graffiti. He just shook his head and pointed to his watch, so I pounded again. And he was so slow, so slow laying down the ball of paper towel, slow to the door, opening it just a crack and the waft of lemon-ammonia from inside.

He said, "School's closed. Closes at three-thirty." Like I didn't know. How could I not know that. I told him that I was late. There'd been an accident and I wanted to make sure my kid wasn't in there waiting for me.

"Just a couple teachers left. I might have seen him though. Whose class he in?"

"Miss Thompson's. He's wearing a red toque, blue ski jacket with red stripes down the side?"

"Okay yeah, I seen him. He was waiting outside a while and must've left after the last kid got picked up."

So sit with that. Sit with that a while.

On the drive back home, I knew something had gone wrong. There's a kind of jangling that happens, an alarm that goes off inside of you and you can't think of anything else but your kid.

Three blocks to home. That's it. It isn't far. It's two mailboxes, two stop signs, one set of lights, one alleyway, four fire hydrants. It's one snow fort. It's one melting snow man. It's seven minutes walking together and twelve minutes with him walking alone, over curbs, up on lawns, stopping to look inside the mailbox slot.

I looked down the alley with its speed bumps and high wood fences, glanced down the one-way streets and for some reason, because I knew, I stopped the car to look through spaces between the narrow houses. I accelerated for the last half-block.

Jammed the keys in the front door lock and started apologizing to him before I was even in the door. "I know, I know, I'm sorry!"

Warm and quiet. There were sounds of the whimpering puppy who had wet a circle around himself on a step halfway up to the second floor.

I called for Joe.

I ran double-stride up the staircase past the puppy.

His bedroom door was closed and when I barged in telling him to get moving I saw his comforter pulled over a lump in the middle of the bed. "Baby, I'm sorry," I said, and flipped the comforter back to see his sheets there, balled-up since morning.

Things you remember: the balsam wood airplane hanging over his bed was slowly turning on its fishing line.

I threw open my closet door even though he'd never be in there, I knew he'd never be in there. Dust. Shoes. Books.

Flung the curtains from the windows. No breath now.

Down the staircase, past the puppy.

I remember the kitchen, calling Mother at Gloria's. Mother answered, annoyed. "Hello." Sounding like she'd just swallowed a bite of oatmeal.

"Do you have Joseph?" Stretching the cord so I could open the back door. The snow in the yard was undisturbed. Squirrel on the back fence, twitching its tail.

"Well, no. Today's Friday." Friday, she said. Like I could have forgotten the days of the week as easily as she did items on her grocery list.

I don't know what I said then. I don't know what I did. Blank spots start.

"Well, where is he, Abigail?" I remember her saying that. All close to the mouthpiece. All buzzy. I remember saying, "I can't find him." And I must have called others, it seems. Phone cord slackened and coiled around itself like intestines.

Call Brenda. Call the babysitter. Call the neighbour. Call Mrs. Commetti.

She said, "Is something happened, Abigail?" while the kitchen spun in wide, wild breathless circles and I couldn't speak. "Joseph is not home?" she was saying. And I was saying, "Oh my God. Oh my God." I managed to tell her to call the police before I hung up.

Then you're just a pair of eyes. They dart everywhere as you speed through the neighbourhood, crossing out the faces of drivers at red lights, catching on stray gloves half-buried in snow, a pair of eyes speed-reading strangers' backyard swing sets.

You say, Jesus God help me ... You recite it.

The car window was down and I pulled up to two children tunnelling into a snowdrift in their front yard. I shouted across the passenger's seat, "Did a little boy go by here?" And the kids just glanced suspiciously at each other, and one of them shook his head no, while the other brought a mitt full of snow to his mouth.

Your finger punches doorbells.

"I can't find my son," I said to strangers at front doors. "Please help me. I need to check your backyard. Please help me."

Then were too many streets. Too many basements with small, barred windows, and so many children with woolen toques pulled over their eyebrows.

A woman left her house to help. Someone I'd never met. She pulled on her winter jacket and slipped on a pair of running shoes beside her front door and just like that she came. Rode with me as I parked half on the sidewalk, motor running, searching up and down one-way streets. Door to door. Barging through backyard gates, then another street, another alleyway, our hands pulling back black swimming pool tarps frosted stiff, encrusted with leaves. Our hands pounded on side doors, on garage doors. We called him.

Nothing. Barking behind doors.

Down in Christie Pitts Park, figure skaters were swirling around in their black coats against the ice. Children stepped in short strides on their skate blades, fell down. Not blue. Not red. Keep moving.

I called his name in public washrooms, pushing each stall door open. Strangers ask questions you don't have time to answer. "I can't find my son."

That was the last time I ever came home. Already it looked different; the sky was the colour of a bruise and the bare trees were black ink blown across paper. There were four Ontario Provincial

Police cruisers parked curbside and I was all blood and heartbeat. No thoughts. No breath. Every light in the house was on.

Mrs. Commetti was there, standing on the porch with her thick grey scarf wrapped around her neck and held over her mouth with one hand. She reached out for me as I passed.

"Is he there?" I asked—and didn't wait for her to answer.

Inside, a police officer was descending the stairs. Shoes and shins, navy pants with a red stripe, and then there was Gloria grabbing at my shoulders. Her face looked smudged. She clutched and grabbed, nearly clawing. She was wailing. "He's gone! He's gone!" She just kept saying that over and over in this voice I'd never heard before. Shuddering and sobbing and clinging. Not my sister.

My hands were shaking, fluttering around my mouth, my heart, like there was something there, an explanation.

"Where is he?"

Gloria was leaning into the kitchen doorframe.

"Where is he?"

I tried to get into the kitchen. Peer around the uniforms to see if he was there at the table. Then the officer with deep set eyes and years of laugh lines around those eyes, he started talking and saying absurd things. "Abigail, I'd like for you to sit with us in the living room while we talk to you about what's happened." He touched my arm and I lost my breath and tented my hands over my mouth and nose, trying to breathe. Closed my eyes. Concentrate. Breathe.

When I opened my eyes the corners of the walls disappeared and we were standing in a small rounded room with rounded doorways and rounded hallways and nothing to lean into. Gloria's voice had rounded-out too. She was howling in a tunnel.

I told them I wouldn't go in there. No.

I told them I needed to find my son. I didn't want to talk about what had happened. I needed to find my son. Now. Quickly.

And he took me—"Come this way"—right into the room. And I twisted his sleeve in my hand.

Mother was in there. Her tight mouth and the straightened-out gaze, looking so determined. She stood up from the sofa and took my hand in hers and held it firmly.

There were clusters of Kleenex scattered all over the coffee table.

Mother had been sitting there with a stranger, a woman in a plain grey skirt. And now the stranger-woman was saying my name, saying nonsense, "Abby, I'm here from the hospital. I need to speak with you about your son Joseph." She sat me down and pulled a chair beside me. She smelled antiseptic. Soapy. She was too close, all eyes and mouth.

She said this: "There's been a very serious accident."

Nonsense words. Nod. I was nodding.

She said this: "On his way home from school Joseph was injured very badly. He was struck by a car and was taken by ambulance to Toronto Western Hospital."

No more nodding. Shut up. Throat closed up.

Close your eyes and think it away. Think them gone.

But she kept talking. "They did everything they could, Abby, but the injuries he sustained were severe. His brain was injured very badly, Abby. He died. There was nothing more they could do for him, Abby. I'm so sorry."

Nothing.

Nothing.

Nothing.

I said no. I said I need to see him.

Everything was loose and wobbling.

I said it's not the right boy. I told them he's got a birthmark right here, on his arm. It's a leaf shape. He's missing a tooth, this tooth right here, it fell out two nights ago. I have it upstairs in my jewelry box, I told them. I told them I'd go get it. I'd show them, and the stranger-woman stood with me as I went looking for it and laid her flat warm hand on my arm and I told her, "Don't touch me!"

"Abby ..."

"Get the fuck out of here!"

"Abby ..." She said Abby, Abby, a nonsense name.

"Get out!"

Gloria sobbed on and on in the hallway and everyone was crowding around like I was some kind of wild animal. Circling to trap me. I told them all to get out of there. "Leave!"

Mother told me to sit down. To listen to what the people were trying to tell me. I told her I want my son.

The woman in the grey suit was nodding, "We'll take you to him," she said. She looked right the fuck into me and broke me right in two, but I couldn't look away. "We'll take you to him."

I remember saying "No, no, no, no," and "please," to the woman from the hospital, to God, to anyone who would listen.

Please please please please.

And I didn't know what that word meant anymore. It meant everything all at once. Please leave me and we'll start this all over. Please stop this. Please let it be the wrong boy. Please let me see him. Please give me back my son. Please.

XXV.

I WEPT. And the sobs that originated deep inside were deeper than marrow and pulse, and I sobbed through each of my cells. I sobbed into my arms, knees to chest. I sobbed into my useless fingers, deadened hands. Neck wet with tears and Mojo's arms around me, like heavy ropes I didn't have the energy to throw from me. It was alright. It didn't matter. Mojo wept too. And we sat like that until the sky overhead was thick with cottony storm clouds and we were both empty and mute.

Then as we stood up to go join the line for the *trambilla* she said to me out of nowhere, "He's part of everything now." She said "he's here" and she grabbed my hands and she said "he's here," and she held my face like the face of a child. "He's here, he's in you."

"How'd you get through it?"

"Who says I've gotten through it?"

I wanted, as we boarded the *trambilla*, to say thank you. And I wanted to tell her about the letter. But I didn't. Thunder rolled, far off. A drop or two of rain on the dirty cobblestone. I wanted, as we rattled in the *trambilla* with its rows of chicken crates and crammed-in passengers, to tell her we'd buried him on a Saturday when ordinarily he'd be watching morning cartoons. I wanted, as I watched from the dusty window as a hawk dove from its spiral, to tell her how they'd told me they didn't think he'd suffered. And how the fuck would they know that? They didn't know. But I guess they just had to tell me something, right? So. What were they supposed to say. I didn't tell her any of this. I watched the landscape and she closed her eyes and rested her head back and held my hand the whole way back to Tadeo as we breathed sawdust and sweat and feathers.

As we were walking up the stairs, me feeling like I'd just lost a fistfight, Vula came bounding down in her bare feet with one blackened toenail.

It must have all shown on my face because she said, "Whoa-ah, hey. You don't look good, sister. You alright?" And when I nodded and said I was fine she lifted her sunglasses from her chocolate eyes, and looked at me deeply. "Yeah, you're alright. I know that look. You've just got a broken heart." And she took my hand in hers and swung it. "Right?" Her big, childlike features brightened and made me smile. Vula squeezed my hand and kissed me on the cheek.

"Such is life," she said lightheartedly before taking the rest of the staircase and bounding out the hotel doors. She left a pungent smell of sweat and freshly-peeled oranges behind her.

As I unlocked the hotel room and pushed the door open, I found a slip of paper wedged under the crack. The note was written in blue pen on the back of a bus ticket receipt. It read "A woman's heart is like a needle at the bottom of the ocean." And I smiled at it and folded it in two and dropped it on the bed beside me as I kicked off my boots and lay back, not intending to sleep, but doing so before I'd even unbuttoned my jeans.

Later, the room spun into focus as I came out of this totally inviolable, dreamless sleep. It was darker in the room now that the storm clouds had descended on town. Thunder wasn't far off now. And in the next room, Mojo played her *Canned Heat* album. I patted my jeans and realized that my cigarettes had likely fallen out somewhere on the way back home. I scolded myself and emptied my wallet in search of a ten-peso coin. The photo of Joseph fell on top of a pile of bus receipts, gas receipts and a handwritten one from a diner in Kansas. I held the photo in two hands to study it, then I took it to the shard of mirror over the kitchenette sink and wedged it behind the mirror, and sat back on the bed just to look at it for a minute. Then it seemed right and it seemed time to scoop the pile of clothes from the floor of the room and dump them on the bed so I could start hanging them, shaking them first for scorpions, then lining them up, jeans and all, on the wooden hangers in the closet. I didn't have much to hang, but it was a start. It looked good, tidy.

I'd never tried the radio on top of the fridge, so I did that too. On hands and knees I groped for an outlet behind the fridge and the radio blasted garble. I spun the dial and landed on a station playing some kind of love song—complete with violins and tuba and trumpets.

Who knows what I was thinking then. It might have been the song. I used my buck knife to cut away at the stalks of bougainvillea that crept over the balcony and brought some of those tissue-thin blossoms inside to search the cupboards for a vase. I'd never opened the cupboards before, so it was creepy to feel around in there with all the aluminum pots and terracotta ashtrays. I ended up using a clear soda bottle I found under the sink. I adjusted it so it reflected into the mirror. It made me happy, looking at the petals like painted lips.

The whole place looked better. I wished I had that *What is Home Without a Mother* magnet to stick to the fridge but I think it fell out of the car so I propped the doll on my night table and reached into the knapsack for the tightly-wrapped Christmas gift from the bottom of the bag. Sitting on the edge of the bed, I turned it over and looked at the teacher's precise strip of tape. I opened just a corner then changed my mind and slipped it into my night table drawer.

The heat had become oppressive in that little room, even if you just sat around in underwear. I was sweating across my forehead and nose, and down my chest, and had to towel down before wrapping the bath towel around me to lean out into the hall to see if the bathroom was free. I could see the door wide open, the shower curtain had been flung to one side, and there was Sue drying her legs, a mean-looking bruise on her hip. She wrapped a faded, threadbare beach towel around her waist and left the bathroom bare-breasted. I ducked back in until she'd passed. Some people are just more naked than others.

When the tepid shower leaves your skin smelling as sour as the sweat of some work animal, you have to wonder if it just swirled down the drain and eddied back into some huge communal tank to pour out over someone else who wanted, desperately, to be cooled. But the moment when the breeze blows through the glass slats of the bathroom window and gives your wet flesh goosebumps, it is so worth the stench.

When I toweled off, running the towel up the stubble of my legs, I realized there was barely anything left to pick at. No scabs. Just these faded pink scars. No little blisters. And nothing left of the fever I'd sweated out on the bedsheets. I came close up to the mirror, already beginning to sweat again, my upper lip studded with perspiration. I pursed my mouth to one side to see that my chin had healed nicely into a neat white line. Even the hair on my head had grown some from its awkward tufts. There was flesh to me now. And colour. Not bad, I thought.

When I left for cigarettes, the street outside was static electric. You could taste it, the air was metallic. A dry, skittish kind of wind slid hair across your face. And it seemed like metal was holding a charge like a resentment, hubcaps and sheets of tin leaning against the storefront, telephone wires, junk lanterns, coins, all conductive and dangerous. The earth at your feet was even ready to spring with lightning if you stood around too long looking at the sky.

Jimmy and Ines' children ran toward their house, cutting in front of me and shouting a clipped greeting as they passed. The second-youngest, Jorge, tagged along behind, his knapsack firmly on his back and the flushed baby fat of his cheeks jiggling as he ran as fast as he could to keep up.

"You're so fast, Jorge! Corre! Corre!" I said. His leather soles patted by.

I had to stop myself from insisting the grocery girl hurry up with my change. As she fingered for greasy pesos in the well-ordered register, the two dusty dogs that were forever outside, forever scratching at mites, snarled at each other for some bit of food they'd pulled from the neighbour's trash. My fingers roamed around my wet scalp in circles. Thunder. The grocery girl and I exchanged hopeful expressions. I popped the cap of my beer against the counter and swigged back as much as I could at once. Like breathing deep in winter.

"Y Faros también?" she asked and I silently told myself it would be my last pack.

The grocery girl moved the aerial on her tiny television and the picture shuddered moments before a thunder roll. A fly alighted on the corner of my eye and bit.

By the time I got back to the hotel, Marcella and Delilah were almost ready for the rain. I helped Delilah shimmy the potted plants out from under the colonnade to the open courtyard so they'd get water from the downpour. And Marcella was closing the shutters in the office and arranging rags along the windowsills. Delilah kept picking at the shoulders of her muumuu and sighing and tsking about her heat rash. I nodded and let her finish while I drank the rest of my beer, then we both retreated upstairs behind our doors.

When the rains came, everything changed.

First, waves of heat lightening will tell you it's coming. They're like a trick of the mind the way they make everything shimmer. The radio's like a piss-poor fortune teller, all staticky just moments before the thunder. Then we were drenched, and we were joyful. I could have danced. I could have laughed aloud. I let it soak me through. Once everything was drenched, bathed and dripping, is when Mother showed up, like she'd brought her very own weather system.

And there she was. Plain and as unavoidable as the 'x' in the middle of Mexico.

She looked thin and pale as the tender meat inside a willow branch. There was no husk or leather about her, now. No vigorous flush of red to her skin, nothing brash or hurried. She was wet from the rain and she looked like she was made of bible paper, skin translucent. I was afraid to touch her, afraid she might come apart in my hands.

I barely noticed Marcella coming out of the office as I unbolted the door for my mother.

We stood there assessing each other's expressions, each other's thin and emptied faces. "Esta es tu mamá?" Marcella asked. "She looks like you, very similar, in the eyes." Marcella smiled and extended her hand in welcome, helping my mother over the threshold. "Come in, come in, it's raining pitchers," she said in Spanish.

So there she was, heavy vinyl suitcase by her side, the rain streaking the arms of her stiff cotton blouse. Marcella struggled with the outer doors, bolting them hard as though barring the rain from the premises.

"So there you are."

"Hi, Mother." I reached out, a little carefully, to touch her arm, then pulled her close. Mother stood with her arms at her side and felt stiff but I held on. After a moment she lifted a hand to my back and kind of leaned her head against mine, saying into my rain-soaked hair, "What were you thinking?"

XXVI.

MARCELLA LEFT a folded towel, two pillows, a blanket and a tiny bar of soap on my bed. It was the first time she'd ever been inside, as far as I knew. I was glad for that. For the privacy, I mean. Mother used the towel to dry her hair as she sat in my saint's chair like she owned it. In minutes, her suitcase was unpacked and she was in dry clothes. She'd lined up her two pairs of shoes, hanging her windbreaker alongside my clothes in the closet. Then she folded her pants—two pairs, again—and laid them in a neat pile on the upper shelf. I sat on the edge of the bed and watched as Mother found drawers for her socks and underwear and hangers for her scarves.

Mother was wearing one of her matching cotton outfits that made her look a little like a nurse. Neat and clean. Her face scrubbed, her wet grey hair combed into a tidy ponytail.

"I got one phone call." Mother produced a green pack of menthol cigarettes from the duty-free carton inside her suitcase. She expertly removed the cellophane in one movement and put a cigarette between her lips. "One phone call." She flicked her lighter and exhaled a cloud of smoke.

"I know."

"Do you?" Mother, with her washed face and combed hair, was inescapable. Her face concealed nothing. Her face demanded answers. She sucked on the cigarette and I watched the wrinkles around her lips cinch tight.

"Do you know how long it's been?" She sat facing me, balancing the ashtray on her knees.

"A while now. A couple weeks."

"Eight weeks," Mother said, nodding.

I lied and told her it didn't seem that long.

Mother looked away. "Well, maybe not to you."

"How'd you know how to get here?"

"You called collect, smarty. There's one San Judas whatever-you-call-it in this state so there you have it." She stared at me. Mother. Ruth. "Then I took a taxi from the airport to here. Then I said, Hotel! Hotel! and he said, Si, señora, si! And here we are."

"But the money, Mother."

This time she didn't look away. "Don't even talk to me about the money. You have no idea what you've put me and your sister through. Absolutely no idea, it's clear to me now."

I told her she didn't have to come. And I was going to tell her that I was about to leave Tadeo, find my way back home but she cut me off with that ripped-tin voice of hers.

"Oh, didn't I?"

She could stare without blinking. Right through you. She could tell if you'd been drinking or if you weren't wearing underwear or if you'd screwed someone the night before. She'd had x-ray vision since I was a kid and I felt her x-ray vision on me as I got up to answer the tap-tap-tap at the door.

When I opened it, Marcella was standing there between two officers dressed in their blue uniforms. Marcella spoke quickly and quietly in Spanish, too quickly for me to really get what she was saying. She used her hands when she spoke, forming them into shapes, then freeing them in this kind of an exasperated flutter. She looked near tears. I got the words Luis and Ilario and distress and very little else. As Marcella prattled on, I caught Mojo taking the staircase to the courtyard. She was mouthing words to me, shaking her head, eyes wide and I got it that I was to say nothing.

One of the officers looked like he could have been the father of the other—same mouth, turned down at the corners. The younger one took a pad of paper and a pen from his breast pocket.

I didn't know whether I was supposed to invite them in or go into the hallway. How do you handle these things?

Mother watched from the saint's chair, smoking. "Now, what's this all about?"

I ignored her and stepped out into the hall, pulling the door closed behind me. The older of the two seemed eager to see what I was keeping out of view and politely asked to go inside. I let him and stayed out there with the little note-taker. He spoke very little English and I think he even got flushed when he couldn't find the right word for what he wanted to say. Anyway, my Spanish prevented me from giving any kind of a complex answer, so between us we had this weird, cursory, even cordial conversation, both of us relying heavily on the polite, rehearsed expressions we'd probably both learned in school.

The officer, of course, asked if I knew Luis Reynosa and Ilario Tristán. I folded my arms, shouldn't have, but did, and told him I knew them only a little.

"From el Toro Rojo," I said. "Met them before."

He wanted to know the last time I'd seen the two of them and I paused to pretend to think about it. I said, "A week ago? Maybe more." The officer nodded. Scribbled. So I asked him if everything was alright, if there was some kind of problem, and he assured me that everything was fine. Finally, he asked me if I'd given them any money. I acted confused and said, "No. Why would I do that? No." And then he apologized for disturbing me and my mother.

The older of the two officers came out of my room pushing a pack of Canadian cigarettes into his uniform pocket. He looked pleased. As they were leaving, the older officer boasted to his partner that they were a gift "from the girl's mother. They're Canadian." He tapped the top of the pack.

"Is this a normal, everyday thing around here? Police at your door?" She looked nervous and was putting on a sweater as if, despite the heat, another layer of clothing would somehow keep her safe.

"Some friends of mine were having some trouble."

"Police trouble."

"No. Relationship trouble. Love trouble."

"And the police came? Was it a domestic dispute?"

Mother knew from the way I looked at her that I wasn't going to talk about it.

"Anyway, it's none of my business what people do," she said. But I knew she didn't mean it. I stifled a laugh. Everything was her business, all the time.

Then the sound of Vula racing up the flight of stairs, laughing. Someone running after her, up the stairs, past our room. Vula screeched and laughed and slammed a door at the end of the hall while whoever was chasing her rattled the handle and banged on the door, shouting in Spanish. I could hear both Vula and Sue laughing like mad. Mother shook her head.

"This is not a safe place, Abby."

I shrugged. "I like it."

"It's a very unsafe place for a young woman," she said. "You're lucky nothing terrible has happened to you. Has it? Has something gone on I should know about?"

"No, nothing terrible," I said.

"Well, you're lucky."

Mother stubbed out her cigarette and put the ashtray on the kitchenette counter. She opened the fridge and actually said, "Tsk, tsk!" She started sorting through whatever was left in there, stale tortillas in their paper wrap, beer bottles, leftovers from the café, some grapes. She found a cloth under the sink and started in on the fridge, wiping shelves, rearranging.

"What I want to know"—her tone telling me a lecture was coming—"is what you've been doing here all cooped up for eight weeks? Far as I can see there's not much to this town, so how've you managed to whittle away two whole months of your life in a place where there's nothing to do? That's what I want to know."

I lit a cigarette and lay back on the bed. I'd ash it on the floor just because I could. That would really get her going. Disgusting, she'd say.

"I was taking a vacation, Mother. A holiday."

"A holiday's a week in Florida with a bikini and a sunburn," she said. She held up a mangled clump of tinfoil with shrivelled leftovers inside. She gave it a shake. "This is not a holiday,"

"How would you even know? Have you ever taken a holiday in your life?"

"Well, tell me how've you spent your time."

"I'm not answering that. I don't have to answer that."

Mother finished with the fridge. Made quick work of it and made a show out of throwing the rotten food into the garbage can.

Scrubbing the counter was next. "Anyway, I figured you'd take the weekend to get things wrapped up here, then you could show me how to catch the bus since you're the one with the Spanish, and we'd fly out on Monday."

She had to be kidding.

"No. Nope. I'm not ready."

"Ready for what?"

"For anything."

"Stop being stupid."

"I'm staying, Mother."

"Stop being absurd."

"Just for a bit."

"And who gets the privilege of sorting out the mess back home, Abby? Me? Am I responsible for paying your rent or is it Gloria, who's done it for the past two months and who, by the way, since you asked, is planning on getting married to Bruce next spring and would like very much if her only sister could be there to be her maid of honour?"

"Oh, Jesus. Bruce? Come on."

"He loves her. He'd do anything for her."

"So she'll be trapped at the tavern for the next thirty years slopping shitty food from the kitchen and wishing she'd gone back to school. Great. Bruce."

"You're one to talk, Smarty."

"Oh please."

"You were the bookworm with all the promise. You could go back to school, you know. Get a good job. One that suits you."

"I'm staying. That's it. And it's not that I don't appreciate this over-the-top, melodramatic gesture of yours, but I want you to go."

"Answer me this, Abby. What's life got for you here that you can't have back home?"

How do you answer that? How do you begin to explain to someone who doesn't see it, doesn't feel it, the moment they step onto the streets of this town? I wanted to give her an alphabetical inventory of all the things Tadeo gave me, things home never could—from *alacrán* to *zapateado*—but I'd just end up sounding like Lucky with his endless list of foods and prices. Ludicrous.

Mother sat on the edge of the bed. "How're you going to survive here?"

My mind flipped through the possibilities of taking care of kids, serving food, working for rich housewives, digging graves, pouring booze, cleaning houses. Mother wouldn't appreciate hearing any of those things so I just said, "I'll figure it out."

"Well I hope to heaven you do." She zipped up her empty suitcase and shoved it under the bed. "And here's you, wandering through the world like you're the only one who's ever suffered. Wake up, Abby. Everyone's got something."

Outside our heated little room was the sound of the clop-clop of the burros and the bells ringing six o'clock. I was grateful for the passing of time.

When Mojo showed up at the door to go down to the café, Mother and I had survived our silences and were now listening to the radio and playing a game of gin rummy on the bed. It was better than yelling at each other, even though Mother was frustrated with me for making so many mistakes in my scoring. She'd borrowed the deck from Gloria so she could play solitaire while waiting for her flight connection in Houston. To think of Mother alone in the airport made me all achy with pity. Then she told me there'd been a man there in the airport bar, a man with a real "honest to goodness" cowboy hat and "the kindest eyes" and they began talking about cards and ended up playing a game of rummy together, "laughing and carrying on like old friends."

"You may have a new beau."

She shook her head. "I'm too old for that."

Mojo was in a purple crêpe one-piece outfit, cinched at the waist with a braided leather belt. It billowed around her wrists and ankles and she'd put on a little extra mascara for our dinner out. The whole effect made her look even more like a cheerful clown.

She hugged Mother when they were introduced, which was even more awkward than I could have imagined, then held her by the shoulders while she gushed all the stuff about what a beautiful, gentle soul I was and how she must be so proud of me.

"She's a good girl." Mother gathered her purse and slipped on her walking shoes. I shot Mojo a look as Mother licked her thumb and removed a scuffmark from her beige leather purse. Mojo shrugged and smiled and mouthed the word, "Mom."

On the way to the café Mojo linked arms with Mother and pointed out little things she thought might be of interest to her. Mother must have just been reeling to be so close with Mojo. She released herself to take a tissue from her purse to wipe her nose. As Mojo pointed, Mother nodded at the carvings of angels with swords and the girls who sat on the church steps selling stone rosaries and medals of St. Jude Thaddeus.

"Is that so," and "my goodness" was all Mother said about anything Mojo told her.

At the cathedral, Mother stood tutting her tongue and repeating the words, "Just gorgeous." Every time she looked as though she was about to walk away, she'd stop, shake her head at the church and repeat the words.

Before we moved along, I stopped to buy Mother an agate rosary from a woman seated on the church steps. I watched as she tucked it into a little zippered compartment inside her purse, smiling.

"You didn't have to do that," she said, and it made me swell inside to see my mother's precise movements again, to smell the purse, its scent of spilled perfume and to see her clutch it at her side and gaze about like a little girl. I never imagined in a million years that Mother could look so out of place anywhere. And in Tadeo, she looked so small. If she stayed much longer she might soon be pocket-sized.

As we crossed the *zócalo*, the streets were warm and wet and the humidity made the cobblestones feel slippery underfoot. There was a kind of wet forest atmosphere after the rain, with the trees holding moisture in their fists of leaves. The grackles cackled happily and the benches were still slicked with rain. Washed new.

Mojo again took Mother by the arm and pointed out the jail, the bank, and then the two of them peered into a red plastic bucket belonging to a young woman selling rock crystal. She had pieces laid out on an oily cotton cloth. Mojo squatted to pick through them while Mother was busy avoiding a street dog that was vying for her attention.

"No," she said. "Shoo now."

For just a minute I closed my eyes and breathed in the humidity. I thought about what I'd told Mother in the hotel room. That I was staying. I wondered if that was even true. What would it feel like to stay put? I held my breath in the town square and tried to imagine how it would feel, day after day, to live amongst those noises: the grackles, the whistles, the children's shouts, the church bells. I breathed out and looked across the square to where Mother was now sitting, purse on her lap, with Mojo. Mojo was gesturing with her hands, telling some elaborate story. I watched the pinwheel man trundle by on his over-sized tricycle. Day after day. How would it be.

Then I called to Mojo and Mother to come to the café.

"Let's eat," I shouted across the square, waving them over.

XXVII.

MOJO CALLED IT a "divine accident."

Mother's fork poked the slippery grey-brown fungus on her plate.

"Everything's got to be timed exactly right," Mojo said, cutting little squares of crepe and squash blossom and *huitlacoche* with the side of her fork. I watched as she stacked a forkful and devoured it, making appreciative noises with her eyes closed. Mojo told us the *huitlacoche* was a product of rain and corn and butterflies. That the butterflies would come and leave stray spores on the ears of corn, then the rains fell, and from those spores this funky black fungus would grow. She used her shadow-puppet hands to illustrate as she spoke. Mother looked amused. I placed a big forkful of the crepe into my mouth and was astonished by the rich, smoky, buttery flavour.

"That's corn smut," Mother said. "My Daddy was a farmer and that's corn smut. You don't eat corn smut."

"It's a delicacy," Mojo said.

"It looks very chewy," Mother said.

Mojo shrugged and wiped the corners of her mouth with a paper napkin. She pushed her plate to the side and looked satisfied only for a moment before her eyes widened and told us she spied something sweet. She slid over to the pie counter to peer in at the shelves of flan and coconut cream pie, banana mousse tarts and small, impossibly shiny tartlettes.

I slipped another forkful between lips and thought of rain-broken fields, the filigree legs of the butterfly. It was like a foreign language on the tongue.

Mother ordered coffee and when it came she stirred loudly.

"She's very theatrical," Mother said. An observation as good as an insult.

"I like her," I said, surprised at how protective I was of Mojo.

She sipped her coffee.

"Gloria's taken Seymour to the park every day. He's stopped chewing shoes."

I smiled and didn't mean it. "I knew Gloria'd be good to him."

"She's worried about you. Like everyone. She wants you back."

"Everyone. What does that mean? You and Gloria?"

"Isn't that enough? Some people don't have anybody to worry about them, Abby. You ever stop to think about that?"

I said I'd call her. I said that I'd let Gloria know I was going to be here a while longer. I pushed the plate away and rested my elbows on the table while Mother exhaled a deep, exasperated breath through her nose. We just sat there staring at each other. Who would crack first. Not me, that was for damn sure.

"So I came for nothing, in other words," Mother finally said.

"I didn't ask you to."

"All that money, my savings."

I lit one of her disgusting menthol cigarettes.

"You can't hide from life forever," she said. "Here or anywhere."

Quiet, defiant, tap-tapping the cigarette, I said: "You may not believe this, but life followed me here. I never shook it."

I looked as directly and as bravely as I could into Mother's grey eyes and I knew she understood. I knew she got it. And she pressed her lips together into something like a smile.

"Alright," she said, all clipped, finally resigned. "It's up to you now."

Then Mojo came back to the table with a stainless-steel bowl of jiggling flan and three spoons.

"What'd I miss?" she asked, grinning.

That night, the *posada* was quiet as a crypt. We were tired of endless hands of gin rummy on the bedspread, so I took Mother all the way up onto the rooftop to sit beneath the stars and laundry wires. The guard dog was curled atop a heap of hotel bed sheets waiting for laundering. Mother hauled a rust-flecked folding chair from some forgotten corner of the roof and wiped it down with a tissue she magically produced from her pajama top. I settled on the gritty concrete and leaned against the frame of her chair.

There would only be an hour or so of starlight before the clouds would gather, accumulating for the next day's rain. The stars were glittering coolly in the murky, shape-shifting skies, and I could still remember all the names of the constellations from growing up in someone else's cottage country.

I traced a finger over the Queen's zigzag of little stars. "Cassiopeia."

Mother nodded and smiled to herself like she remembered our game, like she remembered a child so full of promise.

"Ursa Minor," Mother said, her index finger circling above on the black screen.

"That's an easy one. Little Dipper."

"Alright. Perseus, how's that, Smarty?"

"Andromeda."

"You were always so good at this. Did you ever want to become an astronomer?"

I laughed and leaned against Mother's leg. She stroked the side of my hair with the very tips of her fingers.

"So what's with this haircut, anyway?" she asked, relaxed now after the two beers she'd had at dinner. She tugged at the ends and I tried to duck away from her hand.

"You should have seen it before. It's grown out."

"Let's see," Mother said. "It's not the tin man, it's not the lion ..."

I swatted her hand and we both laughed. I'd never really noticed how similar our laughter was until it blended together like that. Then Mother looked at me with this bittersweet expression on her face, somewhere between a smile and a frown. She used to smile a smooth, big smile, no teeth, but a loose smile, a real smile. Not any more.

"When's the last time we laughed, you and me?" I couldn't think of an answer but she could. "A long time ago."

I nodded. Didn't want to think about it. My throat was getting tight and I swigged some beer. Warm. Like everything else. Like the aluminum chair. Like the concrete. And my mother.

She lifted the bottle from my hand. "You drink too much." A pause. "You do, Abby."

"Well, you talk too much."

Smacking her lips, Mother took a generous swallow and handed it back. "That may be so."

We sat quietly for a long while, watching the clouds blot out the stars.

"It's when it's quiet that I think about him most." She nodded to herself.

I could still see the man in the moon, veiled in clouds. I looked at the 'o' of his wordless mouth. He's howling, I thought.

"He was the happiest noise of my life." I handed the bottle over.

"First there was Gloria, then you, then him." She took a deep gulp and straightened her pajama sleeves.

"Sometimes I just can't take how quiet my life has become."

I took her hand and held it firmly. Amber ring. Blue veins. Her thin skin. I don't know why it was that I could see her age for the first time in the half-light of the moon and a few faltering stars, but I did. Mother with all the decades and all that grief upon her.

She took it away and wiped her face with her hands. "I've run out of Kleenex," she said, which seemed impossible. She was probing her sleeves.

"I want you to know I still visit him every week," she said. "On Saturdays, so he's not lonely."

And that was it. A sucker punch.

"Jesus, Mother. He's not fucking lonely. He's not even there."

"Watch your mouth."

"Well, he's not! He's not in some grave. He's not waiting for visitors. He's not even fucking there, Mother! You believe in heaven, right? All that shit you told us growing up. You believe in all that, right? Dad's there and we'll all be together some day? Well then why the fuck are you looking for him there?"

"Why are you looking for him here?" she said.

And I had absolutely nothing to say.

"It helps me, it helps me to be there. To plant snapdragons and keep it looking good. To bring him things. It gives me something to do."

"Okay. I'm sorry."

"It helps me."

"I know, I'm sorry." And I really meant it. Jesus, of all things to say to her.

Mother lit another cigarette. There were so many of these tiny failures between us now. Moments that afterwards made us stiff and foreign with each other. Moments that hardened us to each other. Mother blew a screen of smoke in front of her and broke our silence.

"Abby I might as well tell you. Now, you're going to hate me I know, but I read the letter."

"What?"

"I read it and I shouldn't have but I did."

I guess I got up then and started walking, where, I don't know. To the edge of the roof, back to Mother, to the far side of the roof. I just remember saying, "Oh my God."

"You can tell me off," she said. "I deserve that, but I can't undo it."

"Oh my God."

I was underwater, sucked in and rolled over by the tide. I was slammed against the sandy ocean floor. I was dragged back out again and tossed into a swirling current. Mother. She dragged me underwater into that curling ocean tide.

"I can tell you about it, if you want me to. Or you can read it sometime. But I think you should know what it said."

"I don't want to know," I said, loud or quiet, I don't know.

"Well I think you should know."

"No."

I thought I'd leave the roof. Step off the roof. Or down the steps, retreat into the room, the barroom, the street, anywhere I couldn't hear her, but the dizziness, the lack of air. I tried to breathe deeper but that didn't seem to help then I thought I would honest-to-God pass out if I didn't put my head between my knees so I did that and it didn't help. So I laid flat on my back and closed my eyes to the spinning world. I told her I didn't need to know. I think I told her that.

And she told me anyway as I lay there on the roof. She told me this man was praying for us, for our family, every day. That's what she said. That he was praying for us, which holds a lot of weight with Mother. She said he'd written that he'd been over and over it in his mind a million times but he couldn't have changed anything. So, not his fault, I thought or said. My son's fault. Was that what I was supposed to presume? No. My fault, I thought or said. My fault for letting him go home on his own. My fault for not knowing that one day after a snowfall he would slip from the ridge of a snow bank because when you're nine why shouldn't you walk there, and that he would slip right off and onto the road. This guy, he said he'd think of us every day for the rest of his life, for what that was worth. That he'd been in treatment for depression since, and that he still could never forgive himself. Ever.

My mother's great trembling unburdening, the telling of this letter. I lay on the gritty roof with its invisible stars behind the heels of my hands. I lay there with my hands over my eyes when it should have been my fingers in my ears to Mother's swirling, dizzying editorial. It was the first honest-to-god dizzy spell I'd ever experienced and I wasn't sure if I would throw up or spin right off the roof into the wobbling street if I stood up. So I lay there until she was finished.

"He needs to be set free from all of this," Mother said. "He's a suffering man. And he needs you to forgive him. But you need to forgive yourself first, Cookie."

I took my hands off my eyes and in the dark of the roof I could see the cherry of her cigarette glow as she drew on it. She was looking out over the street. That was her best. What she said, she meant and she didn't need to look me in the eye. Mother always told me the truth while she was looking in some other direction.

"Well,"—turning to me now—"the stars have gone in for the night. Maybe we should too."

XXVIII.

I WAS SITTING in the dim glow of a candle stub in a beer bottle and I had the letter in my hand. "Of course I brought the letter," Mother had said. She had it folded in some inner zippered compartment of her purse normally reserved for corn cushions and maybe a tube of Almay lipstick. I think that's where she kept the rosary I bought her. She seemed to sleep deep after she handed the letter over. Her breathing was rhythmic. She'd done what she needed to do and now she could sleep deeply.

I held the corners of the letter to inspect it. Straightened it out on the night table. The crooked handwriting was like little falling fence posts, leaning back on themselves. It was the writing of a man who never did well in school. Backwards slant of an introvert. I found myself thinking these things like I knew, like some kind of a handwriting analyst. A boy who tripped a lot. Spoke slowly. I could see him. He became a man who struggled in the world. Everyday things just a little bit harder for him. A man who led a simple life with a shitty job and a wife who loved him but not enough and he was contented with it all until now, until this great sorrow. And then there were all those things he said, specific things that Mother had left out, or maybe it was just the way this man put it that made it sound new to me, I don't know. It was a longer letter than I thought. Mother had made it sound so brief and factual.

"I have two children," he wrote, "girls, not much older than your son." Children not kids. Children you cherish. Had Mother told me that? Had she said the man was a father? That his name was Tim.

That Tim was a father. He wrote: "I try to imagine what you're going through. I think about my girls and I can't imagine the agony." He used that word. He wrote that he felt a little bit of that agony every day but he knew that telling me that "wouldn't change anything either." There was something about his frankness, something in the fact that he didn't have any fucking answers and didn't write to be forgiven, like I'd thought he had. If you flipped it over you could see that on the second side he was writing fast, the little fences of words stretching out like wires. He wrote: "Maybe to know I think of you and your son every day might mean something. I'm not sure just what." He said other things. About images of that day. How he couldn't shake them.

I wrote him back.

I wrote him back on a pad of paper I stole from the hotel office. It had some other hotel's address on it. Some other place with a proper name.

Here's what the letter said:

Tim, You need to forgive yourself. There's no sense in ruining your perfectly good life with sadness and regret. I never blamed you, if that matters. Not so much as I blame myself. You were an unfortunate victim of fate, I think. It could have been anybody else, which doesn't help you, I know, but it could have been anyone else who turned down that street. When you think of that day, when those images come to you, try thinking of this instead: it is summer and Joseph is swimming underwater in the lake up north. He swims a long time underwater. His limbs are strong, silver bubbles trail from his nostrils like he's full of magic and not just breath. His skin is brown with sun. When he surfaces he takes a deep, exultant breath and wipes the lake water from his eyes. He is grinning. That is the way I think of it. That Joseph has surfaced someplace else, from one world to another. Maybe it will help you to think of him that way too. I hope so.

Sincerely, Abby

I was contemplating the letter on the night table, had just folded it over, when Mother awoke from the heat. She shuffled to the balcony in her pajamas, tattered at the hem, a bit of lace trim hanging from its stitches. Mother stood in the open air, which was only a little bit cooler than the air inside the hotel room.

"Oh,"—her voice hoarse with sleep—"you've got a little bird out here." She leaned down to look into the rickety bamboo cage where the bird roosted and tapped at the bars.

"It won't leave," I said, putting our letters into the night table. "I mean it leaves but it comes back again."

Mother came inside and opened the fridge and organized the beer bottles on the wire shelf. She opened the door to the freezer and brought her face to the whirring fan inside. I watched her.

"You alright?"

"No," she said. "This heat's killing me. It's no wonder neither of us can sleep. I'll bet you nobody's sleeping in this whole town." She fanned the room with the tiny freezer door. I asked her if she wanted a pitcher of water from the lobby, and she nodded as she stood rotating her arms in the cool of the open refrigerator.

"I don't know how you stand it."

I went barefoot.

In the lobby, Delilah sat fanning herself on a wrought iron chair by the fountain. Her dog lay panting on its side beside her, its tongue lolling against the flagstone. Its tongue looked like it might stick to the stone if it suddenly raised its head.

"Your mother brought the rain," she said, wafting the words out into the courtyard with a Chinese paper fan.

"Let's hope she doesn't take it with her when she goes," I said, slopping a little bit of water onto the tile as I filled the jug. "She's leaving tomorrow." Saying the words made me sadder than I thought they would.

Someone was tugging on the string through the front door of the hotel and the door lock popped open. There was that necessary thud against the wood with a hip or shoulder and the door came open with Vula tumbling in, dropping the satchel she had over her shoulder. She looked both bedraggled and sparkly as ever, a silver-threaded scarf wound around her dreadlocks. Glass beads tinkled from all her edges.

She entered like a first frost.

Then she looked out from under her heavily-glittered lids and took a long, deep drink from the pitcher of water in my hand. She closed her eyes as she drank, water dripping a little from the corners of her mouth. I felt weird about the whole thing and looked at Delilah who just shook her head. Vula thanked me and, sauntering up the staircase, she recited: "I am the poem of Earth, said the voice of the rain, eternal I rise impalpable out of the land and the bottomless sea." She dragged her fingers dreamily along the banister.

Delilah wilted, made visibly weary by Vula's passing. "They'll never leave me. Never."

As I refilled the pitcher I could hear Vula rattling the door handle to her hotel room. Delilah tsked her tongue and fanned a little faster, the painted paper making the sound of a bird's wing in flight.

After a moment Vula began to call through the crack of the door, her voice all muffled. I wondered if Mother would hear and check to see what all the commotion was about. Then she began pounding with both fists. In something like a stage whisper Delilah told the girl to hush. Vula ignored her and began to hip-check the door, her voice rising in panic as she called Sue's name.

Delilah was on her feet. "What in heaven ..."

And I could see that upstairs Mother had come out onto the colonnade along with a handful of others who had been inside their hotel rooms in an uneasy sleep. Mojo emerged last, when Vula began to shriek for Sue.

I left the pitcher and lunged up the stone staircase, a metallic taste singing through my mouth. Delilah followed as quickly as her heavy legs would allow, up the staircase, pulling herself along with the banister in one hand, her dressing gown in the other.

Now Vula was crouched over, stuffing her fingers under the crack of her hotel room door.

Now she was shrieking for her friend to open up and for someone to help.

She turned to her half-clothed neighbours who stood in their doorframes, afraid, bewildered, maybe wondering if they were half-asleep still from the opiate heat.

"Get it open!" Vula shrieked as she shoved her fingers under the door and leaned down to smell the air. "It's gas! Get it open!" The neighbours stood back with hands to their mouths, a couple rushed downstairs. Vula clawed, trying to remove whatever it was that had been stuffed there. Other guests rushed out the front door of the hotel in little more than their underwear or a bedsheet as Vula's hands were quickly becoming bloody. So I wasn't thinking about it and I just pulled her out of the way as Delilah slammed her whole weight against the door in this surprisingly athletic gesture. I tried too, ramming it shoulder first and it finally buckled under our combined force after the third or fourth try, capsizing whatever it was that had been pushed up against it on the other side.

Once we pushed inside past the upended dresser, there was the overpowering raw-sweet stench of gas so thick and pungent you could almost see the vapors emanating from the gas elements on the far wall of the suite. Across the bed, in a sleeveless T-shirt and a frayed pair of men's underwear Sue lay unmoving. There was a blue cast to her skin. It seemed to have seeped from her lips, which were parted, deeply stained.

Frostbite blue. Suffocation blue.

I held my breath and used all my strength to try to lift her body from the bed, get her out, but she was too heavy and I buckled. Vula helped, and together we half-dragged, half-lifted her to the hallway while Delilah shut the burners off and flung open both windows, pushing the pillows out of the way. She held her hem to her mouth as she rushed around the room.

As we pulled her into the colonnade, we stepped over the crumpled newspaper, the pillows and pillowcases Sue had stuffed against the crack of the hotel room door. I don't know where Mother was. I don't know about Mojo either. It's strange how everything comes into this kind of narrow focus in moments like that.

We laid the girl on her back. Put an ear to her chest. Bone and heartbeat. I couldn't hear breath but maybe it was shallow, I don't know. My head was whirling from the gas and my thinking was all a mishmash. Delilah told us to move her outside, away. Then she slipped her hands under the girl's arms and hoisted her so she appeared to be upright. Standing. Then Delilah backed down the staircase while I kept a hand at her back, guiding her. Sue's bare feet slid lifelessly down each step, Vula crying while saying "I love you, I love you!" and "wake up, you asshole!"

We laid her down at the entrance to the courtyard and I pinched her nostrils, gently closed her jaw and sealed my lips over the blue mouth.

Breathe.

I exhaled from the very bottom of my lungs.

Delilah was speaking Spanish on the office telephone.

Breathe.

The girl's mouth was an airless place of whiskey and vomit. I counted. I tried. Tried to bring her to life with my own spent breath.

"You're doing good, Abby." Mother's voice trembled. She said it over and over. "Good, that's it. Keep trying."

Her face wasn't the right temperature, but the blue cast was washing out to pale. I kept trying. Vula rubbed her leg and sobbed, "Please, please."

The *ambulancia* had a different kind of siren but it sounded just as desperate, just as panicked as the ones back home. Mojo met it as the light flashed blue against the stone facade of the hotel. She rushed ahead of the three attendants saying, "Okay let's hurry, let's go guys." They were carrying a tank of oxygen along with an assortment of other devices in their hands; cords, tubes, paddles and wired machines. At the doorway I watched as they tried to resurrect the girl with a ventilator they squeezed by hand.

I prayed my novena with jumbled-up words.

The police arrived within minutes and evacuated all of us to the sidewalk down the block. They evacuated Ines and her gravedigger husband and their sleepy children. All of us down the block where we speculated in Spanish, in English, in German and French, about what may have happened, and worried, in Spanish, in English, in German and French, about the belongings we'd left inside and what would happen if the place blew up. Someone had a very expensive camera they were worried about and it made me snap at them. Ines' baby was crying and her husband sat on the curb with a kid on each knee. A man with a thick German accent asked me if it had been a suicide attempt and what the hell could I say? I lied and said I didn't know.

In minutes, they were sliding her into the ambulance and I watched Sue's entire body spasm from retching. Vula clung to the open door and then very deftly hopped up into the back after the attendants.

The doors slammed shut, the siren started up, and the ambulance pulled away from the hotel and its half-naked crowd of onlookers.

"I'm shaking," Mother said to no one in particular, holding her hands out in front of her. "I need a cigarette."

"Don't!" Delilah overheard her. "The gas."

"I wouldn't." Mother's tone was just as sharp. "I'm just saying."

When the police officers emerged from the hotel they said the place was fine to re-enter. They waved their hands in a universally-understood gesture. Not to worry, their hands said. Everything's alright, their hands said. They nodded with serious mouths that pulled down at the edges. A pilot light had gone out, they explained, but the problem was rectified and no one should worry. The smell of gas will go, they said. Not to worry.

Mother was not convinced. She wanted her clothes and to go for a walk while the hotel aired out.

"I can't sleep, Abby. Not after all this. With the heat and the smell, forget it."

"We could all use a drink," Mojo said.

And Delilah said she'd like nothing more than a nice bourbon but that she should stay behind. Her face was flushed and trickles of perspiration left trails across her ample cheeks. She pressed her sleeve to her face, dabbing it. Still breathing hard she said, "I'll go calm the guests." She produced her fan and aired herself with useless little flutters at her chin.

The crowd trailed Delilah back into the hotel, where she stood at the gates of her little *pension* with the soothing air of a den mother.

"My, my, my," as she ushered the last stragglers through the doorway, "Look at all those sleepy heads in need of some dodo." She fanned on and on nervously.

We barely spoke as we sipped sangria from our sticky glasses and watched the *toro* buck and reel. We looked on quietly as it threw a cowboy from its back and his friends cheered and gave each other *palmadas*, macho claps on the back. Then the *toro* was motionless. Cocked forward mid-buck.

It was a slow night at the cantina. The bartender leaned on his elbows. The jukebox played the same 45 over and over again. And Rubia, the prostitute, sat alone sipping her blue drink. There was none of the commotion of my first night there and that was fine by me. I just didn't want Mother to be exposed to any more scenes that night. She wouldn't sleep a wink.

Across the table, Mother looked overheated and disheveled and tired. I thought with a few more sleepless nights and some clattering jewelry, some beads made out of bone, she could blend right in with the expatriate crowd. Her gaze was fixed on the *toro*, her lips around a straw.

She watched a rider board the bull. "They do this for fun?"

I couldn't get the girl's blue lips out of my mind. The taste of her mouth. The hospital might release her in a day or two but what after that? What does a girl like that do? I wondered if she had family back home. If she had a back home.

So I asked Mojo out of nowhere: "What do you think's going to happen to them?"

Propping her elbows on the table she scratched her curls like the answer slept in there among the ringlets. "You know, I hate to speculate about another person's destiny but if I were to guess, I would say that Vula will probably end up marrying some rich Mexican soap star and living in Mexico City."

It was true. Vula was charmed. Someone would write about her life someday. She'd have a ranch with jaguars and cheetahs. She'd live to be a hundred and three. They'd name a colour after her. But Sue might not get out.

"What about the other one?" I asked Mojo like she was a party oracle, like Mojo could turn the question over in the green oil of her mind and a little triangle answer would emerge saying, ask again later or outcome favorable.

Mojo looked serious and Mother wanted to know what would happen to the girl so she took her eyes, momentarily, from the *toro* to listen.

"I get the sense that she could just drift away one day, you know?"

Mother shook her head as though Mojo was talking gibberish, but I thought I understood. Mojo smiled and her eyes went wide. "But who knows. I mean, around here she could end up mayor."

"I think you're both bonkers," Mother said as the needle lifted from the 45, dropped and played the same song again.

XXIX.

WHEN MOTHER GOT in the taxi that Sunday, her vinyl suitcase was heavier with little curios wrapped in newspaper: a bronze angel doorknocker, two ashtrays from the *posada*, a wooden carving of the Virgin of Guadalupe, and the package I'd been keeping in the night table. That morning we had opened it. I had released it from the never-neverland of what it could be, what it might be, and watched as it, bit by bit, became something fixed and concrete.

It lay on the tissue paper in my lap: an imprint of Joseph's hand in clay. He'd painted it green and red and white, for Christmas, and, I thought, somehow, for Mexico. Then he'd painted his little fingers into tiny snowmen with orange noses and black scarves and buttons.

Mother cried when she held it. She rubbed her thumb over the imprint of his.

"Oh what I'd give, Abby, to hold that little hand again."

"Take it home, Ma. Keep it." And she nodded, her thumb rubbing over and over the imprint of his. She'd take that with her. And she'd get the letter to Tim. She promised to mail it as soon as she was home.

I strained to swing Mother's full suitcase into the trunk of the car, the driver helping, of course. "Careful! Careful! Permit me." Mother thought he was very polite and told him so in loud, slow English.

As the taxi trundled along the road to the bus station, Mother fidgeted with the edges of her ticket. I nudged her and told her she didn't have to leave so soon. She could stay longer, change her ticket.

Mother looked agitated by the suggestion and slipped the ticket into the pocket of her short-sleeved blouse.

"No." Her answer was swift. "I've got to get back to Gloria and take care of that dog of yours. And the heat's too much for me besides." She held her purse, hands over the clasp, like it would fly away or open its mouth or someone might snatch it. I was suddenly afraid for Mother with her posture and her cheap purse, her nervous hands.

"You have to be careful getting home."

"You're telling *me*, Smarty?"

As the taxi neared the station, there was the overwhelming impulse to direct each other, to make promises, to say everything. I promised Mother that I'd use the hotel phone to call back home every two weeks, and I'd even sit and try to write a letter once in a while. Mother would write back, she said. She would write even if I didn't, she said. She checked her notepad to make sure she'd taken down the address of the *posada* just below our Gin Rummy scores.

"Yep. Got it."

Mother made me promise I'd brush my teeth with bottled water. And that I'd watch my drinking. And not ride on the back of pickup trucks. And at least think about going to church. I told her not to push it. I told her to give Gloria a big hug and tell her I loved her and that I was sorry I left Seymour like that, really sorry, and I'm going to come and get him soon.

"Make sure she tells Seymour he's a good boy, would you?"

"Okay." Nodding like it was going on her mental checklist.

"And make sure you tell Gloria I miss her."

"Fine, I will."

"Don't forget."

As the taxi pulled into the station driveway Mother looked right at me. "You be good. Okay? Don't get stuck." I understood exactly what she meant but could never have put it into any other words. I felt it right in my gut.

Mother paid the driver and bought a bottle of water for the ride at the bus station. Out on the sunny platform were the comic vendors and a cart of candy topped-off with a field of bright foil pinwheels. I was drawn right to that beautiful spinning garden and asked the vendor how much. I took five pesos from my jeans pocket and the vendor told me to choose whichever I wished.

"Gracias," I said and thought about it carefully. Which brightest. Which most cheerful. I thought about it twirling on Joseph's plot, bright red and gold, red and gold. I pulled one from the patch.

Mother approached me but didn't ask what I was doing, like I thought she would. She just looked at the pinwheel and smiled in that new way she had.

"Will you put this there for him?"

Mother nodded. "Of course." And she tucked the stem of it into the pocket of her beige purse.

The first-class bus to the regional airport handed out little bagged lunches and Mother looked pleased as she accepted hers from a neat but scantily dressed attendant at the bus door. Holding it tightly she held the line up to turn and blow a kiss from her hand. I waved from the platform and watched her moving behind the brown-tinted windows as she found a seat. I wanted to wait until the bus pulled from the station and then until Mother was safely on her way down the highway past the ranches and the rain-soaked fields. If Mother should turn in her seat she would see me there, still waving, not leaving, not running. That's how I wanted it.

I could see that Mother was looking back at me through that tinted window so I raised my hand to wave one last time. Mother touched her hand to the glass, just for a moment.

The bus chugged exhaust as it took my mother from the station. Watching it round the corner out of sight, I hoped Mother would look down into the valley as the sun sank, that everything would be timed right so that she'd leave with everything still glowing golden. She'd like that. She'd think it was just gorgeous.

I hitched a ride to *centro* in the back of a white pickup truck with the intention of wandering around in the blue twilight. That was when the town seemed most inspired, when everything was so thankful for breath that it sang. I wanted to eavesdrop on the grackles in the sculpted trees, to hear the whistles of the balloon vendors, to wrap myself in the sad ballad strummed at the café.

By the time the truck dropped me off at the town centre, crowds surrounded its bandstand, chatting as they waited for the band. A man pulled a bow over his fiddle's strings, tuning it. A barrel-chested man plucked at his upright bass. Fingers skittered across the guitar strings. Then all at once the instruments struck up a spirited song and in three-part harmony the musicians began to sing.

I was filled with a sweet kind of melancholy as I made my way through the square watching families buy bags of hot chestnuts and chocolate for the little ones. The teenagers were out too, the girls trolling in pairs pretending not to notice the boys watching them as they sat, side-by-side on benches, nudging one another. People were milling about in the street, hand in hand, with children zipping between them like quick stitches. All around were neighbours who had left their homes to revel in the ephemeral cool the rains had left behind.

I wandered toward the singing, toward the three men creating one perfect note between them. Winding my way through the chatter and the perfume I drew in closer to the music, and by the time a new song had begun, I had completely disappeared into the crowd.

"You'll see why a person would want to live there forever. Dawn, morning, mid-day, night: all the same, except for the changes in the air. The air changes the color of things there. And life whirs by as quiet as a murmur ... the pure murmuring of life."
— Juan Rulfo, Pedro Páramo

ACKNOWLEDGEMENTS

My gratitude to the following people for their generous support:

Guernica Editions: for providing a platform for new fiction and for giving *Blessed Nowhere* a true literary home. Special thanks to the editors of the sixth annual Guernica Literary Fiction Prize, especially Nazanine Hozar, for choosing to shine a light on this book.

Editor Lindsay Brown: for your critical insights, your keen eye and your humour (notice, Lindsay, I didn't use an oxford comma there). You made this process an absolute delight.

Designer Rafael Chimicatti: for your willingness to work with my vibes and vagaries to design a cover image that felt like it had always been.

Mary Cross: for so lovingly midwifing the earliest draft of this book into being. You were the first to meet "Abby," and your voice has been with me throughout this entire process.

To the women whose friendship is nourishment: Ainsley Burns, Charlotte Osborne, Jennifer Wai-Lan Huang, Lisa Pennycook, Melanie Janisse-Barlow, Amy Culberg.

My siblings, Stephanie, Paul, John, Gregory: thank you for lifelong love and encouragement.

Andrew. Andrew. Andrew. Thank you for being the best supporter, safe harbour, trail walker, pep-talker I could ever ask for. *Gracias, mi amor.*

Liam and Gabe: thank you for being patient with me while I write and for being so loving and encouraging. You teach me everything about life.

My mom: thank you for surviving and continuing to love despite living with unfathomable grief. This book is for you.

Mexico: thank you for shelter and inspiration, then and now. You hold half my heart, always.

ABOUT THE AUTHOR

CATHERINE BLACK is an Associate Professor at OCAD University, where she was a co-founder of the Creative Writing BFA program. She has published two collections of prose poetry: *Lessons of Chaos and Disaster*, and Pat Lowther Award-nominated *Bewilderness*. Her lyric non-fiction novella, *A Hard Gold Thread*, was nominated for the ReLit Award. This is her first novel.

Printed by Imprimerie Gauvin
Gatineau, Québec